ALL
THOSE THINGS
WE NEVER
SAID

ALSO BY MARC LEVY

ALL
THOSE THINGS
WE NEVER
SAID

MARC LEVY   TRANSLATED BY
CHRIS MURRAY

amazoncrossing

Text copyright © 2008 Marc Levy

Translation copyright © 2017 Chris Murray
All rights reserved.

Previously published as *Toutes ces choses qu'on ne s'est pas dites* by Éditions Robert Laffont in France in 2008. Translated from French by Chris Murray.

Published by AmazonCrossing, Seattle

www.apub.com

Amazon, the Amazon logo, and AmazonCrossing are trademarks of Amazon.com, Inc., or its affiliates.

ISBN-13 9781542045988
ISBN-10 1542045983

Cover design by Kimberly Glyder

Printed in the United States of America

For Pauline and Louis

There are only two ways to live your life.
One is as though nothing is a miracle.
The other is as though everything is a miracle.

Albert Einstein

1.

'What do you think?'

'Turn around and let me see.'

'Stanley, you've been looking me up and down for half an hour. I really need to get off this platform.'

'First off, we should bring up the hemline. It would be a crime to cover up legs like yours.'

'Stanley.'

'What, you want my opinion or not? Turn around, show me the front again. Yes, just as I suspected. Same plunging neckline in the front and back. On the bright side, if you spill something on it, you can just put the thing on backward. No one will be able to tell the difference.'

'Stanley!'

'The mere notion of purchasing a wedding gown on sale gives me hives. You might as well just find one on eBay! Sorry if that sounds harsh, baby doll. Just telling it like I see it.'

'Well, excuse me if it's the best I can do on a graphic designer's salary.'

'Come on now. Just say *artist*. Lord, twenty-first-century vocabulary makes me shudder!'

'It's not like I use oil paints, Stanley. I work on a computer.'

'You're my best friend, and I won't listen to you sell yourself short. You draw amazing characters and make them come to life. Computer or not, you're an artist.'

'Fine, fine . . . So do we hem it or leave it be?'

'Two inches higher and we would have to work on the shoulders . . . and bring it in around the waistline.'

'Okay, I get it, you hate the dress.'

'I didn't say I hated it!'

'Not out loud.'

'If you'd just let me help foot the bill, we could go to Anna Maier. I'm begging you here, baby doll, please. Listen to me just this once.'

'Ten thousand dollars on a dress? Are you insane? It's too much, even for you. It's only a wedding, Stanley.'

'Only *your* wedding!'

'That's right. My wedding.' Julia sighed.

'I mean, with the fortune your father's sitting on, you'd think he could at least—'

'The last time I laid eyes on my father was six months ago. At a red light. I was on my bike. He was in his limo, heading down Fifth Ave. And that's that, end of story.'

Julia shrugged and stepped down off the fitting platform. Stanley took her gently by the hand and pulled her in for a hug.

'Baby doll, any dress on you would be a masterpiece; I just want yours to be perfect. And what about Adam? Couldn't he help?'

'I don't know, with Adam's parents already paying for the entire reception, I'd rather not have my future in-laws gossiping about how cheap the bride is.'

Stanley crossed the small boutique discreetly, straight past the sales staff, who were leaning against the counter and chatting away. He grabbed a hanger with a white satin sheath off the rack and brought it back to Julia.

'Not a word! Not even a syllable. Just try it on.'

'It's a size two. How do you expect me to fit into—?'

'Hey! Quiet. What did I say?'

Julia rolled her eyes and made her way into the changing room, closing the curtain with dramatic flair.

A few minutes later the curtain whipped back open just as abruptly.

'Now we're talking! I look at you and I think, *that* could be Julia's wedding dress,' exclaimed Stanley. 'Now get your ass back up on that block.'

'It's so tight in this thing, we're going to need a crowbar to pry it off.'

'Totally worth it. You look drop-dead gorgeous!'

'Except that I feel like it's about to burst at the seams. If I eat one little hors d'oeuvre, it will!'

'One does not eat on one's wedding day. All we need to do is let it out a tiny bit around the bosom, and we're golden. God, are the employees here on strike or just total assholes?'

'Shouldn't I be the one acting all stressed out right now, not you?'

'Stressed out? I don't know, should I be? I mean, we've got a whopping four days until you tie the knot, and yet I have to twist your arm just to get you to try on dresses.'

'You know how buried I am at work right now. And I can't say a word to Adam. I've been swearing up and down that everything has been set for at least a month now.'

Stanley found an abandoned pincushion on the armrest of a chair and knelt at Julia's feet.

'Your future husband has no idea how lucky he is getting hitched to a superstar like you.'

'Again with the jabs at Adam. I don't get what you have against him.'

'Honestly? He reminds me of your father.'

'Are you crazy? Adam is nothing like my father. And he hates him, by the way.'

'Adam hates your father? Maybe I should give him another chance.'

'No, no, no. My father hates Adam.'

'Big surprise. Your father hates everyone you're close to. If you had a dog, he'd probably bite him.'

'Any dog of mine would definitely tear my father to shreds,' Julia said with a laugh.

'Actually I meant your father would bite the dog.'

Stanley rose and took a step back to admire his work. A quick little nod, and then a deep breath.

'What? What is it now?' Julia asked.

'It's perfect. Or rather, you're perfect. Let me adjust the sash a bit, then you can take me out to lunch.'

'Oh, can I? Where am I taking you?'

'Anywhere – as long as there are outside tables and enough shade, I'm a happy camper. Now if you'd just stop squirming, I can finish. Flawless. Well, almost.'

'Why almost?'

Stanley winced. 'Because this gown . . . is on sale, darling.'

A sales assistant finally approached and asked if they needed help with anything. Stanley sent her packing with a flick of his wrist.

'So what's the verdict? You think he'll come?'

'Who?' asked Julia.

'Who do you think? Your father!'

'Him again . . . Forget about it. I told you I haven't heard from him in over a year.'

'That doesn't mean a thing.'

'He won't come!'

'Have you even tried to reach out to him?'

'I gave up pouring my heart out to his personal assistant a long time ago. Talking to the man himself is damn near impossible. Always on a business trip or in a meeting. No way he'd make time for his daughter.'

'But you sent him an invitation?'

'Are you done yet?'

'Getting there. You know, you and your father are like an old married couple. He's just jealous. All fathers are. It'll pass.'

'That's the first time I've ever heard you stick up for him. And if we're an old couple, we're a divorced one. Been that way for years—'

Right on cue 'I Will Survive' started playing from inside Julia's purse. Stanley threw her an inquisitive look.

'Are you going to get that?'

'Oh, it's probably Adam. Or the office.'

'You know what? Let me get it. If you move an inch, you'll mess up everything.'

Stanley dug into Julia's bag, pulled out the phone and handed it to her. Gloria Gaynor fell silent.

'Too late, missed it,' said Julia, glancing at the caller ID.

'Adam? Or work?'

'Neither,' she replied with a frown.

Stanley glared.

'What, do I have to guess?'

'Believe it or not, it was my father's office.'

'Call him back!'

'No way! He wants me, he can pick up the phone and call himself.'

'Wait, you lost me. Isn't that what he just did?'

'No. That was his personal assistant's extension.'

'Cut the pouting-child act. You've been waiting for that call from the moment you dropped his invitation at the post office. Baby doll, four days before your wedding you should be minimizing stress at all costs. If you don't relax, you could get a cold sore or a rash on your back! Just call the man already!'

'Why? Just to listen to Wallace explain that my father sends his sincere regrets, but he'll be unable to attend? That the wedding is unfortunately the very same day as a major business deal and my father will be abroad, tickets are nonrefundable and the trip has been planned for months. Something like that?'

'Or maybe that your father would be delighted to give away his daughter, and he hopes that despite their past differences, she has a seat reserved for him at the head table.'

'Ha! Like he cares about that. Give him a seat next to coat check, as long as there's a pretty girl handing out the tickets.'

'Would you stop hating him for just one minute? Or don't, and you'll spend the entire reception in suspense, worrying about whether he's coming instead of enjoying your own wedding day.'

'Well, at least it'll take my mind off the fact that if I take a single bite, this stupid dress is going to burst!'

'Then have it your way, baby doll!' hissed Stanley as he turned to leave. 'Let's have lunch some other time when you're feeling better.'

Julia took a reckless leap from the platform and ran straight across the boutique after Stanley. She caught him by the shoulder and pulled her friend in for a hug as her eyes welled up with tears.

'I'm sorry, Stanley. I don't know what got into me. Really, I apologize.'

'About your father? Or about the dress? Cos I could point out neither that narrowly diverted disaster of a jump, nor running like a fool across this hellhole, has burst one single stitch.'

'Stanley. I love this dress. I do. And I couldn't imagine anyone but you there beside me when I walk down the aisle.'

Stanley took a silk handkerchief from his pocket and dabbed softly at Julia's tears.

'You really want to walk down the aisle with an old queen like me? Or is this another cockeyed scheme to pass me off as your bastard of a father?'

'Don't flatter yourself. Sorry to say, but I don't think you could pull it off. Not nearly enough wrinkles to play my dad.'

'On the contrary it was a compliment. I was casting you as a woman young enough to play *my* daughter.'

'Stanley, I want you to be the one who gives me away. Who better, huh?'

With a tender smile, Stanley motioned down to Julia's cell phone and said, 'Call your father back. I'll make arrangements with that mouth-breathing clerk, who wouldn't know a customer if it bit her in the ass, to have everything ready for the day after tomorrow. Then off to lunch. Hurry up! I'm starving.'

Stanley turned and headed towards the counter. He looked back and saw Julia hesitate before picking up her phone to call. Stanley took advantage of the distraction to put the whole thing on his card – the dress, the alterations and the forty-eight-hour rush fee included. He slipped the receipt into his pocket and walked back to Julia, who had just got off the phone.

'So?' asked Stanley impatiently. 'Is he coming?'

Julia shook her head.

'Go figure. What's his excuse this time?'

Julia took a deep breath, then looked Stanley in the eye.

'He's dead.'

The two stared at each other in silence, not a single word uttered between them.

'Well, as far as excuses go, that one is airtight,' whispered Stanley.

'You really are an ass, you know that?'

'Shit. That's not what I meant to say. I'm all mixed up – I don't know what I'm saying. I am so sorry for your loss.'

'I . . . really don't feel a thing, Stanley. Not a thing. No tears, no sting, nothing.'

'It'll come, don't you worry. It just hasn't hit yet.'

'I think it has. I think this is it.'

'Do you want to call Adam?'

'No, not now. Later.'

Stanley studied her, the concern leaking through in his voice.

'You . . . don't feel like telling your future husband that you just lost your father?'

'Thing is, he died yesterday. In Paris. So they have to fly the body home. Which makes the funeral . . . four days from now,' she said in a voice that was barely audible.

Stanley counted the days on his fingers – just to be sure.

'Saturday?' he asked, his eyes widening.

'There goes my wedding,' murmured Julia.

Stanley turned on his heel and strode to the cash till, where he had a refund for the rush fee issued to his credit card. Leading Julia out of the store, he patted her softly on the back and declared, 'Lunch is on me.'

The golden light of June bathed the streets of New York as the two friends crossed Ninth Avenue towards Pastis. The French brasserie had become an institution in the fast-changing neighbourhood. In recent years the slaughterhouses of the Meatpacking District had been replaced by top-end stores and the city's most popular designer boutiques. Luxury hotels sprouted from the ground as if by magic. The former overhead railway had been transformed into a broad swathe of green that extended all the way to Tenth Street. A once-renowned cookie factory now housed a bustling organic market on the ground floor, with production houses and PR firms renting the floors above. Julia's office was on the sixth floor. Just to the west lay the banks of the Hudson River, which had become a promenade for bicyclists and joggers, who zipped past couples lingering on park benches – scenes straight out of a Woody Allen movie. From Thursday evenings till the end of the weekend, the area brimmed with the bridge-and-tunnel crowd, who crossed the river to hang out in the fashionable bars and restaurants.

Seated at a table on the outdoor terrace, Stanley ordered a cappuccino for himself and an Earl Grey for Julia.

'I should have called him by now,' said Julia with a guilty groan.

'Yes. You should have called Adam to let him know about your father dying. But if you're worried about announcing that the wedding is postponed, that everyone has to be informed – the priest, caterers, guests and most of all, your future in-laws – I think that can wait awhile. It's a gorgeous day. Give him another hour before you ruin it for him. Besides, you're in mourning – it's the best excuse. Make the most of it.'

'I have no idea what to say.'

'Just tell him, baby doll. It's kind of tough to bury your father and get married on the same day, even if it is tempting to try. My God, what a mess!'

'God's got nothing to do with it. This whole thing has my father written all over it, dying right at that precise moment . . .'

'I'm guessing your father didn't choose to kick the bucket in Paris for the sheer pleasure of derailing your wedding. Though, I must admit, as far as dramatic locations go, impeccable choice.'

'You don't know him like I do. He'd go to the ends of the earth just to interfere with my life.'

'Drink your tea and bask in the sun for five more minutes. Then we're calling your ex-soon-to-be husband.'

2.

The wheels of the Air France cargo jet screeched on to the runway at JFK. Julia watched from behind the tall glass of the main terminal as a long mahogany casket descended the conveyor belt from the cargo hold and continued on towards the hearse parked nearby. An airport security officer came into the waiting room and called for her. Julia got in a minivan and was driven to the plane, accompanied by Adam, Stanley and her father's personal assistant, Wallace. A customs officer handed her an envelope containing some paperwork, a watch and a passport.

Julia flicked through her father's passport, eyes trailing over an array of stamps that told the story of Anthony Walsh's final months on earth: Saint Petersburg, Berlin, Hong Kong, Mumbai, Saigon and Sydney. A whole host of cities Julia had never seen. Destinations she could have only dreamed of discovering with her father.

While four men took care of formalities around the coffin, Julia thought of the long trips her father had always taken, all the way back to when she was just a little girl.

She remembered the endless nights spent waiting with bated breath for her father to come home to their Upper East Side town house. Or the countless days when her morning walk to school became a high-stakes game of sidewalk hopscotch, where only flawless jumps and landings would assure his return. On rare occasions her prayers would be answered. The door of her bedroom would inch open, and an enchanted beam of light would cut across the floor, with Anthony Walsh's silhouette appearing in the doorway. He would sit at the foot of her bed, leaving a little present on the bedspread for her to find in the morning. Her father would bring her a special memento that told the story of the trip he had taken – a doll from Mexico, a calligraphy brush from China, a small wooden figurine from Hungary, a bracelet from Guatemala. These were the hallowed treasures of Julia's childhood.

Then her mother's health started to decline. The earliest episode Julia could recall took place at the movies on a Sunday. In the middle of the film, her mother looked at Julia and asked who had turned all the lights out. The holes in her mother's memory grew insidiously. What began as confusion between the kitchen and the music room grew into frantic screams that the grand piano had disappeared. The vanishing of objects slowly morphed into forgetting the names of her nearest and dearest, and at last descended into the deepest darkness when she looked at Julia and asked, 'What is this pretty little girl doing in my house?' One dreary December day she set her dressing gown on fire, and she was taken away by ambulance soon after. She lay perfectly still all the while, marvelling at the hypnotic power of lighting a cigarette – this from a woman who had never smoked in her life.

Her mother almost never recognized Julia again. She died at a New Jersey clinic a few years later. As the period of mourning gave way to real life, Julia's adolescence became locked into a tightly packed routine, with evening after dismal evening spent studying under the supervision of her father's personal assistant. Her father's business trips became longer and more frequent. High school passed by in a flash. In college, life came to a halt when for the second time she lost someone she loved. After leaving school Julia devoted herself to her passion: creating characters, sketching them on paper and bringing them to life on a computer screen. Her animals became almost human to her. They were her companions and faithful friends, whose smiles she conjured with a stroke of her pencil and whose tears she dried with her eraser.

'Miss, can you confirm that this was your father's passport?'

Julia was jerked back to reality by the customs officer's voice. She nodded in response. The man signed a form and brought a stamp down over Anthony Walsh's photo, the final mark in a passport whose many destinations told of a life spent far away from his daughter – a life of absence. The casket was loaded into a big black hearse. Stanley climbed into the front seat beside the driver, while Adam opened the passenger door for Julia, being especially attentive to the woman he was supposed to have married that very afternoon. Anthony's personal assistant sat astride a fold-out seat in the back, closest to the body. The funeral procession rolled on out of the airport and straight on to the expressway.

The passengers rode in silence as they continued further north. Julia cast a glance around the hearse. Wallace's eyes remained fixed on the box containing the remains of his former employer. Stanley stared down at his hands. She caught Adam looking at her before she turned away to gaze at the grey sprawl of New York City's outer reaches.

'Excuse me, can I ask which route you're taking?' Julia asked the driver as a sign for the Long Island Expressway appeared ahead.

'Whitestone Bridge, ma'am,' he responded.

'Could you take the Brooklyn Bridge please, if you don't mind? Thanks.'

The driver put on his indicator and changed lanes.

'That's a huge detour,' whispered Adam. 'Whitestone would have been the fastest way.'

'Today is a lost cause anyway. We might as well try to make him happy.'

'Who?' Adam asked.

'My father. I think he would have liked the idea of one last drive through Manhattan.'

'Sure, fair enough,' Adam said. 'But we should give the priest a heads-up to let him know we're going to be late.'

'Are you a dog person, Adam?' asked Stanley.

'Sure, I guess. I like dogs. They don't always like me. Why?'

'No reason. Just wondering,' responded Stanley, rolling down his window as far as it would go.

They drove the length of Manhattan and arrived at 233rd Street over an hour later.

The main gate of Woodlawn Cemetery opened, and the hearse turned on to a narrow road, went round a roundabout, passed a row of mausoleums and crossed a bridge overlooking a lake, finally coming to a stop on a tree-lined lane, where a freshly dug grave lay waiting to greet its brand-new tenant.

The priest stood waiting for them. While the casket was being readied, Adam went over to greet him and explain the final details of the ceremony. Stanley put his arm around Julia's shoulders.

'What are you thinking about, baby doll?' he asked.

'What am I thinking about as I bury my father, whom I haven't talked to in over a year? Take a wild guess. You and your sense of timing, Stanley.'

'That's not what I meant. I'm serious: what are you thinking about right now? Whatever it is, you'll remember it for a long time. This moment will always be part of your life, believe me.'

'I was thinking about Mom. I was wondering if she would recognize him up there in the clouds, or if she's spending eternity wandering around in a confused haze.'

'Wait, you're suddenly signing on to God and the afterlife?'

'Not necessarily. Just wishful thinking.'

'Well, I have to admit – and don't laugh – as time goes by, God does seem more and more real, even to me.'

Julia smiled sadly.

'If there is a God, I'm not sure that would be the best news for my father to be honest.'

'The priest would like to get started,' said Adam as he returned, eyeing his watch. 'He just wanted to make sure this is everyone.'

'It's just the four of us,' Julia replied, motioning for her Wallace to come and join them. 'The price you pay as a globetrotter. Family and friends are nothing but a cluster of vague acquaintances scattered to the four corners of the earth. Not the type of people who make the trip for a funeral, and it's not like the departed can call in any favours. You're born alone and you die alone.'

'Didn't Buddha say that? Your father was a staunch Irish Catholic, honey,' Adam replied.

'A Dobermann. I can just see you with an enormous Dobermann,' Stanley said with a sigh.

'What's the deal with you wanting me to have a dog all of a sudden?'

'Nothing. Forget it.'

The priest came over to tell Julia how sorry he was to be there officiating at a funeral when he had originally been brought on for Julia's wedding.

'Too bad you can't just kill two birds with one stone,' Julia said. 'When you think about it, who cares about the guests? It's the thought that counts as far as the man upstairs is concerned. Am I right?'

Stanley fought to stifle a giggle, and the priest glared at him before shifting his disdain back to Julia.

'Really, miss . . .'

'Hey, it's not the worst idea in the world! I mean, in a way my father could still attend.'

'Julia!' Adam reproached her.

'Okay, I get it. Survey says: bad idea,' she conceded.

'Do you have a few words you'd like to say?' asked the priest.

'I wish I did. But I don't think so.' Julia just gazed at the casket. 'What about you, Wallace?' she asked her father's personal assistant. 'After all, you were his most trusted friend.'

'I don't think I'm quite capable, ma'am,' responded Wallace. 'And come to think of it, the relationship between your father and I was a sort of . . . silent camaraderie. But I do have something to tell you if I might. I'd like to say that despite all his faults, despite his sometimes hardened demeanour, your father was a good man. A good man who loved you very dearly.'

'How perfect. The assistant does the heavy lifting, even postmortem,' Stanley murmured as Julia's eyes started to well up.

The priest recited a prayer and closed his missal. Anthony Walsh's coffin slowly descended into the ground. Julia handed a rose to Wallace. He smiled warmly and handed it back.

'Please. You first, Miss Julia.'

Julia dropped her rose, and the petals came off as it struck the wood. Three other roses fell in turn, and the four mourners started making their way back towards the cars.

Further down the cemetery road, two town cars now sat idling where the hearse had been just moments earlier. Adam took Julia by the hand to lead her along. She lifted her eyes to the sky.

'A few fluffy white clouds and a pure blue sky as far as the eye can see. Not too hot and not too cold. No shadows, no chills. An absolutely *perfect* day for a wedding.'

'There will be other days like this, don't worry,' Adam reassured her.

'You think?' Julia exclaimed, her arms opened wide with exasperation. 'A sky like that? The perfect temperature. Sunlight making the trees greener than green. Ducks gliding along the surface of the pond.

There won't be another day like this for the rest of the year. We'll have to wait until next spring.'

'Fall weddings can be beautiful, too. And since when do you care about ducks?'

'Since they started following me around! Did you see how many were out there just now, right near my father's grave?'

'No, I didn't happen to notice,' responded Adam, not quite knowing how to handle this sudden burst of energy from his fiancée.

'Dozens upon dozens of mallards, all donning picture-perfect bow ties. They landed right there and then flew away as soon as the ceremony was over. They clearly came for my wedding but ended up at my father's funeral instead.'

'Julia, obviously I don't want to nitpick, not at a time like this, but . . . ducks don't really wear bow ties.'

'And how would you know? Do you draw ducks? I do. If I say they were wearing bow ties and suits for the ceremony, then believe me I would know!' she cried.

'Okay, honey. The ducks were in black tie, whatever you say. Let's go home now.'

Stanley and Wallace were waiting for them near the cars. Adam led Julia forward, but she stopped in front of a gravestone, a crooked slab of rock jutting out of the grass. She read aloud the name and date of birth of the person buried beneath her feet.

'That's my grandmother's. My whole family is buried in this cemetery now. I'm the last of the Walsh family line. My line anyway – not counting the hundreds of uncles, aunts and cousins in Brooklyn, Chicago and Ireland, come to think of it. Never met a single one. I'm sorry I freaked out just now. I think I got a little carried away.'

'No big deal. We were supposed to be getting married, and instead you have to bury your father. I think anybody would understand why you'd be upset.'

They continued down the lane, making their way towards the two Lincolns.

'And you know what? You were right about today,' continued Adam, looking skyward. 'It's the perfect day for a wedding. He really did screw things up, right to the bitter end.'

Julia stiffened and pulled her hand away from his.

'Don't give me that look,' pleaded Adam. 'You've been saying the exact same thing ever since he died!'

'Right. Me! I'm allowed to say it as much as I want. Not you. You take Stanley's car. I'll take this one.'

'Julia! Come on. I'm sorry.'

'Don't be. I just want to be alone tonight. I have to put my father's affairs in order, if you don't mind. The same father who had to screw things up right to the bitter end, just like you said.'

'For God's sake, Julia, those were your words, not mine. Yours!' cried Adam as Julia got into the first of the two sedans.

'Oh, and one last thing. I've decided that the day we get married, I want *ducks*. Mallards. Dozens of mallards!' she added, slamming the door.

Her car rolled away through the cemetery gate. Adam got in the second car in a huff and settled into the back seat next to Wallace.

'Maybe what you really need is a fox terrier. They're small, but they sure pack a mean bite,' Stanley concluded from the front seat before signalling the driver to start the car.

3.

Julia's car inched down Fifth Avenue through an unexpected down-pour. The traffic was bumper to bumper, and they were at a standstill for several minutes. Julia stared at the elaborate window display of the immense toy store at the corner of Fifty-Eighth Street. Prominently placed in the window was a creature she recognized instantly: a giant stuffed otter with steel-blue fur.

◆ ◆ ◆

Tilly had been born in the afternoon, on a Saturday not unlike this one, with the rain pouring down so hard it created little streams that glided down Julia's office window. As her mind drifted, the streaks of rain transformed into rivers. The wooden window frame became the banks of an Amazonian estuary. The wet leaves outside, formed into clumps by the rain, became the home of a sweet little otter who would soon be swept downriver by the flood, much to the dismay of the greater otter community.

The rain continued straight through into that fateful evening. Alone in the animation studio where she worked, Julia completed the first sketches of the character. Countless thousands of hours in front of her computer screen would follow, a combination of drawing, colouring, animation and design that would bring the blue otter alive down to the most nuanced details of her facial expressions. A myriad of late-night meetings and weekends were devoted to crafting the rich world of Tilly and her friends. Julia's brainchild had captivated her bosses, who quickly bought into the idea. While they took off running with the Tilly franchise, all Julia received in return for creating the studio's big hit was a promotion and her name in the list of credits.

'This is fine,' Julia told the driver. 'I can walk from here.'

The driver asked if she was sure, reminding her of the downpour still raging outside.

'It's the best thing that's happened all day,' she assured him, closing the door a split second later.

What did the rain matter when Tilly seemed to be smiling at her through the glass, just begging her to visit? Julia couldn't help herself and waved. To her surprise, a little girl standing next to the stuffed animal waved back. The little girl's mother rushed over and pulled her away. She tried to steer her daughter towards the exit, but the girl resisted and jumped into the otter's open arms. Julia watched the girl cling to Tilly. The mother smacked her hand, trying to make her daughter let go of the stuffed animal's giant paw. Julia entered the store and walked over to the two.

'Hi. Did you know that Tilly actually has magic powers?' Julia asked the little girl.

'If we need a salesperson, we'll let you know,' replied the woman, her harsh gaze still fixed on her daughter.

'I'm not a salesperson. I'm her mother.'

'Excuse me?' the woman said, raising her voice. 'I'm fairly certain that I'm her mother, thank you very much!'

'No, I meant Tilly's, the otter that seems to have attached herself to your daughter. I was the one who created her. With your permission I'd love to buy Tilly for your daughter as a gift. It makes me sad to see

Tilly all alone under these bright lights in the window. Under lights like these her colours will start to fade, and she's so proud of her steel-blue coat. It took us hours – longer than you could imagine – to get her colours just right. The nape of her neck, her throat, her belly, her face. She's happy just being who she is, even though her house was washed away downriver.'

'I'm afraid your Tilly will not be coming home with us today. And as for my daughter, she has to learn to stay close to her mother when we come to the city!' the mother replied, yanking at the girl's arm and finally breaking her grip.

'That's a shame. Tilly would be so happy to have a friend,' insisted Julia.

'You're talking about a stuffed animal,' the woman said, dumbfounded.

'It's been a rough day. If Tilly went home with you, she would be so happy. So would I, and your little girl, too, from the looks of it. Just one small *yes* to make three of us happy. Not too much to ask, wouldn't you say?'

'No, I would not. There will be no presents for Alice today, especially not from a stranger. Goodbye,' the woman said, turning to go.

'Too bad! Alice seems like a fine little girl. And considering the way you treat her, it'll be a miracle if that lasts!' Julia blurted out, trying to hold back her anger.

The mother turned and glared at her.

'You designed a stuffed animal. I gave birth to a child. You can keep your advice to yourself.'

'You're right. Children aren't like toys. When something is broken, you can't just patch up the damage and make it all better.'

Outraged, the woman stormed out of the toy store. The mother and daughter disappeared down Fifth Avenue without looking back.

'I'm sorry, Tilly,' said Julia to the otter. 'Not very diplomatic, was it? Oh well, that's never really been my strong suit. Don't you worry. We're going to find you the perfect family. You'll see. A family just for you.'

The store manager, who had watched the whole exchange, at last came over to Julia.

'Well, hello, Miss Walsh. So nice to see you. It's been – what – at least a month?'

'I've had a lot going on at work these past few weeks.'

'Let me tell you, your character has been a huge hit around here. This is the tenth we've ordered. Most of the time we only have to leave one in the window four days before it's sold,' he assured her, putting the stuffed animal back in its place. 'Though with this one it's been, well, just over two weeks if I'm not mistaken. Maybe it's the weather . . .'

'No, it's not that,' replied Julia. 'This is the original, so it's a bit more difficult. She has to take the time to choose the right family.'

'Miss Walsh, you say that every time you come to see us,' the manager said with a chuckle.

'What can I say? They're all one of a kind.' Julia smiled, waving goodbye.

The rain had stopped. Julia left the store and headed downtown, disappearing into the haze rising from the wet, crowded sidewalk.

◆ ◆ ◆

All along Horatio Street the trees sagged with the weight of rain-soaked leaves. The sun had finally re-emerged in the early evening, only to slink down into the Hudson shortly thereafter. The side streets of the West Village glowed with a soft purple light. Julia said hello to the owner of a Greek restaurant as he set up outdoor tables on the sidewalk across the street from her apartment. He returned her greeting and asked if he should save her a table for that evening. She politely declined but promised to come for Sunday brunch someday soon.

Julia unlocked the front door of the small building where she lived and stepped inside. She climbed the stairs to the second floor and was surprised to find Stanley waiting for her, sitting on the top step.

'Hey. How did you get in?'

'The guy who runs the store downstairs, Zimoure. He was hauling some boxes down to the basement and I lent him a hand. We talked all about his new shoe collection. It's really something! But I can't imagine many people these days can treat themselves to such works of art.'

'Judging by all the shoppers who flood into his store on weekends and leave with stacks of shoe boxes, I'd say quite a few. So, is there something you wanted?' she asked as she opened the door to her apartment.

'No, I just thought you could use some company.'

'Ha! Me? You're the one with the sad puppy-dog face.'

'Oh, this? It's all an act. That's why I invited myself over, too. All so you can save face.'

Julia took off her jacket and flung it on an armchair next to the fireplace. The scent of the wisteria coating the brick facade of the building wafted in through an open window and filled the room.

'Mmm . . . so cozy!' Stanley commented, collapsing on the sofa.

'That's at least one thing I can claim to have accomplished this year,' remarked Julia as she swung open the fridge door.

'What was, baby doll?'

'Fixing up this dump. Can I get you a beer?'

'I'd call it more of a work in progress. And I'm watching the carbs. Maybe a glass of wine, though.'

Julia quickly set out a cheese platter for two, opened a bottle of wine and put on a Count Basie CD. Stanley whistled with admiration at the label on the cabernet.

'Quite the party,' said Julia as she sat down. 'All we need is two hundred guests and some hors d'oeuvres and you could mistake it for my wedding.'

'In that case, may I have this dance?' asked Stanley.

Before she could reply, he pulled her to her feet and led her into a swing.

'See? Our own private party,' he said, laughing.

'What would I do without you, Stanley?'

'You know as well as I do. You'd be lost.'

The music ended and Stanley sat down.

'Have you talked to Adam since this afternoon?'

Julia had apologized to her future husband over the phone on the long, rainy walk home from the toy store. Adam had been supportive and understanding about her need to be alone. He apologized for having been so awkward during the funeral. He had called his mother during the trip home from the cemetery, and she had scolded him for being so insensitive. Now he was heading to his parents' country house to spend the rest of the weekend with his family.

'Between you and me? Maybe your father's funeral falling on your wedding day wasn't altogether a bad thing,' whispered Stanley as he poured himself a second glass.

'Why don't you just admit it already? You don't like Adam.'

'Honey, I never said that!'

'You should be happy for me. I spent three full years alone in a city with two million singles. Adam is kind. He's generous and thoughtful. He puts up with my crazy work hours, and he loves me just the way I am. How about you try showing a little support here?'

'I don't have anything against Adam. He's perfect. But I'd rather see you head over heels, even if your Romeo is loaded with flaws, than settling for someone just because he has a laundry list of good qualities.'

'Easy for you to say. Why are you still single?'

'I'm not single, I'm a widower. Just because the man I loved is dead doesn't mean he's gone. You should have seen him, my sweet Edward, dashing even on his deathbed. The sickness couldn't take his looks or his sense of humour. Down to his last words.'

'I don't think you've ever told me his last words. What were they?' asked Julia as she took Stanley's hand.

'"I love you."'

The two friends sat in silence for a moment. Stanley got up, put on his jacket and kissed Julia on the forehead.

'You win. I'm off to bed. Guess I am lonely tonight after all.'

'Come on, stay awhile. What's saying "I love you" have to do with a sense of humour?'

'Well, it was the least he could do, considering it was cheating on me that did him in,' Stanley said with an impish smile.

The next morning Julia opened her eyes and found herself on the couch under a throw that Stanley had placed over her. Within moments she noticed a note tucked under a mug that read, *Don't forget, no matter what happens, you're my best friend and I love you. – Stanley.*

4.

At ten o'clock Julia left her apartment to spend the day at the office. The decision had come easily. Not only had she fallen behind at work, but she reckoned that staying cooped up at home in a hapless attempt to organize things that would almost certainly crumble into disorder was the last thing she needed. And Stanley was also a no-go. With the exception of being dragged out to brunch or tempted with cinnamon pancakes, the man rarely got out of bed before mid-afternoon on a Sunday.

Horatio Street was still empty. At Pastis, Julia waved to a few neighbours sitting outside and then quickened her pace. As she walked up Ninth Avenue, she sent Adam an affectionate text. Two blocks later she entered Chelsea Market. The elevator operator took her to the top floor. She slid her security badge across the reader and pushed open the heavy iron door.

Three of her coworkers were seated at their desks. Judging from their weary faces and the crumpled coffee cups overflowing the trash, it seemed they had pulled an all-nighter. Her team had been struggling with the same issue for over a week now. And the bedraggled animators before her were proof that they still had yet to crack the algorithm that would animate a squadron of dragonflies meant to defend a castle from an invading army of praying mantises. The schedule, ominously posted on the wall, stated that the deadline was Monday. If the squadron didn't take flight within twenty-four hours, the citadel would fall into enemy hands and production would fall drastically behind schedule. Neither was an option.

Julia rolled her office chair over to her colleagues. She reviewed their progress and immediately decided to activate the emergency plan. She got on the phone and made call after call, apologizing each time for ruining a perfectly nice Sunday afternoon but insisting her entire team be in the conference room within the hour. By midday thirty-seven people had answered Julia's call. The quiet morning atmosphere of the office gave way to a hive of activity. Illustrators, graphic designers, colourists, programmers and animation experts discussed reports, analyses and far-fetched schemes.

At five a rookie team member's novel idea unleashed a new burst of energy. And soon the first dragonfly began beating its wings in the middle of the screen. The entire room fell silent. Julia was the first to congratulate him, followed by a full round of applause from her team. Now all they had to do was get the other 740 armour-wearing dragonflies into the air. The young man's confidence swelled and he set out a method they might use to reproduce the formula on a larger scale. The phone rang in the middle of his explanation. The assistant who answered gestured discreetly to Julia that the call was for her and that it seemed rather urgent. Julia asked the person next to her to take careful notes and went to take the call from her office.

Julia immediately recognized the voice of Mr Zimoure, who owned the store on the ground floor of her building. She worried that the plumbing in her apartment was causing problems yet again. Water was no doubt streaming through the ceiling down on to pairs of Mr Zimoure's shoes, each of which cost nearly half her monthly salary (or a quarter if they were on sale). The year before the price of the shoes had come as an absolute shock to Julia when her insurer sent a large cheque to Mr Zimoure to cover the water damage she had caused. All Julia had done was forget to close the valve on her archaic washing machine before leaving her apartment. Didn't everybody make that mistake once in a while?

At the time her insurer had insisted the company would never cover a problem like that again. He had made an exception that time, and it was a miracle he had managed to talk his superiors out of simply cancelling her policy on the spot. The extra effort he made was due solely to the fact that Tilly was his kids' favourite cartoon character, and the Tilly DVDs were a savior for him on Sunday mornings.

Reestablishing good-natured neighbourly relations with Mr Zimoure had been a far greater undertaking, one which required significant effort on Julia's part. It took an unaccepted invitation to Thanksgiving dinner at Stanley's house, a gentle reminder of forgiveness over Christmas and a great deal of attention before the icy mood between the two neighbours thawed to its normal chilled state. Zimoure was rather unpleasant, with an opinion on everything, and he only ever laughed at his own jokes. Julia held her breath as she waited for the damage report from the other end of the line.

'Ms Walsh—'

'Mr Zimoure, let me start by saying how very sorry I am for . . . whatever has happened.'

'Not as sorry as I am, Ms Walsh. I have a store packed with clients, and I have better things to do with my time than tend to a delivery that's addressed to you.'

Julia tried to slow down her heart rate and understand exactly what Mr Zimoure was telling her.

'I'm sorry, what delivery?'

'You tell me.'

'I haven't ordered anything. I always have deliveries sent to the office.'

'Well, not this time. Or else how do you explain the enormous truck parked in front of my window? Ms Walsh, Sunday is my busiest day, and I can't have this driving away my clientele. I have two brutes here who have unloaded your crate and refuse to leave until somebody signs for it. What do you suggest I do?'

'Did you say a crate? Are you sure?'

'What did I just say? Do I have to keep all my customers waiting while I repeat everything for you?'

'I just don't understand, Mr Zimoure,' Julia said. 'I don't know what to tell you.'

'How about you tell me when you'll be here? That way I can let these guys know how much more time we'll all be wasting while we wait for you.'

'But I really can't come home right now. I'm in the middle of something very important at work and—'

'And I suppose you think I'm over here twiddling my thumbs.'

'Mr Zimoure, I'm really not expecting a delivery. Not a single box or envelope, and certainly not a crate! There has to be a mistake.'

'Are you sure about that? Because right now, with your delivery sitting on the sidewalk *right outside my store*, I can see your name on the label as we speak, even without my glasses. Right in front of me, clearly printed in capital letters: our address and the word *fragile*. So maybe, just maybe you forgot. Unless I need to remind you about the last time you were forgetful . . .'

Julia had no idea who could have sent her a crate. Could it be a present from Adam? An order for work that had accidentally been sent to her home address? Either way Julia couldn't abandon her team – not after calling them into the office on a Sunday. But given Mr Zimoure's tone, she had to think of something. And quick.

'Okay. I have an idea of how to solve our problem . . . if you'd be willing to help out just a tiny bit.'

'Of course. Your solution couldn't possibly involve just one person, namely *you*, Ms Walsh. That would be a miracle.'

Julia explained that she had hidden a spare key to her apartment under the staircase carpet sixth step up. Count six steps, and he'd find it. Unless it was actually the seventh. Or come to think of it, it could be the eighth . . . Mr Zimoure could then let the delivery men into her apartment. As soon as they were in, she was sure the truck blocking his window would disappear and all this would be behind them.

'Except . . . I will have to wait for them to leave I suppose. And lock the apartment door behind them.'

'Mr Zimoure. Always one step ahead.'

'Yes, well, let me just say if this is another washing machine, Ms Walsh, maybe you should consider having it installed by a professional. Do you catch my drift?'

Julia was about to reassure Mr Zimoure that she had ordered no such thing, but her neighbour had already hung up. She stared at the phone for a minute and then returned to the task at hand.

As night fell the team gathered in front of the massive projector screen in the executive conference room. A few more hours of work and the battle of the dragonflies might actually be ready to go on time. The programmers were adjusting their calculations, the graphic designers tweaking the backgrounds and Julia began to feel superfluous. She wandered into the break room, where she found Dray, an illustrator who was an old friend from college.

As Julia stretched her back, Dray asked if she was feeling sore, then added that she should probably just go home, that she was lucky to live only a couple of blocks away and should take advantage of it. He promised to call and check in with her just as soon as they were finished. As touched as she was by his concern, Julia thought it best to stay with the troops. Dray delicately explained that her pacing from office to office wasn't helping anyone and it really only served to intensify the general feeling of exhaustion.

'Since when has my presence been some kind of burden?' demanded Julia.

'Come on, don't overreact. Everybody's on edge. We haven't had a day off in six weeks!'

Julia herself was supposed to be off for a whole week, and Dray teased her that the staff had actually been looking forward to the break.

'We just all thought you'd be on your honeymoon right now,' Dray went on sheepishly. 'Don't take it the wrong way. It's just the price you pay for being the boss. Ever since you were named creative director, you're not just another team member. You represent management. The *brass*. Look at today. All you had to do was pick up the phone and everybody shows up on a Sunday!'

'I thought the project was important. It was worth it, wasn't it?' Julia asked. 'But hey, I wouldn't want my authority stifling everyone's creativity. So, you win. I'm off. But call me the moment you finish. Because brass or not, I'm still part of the team.'

Julia grabbed her raincoat, double-checked that her keys were in the pocket of her jeans and crossed the space towards the elevator. She dialled Adam's number on the way out of the building, but it went straight to voicemail.

'It's me,' she said after the beep. 'I just wanted to hear your voice. Yesterday was a gloomy Saturday . . . now a depressing Sunday to cap it all off. I'm not so sure it was a good idea being alone after all. At least you didn't have to deal with my bad mood. My own team even kicked me out of the office. I'm going to walk around for a while. Maybe you're already back from the country and in bed. I'm sure your mother must have worn you out, but I would have loved a call or a text. You're probably sleeping now, so no point in asking you to call me back. Anyway, I'm rambling. See you tomorrow. Call me when you wake up. Love you.'

Julia slipped her phone back into her purse and went for a stroll along the river. When she got home half an hour later, she found an envelope with her name scrawled on it taped to the front door of the building. The note inside said:

> *I lost a customer due to your delivery. I put the key back where I found it. PS It was the eleventh step, not the sixth, seventh or eighth! Hope you enjoyed your Sunday!*

There was no signature.

'Why not just post an invitation to burglars?' she grumbled to herself.

As she climbed the stairs to the second floor, she thought about the delivery, and her curiosity grew with each step. She quickened her pace and fished out the key from under the stairway carpet, annoyed that she would now have to find a new hiding place for it. She swung the door open, switched on the lights and stepped into her apartment.

Dead centre in the middle of her living room, dominating the entire space, was an enormous wooden packing crate.

'What on earth?' she muttered out loud, abandoning her things on the coffee table.

The label did indeed bear her name and address, just below the word *fragile*. Julia took cautious steps around the gigantic wooden crate. She pushed against it, but the monstrosity was so heavy she couldn't budge it one inch. And because she owned neither a hammer nor screw-driver, she couldn't begin to think how to open the thing.

Since her call to Adam had gone straight to voicemail, she resorted to her usual backup plan: Stanley.

'Hi there. Am I bothering you?'

'Of course not,' replied Stanley sarcastically. 'What else would I be doing late on Sunday night except sitting by the phone waiting for you to call?'

'Please tell me you didn't have this stupid six-foot-tall box delivered to my house.'

'I don't have the faintest clue what you're talking about.'

'Okay then. Had to ask. Next question: how does one open a stupid six-foot-tall box?'

'Depends. What is said box made of?'

'Wood.'

'How about a saw?'

'Gosh, thanks, Stanley. I'll just grab my saw out of my purse.'

'And what exactly is inside the box if you don't mind my enquiring?'

'I couldn't tell you. I have to be able to open it first. If you're that curious, hop in a taxi and come give me a hand.'

'I'm in my PJs, baby doll.'

'I thought you were on your way out for the night.'

'I'm already in bed!'

'Oh, okay. I'm sorry. I'll manage by myself.'

'Hold your horses. Does the box have any handles?'

'No.'

'Are there hinges anywhere?'

'Not that I can see.'

'Well, what if it's a piece of modern art? *The Unopenable Box*, signed by some famous artist,' Stanley said with a wry chuckle.

Julia's silence let Stanley know she was in no mood for jokes.

'Have you tried giving it a little nudge? You know, just some oomph! A bit of elbow grease like when a door gets stuck.'

As Stanley continued spouting ideas, Julia placed a hand against the wood. All it took was the slightest nudge, as Stanley had suggested, in just the right place and the side of the crate suddenly swung open.

One glance inside and Julia's heart nearly stopped. Flabbergasted, she dropped the phone.

'Hello? Hello?' Stanley called into the receiver. 'Julia! Are you still there?'

Stanley's voice crackled from the phone at Julia's feet. Without taking her eyes off the case, she slowly bent down to pick it up.

'Stanley . . . ?' Julia's voice came out as a croak.

'You scared the shit out of me! Are you all right?'

'I guess . . . sort of.'

'Should I get dressed? Do you need me to come over?'

'No, don't bother.'

'Did you manage to get it open?'

'Yes,' she said, voice gone numb. 'I'll call you tomorrow.'

'You're making me a little nervous here, baby doll.'

'Go back to bed, Stanley. Good night.'

Julia hung up before Stanley could say another word.

'Who could have thought up something like this?' she asked, alone in the middle of her apartment.

Inside the crate stood a perfect life-size wax replica of her father, Anthony Walsh. The resemblance was uncanny. If the eyes had been open, it would have seemed completely alive. Julia could barely breathe. A bead of sweat rolled down the back of her neck. She edged closer. The statue was incredible, the colour and texture of the skin astonishingly lifelike. The clothes – the shoes, the charcoal-grey suit and the white cotton shirt – were all identical to those Anthony Walsh had always worn, down to the last detail. She was tempted to touch its cheek or pluck out a hair just to reassure herself that it wasn't actually him. But Julia and her father had long since lost the habit of any sort of easy, natural physical contact. By the end there were no hugs or kisses to speak of, and even touching each other's hands was avoided. The smallest ounce of tenderness in any gesture was strictly out of bounds. It was impossible to bridge the distance that had grown between them over the years, and Julia wasn't going to start trying now, all alone with this eerie statue.

Julia tried to come to terms with the reality of the bizarre object standing in front of her. Somebody had created a waxwork figure of Anthony Walsh, just like the ones in the museums in Quebec, Paris and London, but even more realistic. The strange thing facing her was like a carbon copy of her father. Julia wanted to scream.

Studying the figure more closely, she noticed a little piece of paper pinned to the outside of its sleeve. A small arrow drawn in blue ink pointed to the breast pocket of the suit jacket. Julia unpinned the note and read the three words scribbled on the back: *Turn me on.* Even more disconcerting: the note was in her father's unmistakable handwriting.

Within the breast pocket, the spot normally occupied by her father's signature silk handkerchief, Julia found a small remote control with a white rectangular button in the centre.

Julia thought she might faint. This had to be a bad dream. Any minute now she would wake up and laugh at herself for having believed all this was real. As she'd watched her father's coffin sink into the ground, she had promised herself that the period of mourning was over. She would never again lament his being gone, not after having spent the past thirty years suffering from the void left by his absence. Her father had all but abandoned her, absent night after night throughout her childhood, and there was no way she would let his ghost come back to haunt her by night as an adult.

Then the sound of the dumpster clattering on the street below convinced Julia this was no dream at all. She was clearly awake. Standing in front of her was the improbable statue. With eyes shut tight, it seemed to be just waiting for her to reach out and push the button on the remote control . . .

The garbage truck rumbled off down the street. She wished it hadn't. She could have run to the window and begged the garbage men to take this nightmare out of her apartment. But the street was silent now.

Her finger gently grazed the button of the remote control, but she couldn't muster the courage to push it.

She had to get rid of the ghastly thing. It would probably be best if she closed the crate, looked up the address of the delivery company on the label and called first thing in the morning. She would tell them to come take this monstrosity away and demand the name of the person responsible. Who among her friends could have actually thought up such a prank? Who could be capable of pulling off something so sick and cruel?

Julia opened the window wide and filled her lungs with soft night air.

Outside, the world was just as she had left it. The tables at the Greek restaurant were all stacked up and the neon sign turned off. A woman crossed the intersection walking her dog. The chocolate Lab darted forward in all directions, pulling at its leash and sniffing around the base of street lamps and walls.

Julia held her breath and felt her grip tighten around the remote. She ran through a list of contacts in her head, and only one name came back to her over and over again – there was only one person she could imagine who would be capable of pulling off something like this. Driven by the anger welling up from the pit of her stomach, Julia spun around, determined to confirm her suspicions.

She pushed the button. There was a click. The statue's eyelids opened and its face broke into a broad grin.

Then as clear as day, with the voice of her deceased father the strange object opened its mouth and spoke.

'Did you miss me?'

5.

'I'm going to wake up. None of this is even remotely possible. Say it! Tell me I'm not going crazy.'

'Come now, Julia, calm down,' the thing replied with her father's voice.

The strange figure stepped out of the box and stretched. The accuracy of his movements was astonishing, down to the smallest details of his face.

'You're not going crazy,' he continued. 'Just in a bit of shock. And given the situation that's a perfectly normal reaction.'

'Nothing about this is perfectly normal! "You" cannot be here. This is impossible!'

'Right you are. "I" can't be here. But then again, what's standing before you is not truly "me" at all.'

Julia covered her mouth with her hand, then broke into an uncontrollable fit of laughter.

'Wow. I almost bought it, I really did. Reality check: I must be fast asleep right now. I can't drink white wine. What an idiot! One glass too many and my imagination gets the better of me,' she continued, pacing around the room. 'I have to admit, I've had some crazy dreams before, but this one takes the cake!'

'That's enough now, Julia,' her father commanded gently. 'I assure you you are awake. You're perfectly lucid.'

'That . . . I highly doubt. Cos I'm looking right at you and I'm talking to you. And you . . . are dead.'

Her father looked at her in silence for a moment, before gently replying, 'Yes, Julia. I'm dead.'

She stood frozen, unable to do anything but stare at him, until Anthony put his hand on her shoulder and gestured to the sofa.

'Why don't you take a seat for a moment and hear me out?'

'No!' she said, pulling away.

'Julia, listen to me. For one minute.'

'But what if I don't want to? You think you can always have things just the way you want them?'

'No, that ship has sailed. You're in full control. All you have to do is push that button once more and you'll turn me straight off. But you'll never get an explanation as to how or why this came to be.'

Julia looked at the remote in her hand, thoughts racing. With all her instincts screaming at her to push the button, she gritted her teeth and sat down, obeying the strange being that so eerily resembled her father.

'Fine. I'm listening,' she muttered.

'I can understand how all this could be a bit . . . disorienting. Frankly I can't even recall the last time we were in touch.'

'One year, eight months—'

'That long?'

'And twenty-two days.'

'That's terribly precise. How can you be so sure?'

'Well, it's kind of tough to forget your own birthday. Last year I got a lovely call from your personal assistant saying that you were running late and we should start dinner without you. Then you never showed.'

'I don't remember that.'

'I do.'

'Anyway, it's certainly not the question at hand, now is it?'

'I don't recall asking a question,' Julia replied dryly.

'Let's see, where to begin . . .'

'Try the beginning. "Every story has one." Isn't that one of your little catchphrases? Start there and tell me what the hell is going on.'

'Very well. It started a few years ago when I became a shareholder at a company specializing in cutting-edge technology. A few months in there was already a serious uptick in revenue, and the value of my shares followed suit. I found myself chairman of the board of directors.'

'So your conglomerate swallowed another fledging company.'

'No, on this occasion my investment was strictly personal. I was just one of many shareholders, but with a significant stake.'

'And just what was this cutting-edge technology you personally invested in?'

'Androids.'

'What?' Julia exclaimed.

'You heard me. Humanoids if you prefer.'

'What in the world for?'

'Well, it wasn't exactly reinventing the wheel. They were developing robots in human form to perform the menial tasks people would just as soon pass on doing themselves.'

'Okay. So, you're back from the dead to vacuum my apartment.'

'Shopping, home security, answering phone calls, providing useful information – all this falls under the umbrella of potential functions. But at my behest the company set about launching a far more ambitious undertaking.'

'Meaning . . . ?'

'Meaning our aim was to provide loved ones with the impossible: a few more days with the dearly departed.'

Julia was taken aback. She was having difficulty processing what he was saying.

Anthony continued: 'A few extra days. Postmortem.' He stared at her, eyes full of meaning, waiting for her to catch on.

The moment dragged on in silence. Then Julia finally exploded, 'This is all a gag, right? A big joke!'

'A "big joke" powerful enough to stop you in your tracks, judging by the look on your face when you switched me on,' Anthony responded as he examined his reflection in a mirror on the wall. 'Admit it. It's my spitting image. Close to perfection! Though I have to say they went a bit overboard with these wrinkles on the brow.'

'You've had those wrinkles since I was a kid, so unless they threw in a facelift, I don't know where they would have gone.'

'Thank you I think,' replied Anthony with a smile.

Julia rose to inspect the figure more closely. If she truly was looking at a machine, it was undeniably a remarkable piece of work.

'This is ridiculous, not to mention technologically impossible!'

'Ah, and haven't you accomplished things at your computer in recent days that a year ago you thought were impossible?'

Julia sat at the kitchen table with her head in her hands.

'We invested a great sum of money to achieve this result. And I'm still just the initial prototype! And you, my dear, are our very first client. Nonpaying of course. It's my gift,' Anthony added affably.

'A gift? Who in the world would be crazy enough to want a gift like that?'

'How many people say to themselves in their final moments, "If only I had known! I would have listened more. If only I could have told them! If only they knew."'

Julia just gaped, so Anthony went on. 'We're talking about a massive untapped market here.'

'So right now, am I talking to you or to a machine?'

'One and the same. This machine contains the lion's share of my memory, as well as my cerebral cortex, all housed within a highly resistant mechanism consisting of millions of microprocessors, equipped with technology that perfectly reproduces human skin tone and texture, and impeccable mobility.'

'But why? For what?' asked Julia, stunned.

'So that we can share a handful of days together, time we never had, precious moments snatched from the jaws of eternity. One last chance for you and I to say all those things we never said.'

◆ ◆ ◆

Julia paced back and forth across the living room, running mad theories through her head to try to explain the situation, but every theory fell apart under scrutiny, one after the next. As gut-wrenching as it was to admit, her father's explanation was the most plausible of all. She went to the kitchen for a glass of water, downed it in one go and returned to Anthony's side.

'Nobody will ever believe me,' she said, breaking the silence.

'I wonder, isn't that the same little voice in your head you hear when you come up with your stories at work? The very problem you face every time you pick up your pencil and struggle to breathe life into one of your characters? I seem to recall you telling me, when I refused to support your chosen career path, that I was ignorant and had failed to comprehend the raw power of imagination. How many times did you try to explain it to me, why thousands of children would drag their parents into these imaginary worlds that you and your friends invent on your computer screens? And if memory serves, you were more than happy to remind me of my lack of support the day you received that promotion. You breathed life into a ridiculous Technicolor otter, and you believed in her. Are you telling me now that an impossibility has come to life before your very eyes and you refuse to believe in it merely on the grounds that it resembles your father and not some imaginary animal? If the answer is yes, by all means go ahead and push that button!' concluded Anthony, gesturing towards the remote control, which Julia had left on the table.

Julia gave him a sarcastic round of applause. Anthony's face darkened.

'Now, don't think your insolence will be tolerated just because I'm dead.'

'If one button was all it took to make you shut your trap, I would've pushed it a long time ago.'

As her father's face suffused with rage – an all-too-familiar sight – the moment was interrupted by two short honks from a car outside.

Julia's heart leapt into her throat. She could hear the gears of Adam's car grinding as he put it in reverse. The sound was unmistakable, leaving no doubt: he was parking his car in front of her building right now.

'Shit!' she muttered, running to the window.

'Who is it?' her father asked.

'Adam!'

'Who?'

'The man I was supposed to marry Saturday.'

'Supposed to?'

'Saturday? The day you were buried?'

'Ah, yes.'

'"Ah, yes" is all he has to say,' Julia said, rolling her eyes. 'That can wait. In the meantime, back into your box!'

'I beg your pardon?'

'As soon as Adam manages to parallel park – which gives us I'd say another two minutes max – he'll come straight up here. We had to cancel our wedding to attend your funeral. Maybe it's best he doesn't find you just hanging out in my apartment.'

'Oh why keep pointless secrets? You were considering marrying the man. I have every reason to trust him. I'll simply explain the situation to him, as I did to you.'

'I'm not just "considering" marrying the man; I am going to marry him. The wedding is temporarily postponed, that's all. And forget about explaining the situation to him. I can barely wrap my head around all this, so there's no way Adam will be able to process it.'

'Perhaps he's more open-minded than you think.'

'Adam can't even take a picture with his smartphone. How could he handle an android? For God's sake, get back in your box!' Julia pleaded in pure exasperation.

'No use making that sour face,' he replied. 'Besides, whether I'm here or not, you don't think he's going to find the six-foot crate in the middle of your living room just a little bit bizarre?'

When Julia failed to respond, Anthony added with satisfaction, 'I rest my case.'

'Please,' pleaded Julia, leaning over to get a look out of the window, 'just hurry up and hide somewhere. He's out of the car already!'

'I would hide. But there's really not much extra space in here,' Anthony said, glancing around with thinly veiled disgust.

'It's all I can afford, and it's all I need.'

'I can't imagine how. These apartments with just one bedroom . . . How can you find even the slightest degree of privacy? If there were . . . I don't know, say, a billiard room, a laundry room, or a study, I could easily hide there, but in here it's just too—'

'You know, most people do not have a library or billiards in their apartment.'

'Maybe not *your friends*, my dear.'

Julia shot him a withering look.

'How nice. You tore my whole life apart while you were alive; now you spend three billion dollars on this machine just so you can keep at it even after you've died.'

'Even though I'm merely a prototype, this machine, as you call it, is not nearly as expensive as all that. Who could afford it?'

'Maybe *your friends*?' quipped Julia.

'Temper, temper! Same old Julia. Now, let's stop the bickering and focus on hiding away the father who just miraculously came back into your life. What's above us, an attic?'

'Another apartment.'

'If you know your neighbour well enough, I could go ring the bell and ask for a cup of sugar while you get rid of your fiancé.'

Julia began to rifle frantically through the kitchen drawers.

'What are you looking for?'

'The key,' she whispered, hearing Adam's voice outside on the street as he called out her name.

'I hope it's for upstairs. I'm sure it crossed your mind that if you send me to the basement I might very well run into your fiancé.'

'I own the apartment above us. I bought it with my bonus last year. But I haven't had time to fix it up, so it's kind of a mess up there.'

'As opposed to down here, which is just spick and span?'

'Keep it up and you're going to make me kill you.'

'I hate to split hairs, but I am already dead. And if you kept your life a bit more organized, you'd have already realized the keys are hanging on that hook next to the stove.'

Julia grabbed the keys and shoved them at her father.

'Go up there, and don't make a peep! He knows the apartment's empty.'

'I think you'd better go see what he wants instead of standing here lecturing me. Bellowing your name like that out in the street, he's going to wake the whole neighbourhood.'

Julia ran to the window and leaned out over the railing of the small balcony.

'There you are! I rang like ten times!' shouted Adam, taking a step back on the sidewalk.

'Sorry! Buzzer's sound is broken,' Julia yelled down.

'And you didn't hear me yelling?'

'I did, just now. I had the TV on . . .'

'Can you let me up?'

'Sure,' she said, but stayed planted at the window, waiting for the sound of the closing door to confirm that her father was really gone.

'You don't seem all that happy to see me.'

'Of course I am. Why would you say that?'

'Because you're up there and I'm still down here? You didn't sound so great in that voicemail, so I decided to stop by on my way home from the country. But if you want me to go . . .'

'No, of course not. I'll buzz you in.'

She went to the intercom and pressed the entry button. She could hear the latch opening and Adam's footsteps coming up the stairs. She hurried to the kitchen and grabbed a remote control, then realized she had the wrong one and threw it aside. Julia rifled through a drawer and found the TV remote, praying under her breath that the batteries were still working. The TV flickered to life just as the door opened.

'So you don't even lock your front door any more?' Adam asked as he came in.

'Of course I do. I unlocked it just now for you,' Julia improvised, silently cursing her father.

Adam took off his jacket and placed it on a chair. He noticed the blizzard of static raging across the TV screen.

'Whatever happened to "I hate TV"?'

'Oh, it's just every once in a while,' she responded, trying to gather her wits.

'I can't say this "show" looks all that interesting.'

'Give me a break. I was trying to turn it off, but I hit the wrong button.'

She saw Adam's eyes drift over to the imposing crate in the middle of the living room.

'What?' asked Julia, doing a poor job of feigning innocence.

'Well, Julia. It's just . . . there's an enormous box in the middle of your living room.'

Julia took a gamble, offering a hastily conceived explanation. The box was special packaging to return a broken computer. But the delivery men had got mixed up and sent it to her house instead of her office.

'It must be incredibly fragile to need such a tall box.'

'Yes, it's a very complex machine,' Julia explained. 'And very bulky. But delicate.'

'And they delivered it to the wrong address?' continued Adam, clearly intrigued.

'Yeah. Well, I may have been the one who filled out the form with the wrong info. I've been so worn out these past few weeks.'

'You should be careful. They could accuse you of trying to steal company property.'

'Nobody's going to accuse me of anything,' snapped Julia, betraying her growing impatience.

'Is there something we need to talk about?'

'Like what?'

'Like why I had to ring your buzzer ten times and wake up the entire neighbourhood, shouting in the street just to get you to come to your window. Or,' he added gently, 'why you look like such a wreck, and why the TV is on when the cable isn't even plugged in . . . You're not acting like yourself, Julia.'

'Come on, spit it out. What are you implying? Are you trying to say I'm hiding something?' Julia snapped again.

'I don't know,' Adam replied. 'You said it, not me.'

Julia turned and flung the bedroom door open, then did the same with the closet door behind her. Next she went to the kitchen and began throwing open all the cupboards, beginning above the sink and not stopping until every last one was hanging ajar.

'Can I ask just what the hell you're doing?' Adam said.

'Looking for my secret lover! He's gotta be around here somewhere!'

'Julia!'

'What?'

Just as their uncharacteristic squabble was about to escalate, Julia's phone rang. They both stared at it, stunned, until Julia finally picked it up. She listened for a long time, feeling her shoulders relax, then offered the caller some warm words of praise and gratitude before hanging up.

'Who was that?'

'The office. They finally fixed the problem that had been holding up the project. Production is back on schedule, full steam ahead.'

'See?' Adam said, his tone softening. 'Just in time. In an alternate universe, if we were starting our honeymoon right now, you would've left with a clear conscience.'

'I know, honey, I really am sorry. More than you could know. Which reminds me. I have to give you back those tickets – they're at my office.'

'Don't worry about that – you can throw them right in the trash. Or keep them as a souvenir. No refunds, no exchanges.'

Julia looked at him with raised eyebrows, biting her tongue to hold back her reaction.

'Don't look at me like that,' Adam said. 'Most people don't cancel their honeymoon three days before they leave. And we could still go if we wanted.'

'We'd go . . . because the tickets are nonrefundable?'

'That's not what I meant,' said Adam, taking her in his arms. 'Your voicemail didn't do your mood justice. I shouldn't even have come. You were right: you need to be alone. Let's just drop the whole thing for now. I'll head home. Tomorrow's another day.' He kissed her softly before letting her go.

As he was heading towards the door, a faint creak came from the apartment above. Adam threw Julia an inquisitive glance.

'Adam. That was a rat.'

'Sometimes I wonder how you manage to live in this pigsty.'

'I like this pigsty. And someday, when I'm running my own animation studio, I'll have enough money for a big apartment of my very own, you'll see.'

'Don't you mean "our very own"? I mean, you do remember what was supposed to happen yesterday, right?'

'I'm sorry. That's not what I meant.'

'How much longer do you count on shuttling back and forth between your place and mine?'

'Now is not the time to rehash that old argument. I promise as soon as we can afford renovating we can connect the two floors, and there'll be plenty of space for the two of us here.'

'You're lucky I love you the way I do. Otherwise, I'd insist you leave this place. Sometimes you seem more attached to this apartment than you are to me! But if you really want to stay here, what's holding us back from renovating now?'

'There you go again with the insinuations,' Julia scoffed, changing her tone yet again. 'If you're talking about my father's money, I wanted nothing to do with it when he was alive and even less now that he's dead. I have to go to bed. I'm not going on vacation, and I have a busy day tomorrow.'

'You're right. Go to bed. I'll write off that last remark, and that *tone*, to fatigue.'

Adam shrugged and left. He didn't even turn back to see Julia wave a feeble goodbye from the top of the stairs. The building door slammed shut behind him.

◆ ◆ ◆

'Thank you for that comment about the rat,' Anthony grumbled as he came back into the apartment.

'Right. I probably should have said, "Oh that? That's just a state-of-the-art robotic version of my father pacing around above our heads." You want him to have me hauled away in a straitjacket?'

'Not necessarily. Though it would have been exciting to see the look on his face,' Anthony retorted, not bothering to mask his amusement.

'While we're bickering,' continued Julia, 'let me take this opportunity to officially thank you for ruining my wedding.'

'In that case, am I expected to officially apologize . . . for dying?'

'And thanks for getting me in trouble with the owner of the shoe store downstairs. In addition to everything else, I'll get the stink eye from him every day for the next two months.'

'The shoe salesman? Who cares?'

'I wasn't done. Thank you also for ruining the only time off I've had all week.'

'Please. By the time I was your age, my only night off all year was Thanksgiving.'

'Tell me something I don't know. And finally, – and here I really have to hand it to you – thank you for turning me into a total monster with Adam.'

'Don't thank me for that, thank yourself. I had nothing to do with it.'

'How can you honestly claim you had nothing to do with it?' shouted Julia.

'Fine. Maybe I did play a small part. Truce?'

'Truce? For what happened tonight? Or yesterday? Or for all our fights over the years?'

'I've never wanted to fight with you, Julia. I may not have been around much, but I tried my best to be kind.'

'You've got to be kidding. You did your damnedest to retain total control over my life, no matter the distance. You had no right. What the hell am I even doing? I'm talking to a dead man!'

'You can turn me off whenever you like.'

'It's what I probably should do. Put you back in that stupid box of yours and ship you back to whatever high-tech laboratory you came from.'

'Jot this down: 1-800-300-0001, confirmation pin 654.'

Julia looked at him inquisitively.

'It's how you get ahold of the company that made me. You just dial that number and give them the code. They can even turn me off remotely if you can't bring yourself to do it on your own. One call and I'm gone in twenty-four hours. But think long and hard before you do so. Think about all the people who can only dream of spending a few more days in the company of a mother or father they have lost. This is a once-in-a-lifetime chance. You pass it up, it's gone. We have one week together and not a second longer. Just seven days – well, six, now that Sunday's almost gone.'

'Why one week?'

'It was the duration agreed upon by the ethics committee.'

'Meaning?'

'Well, as you can imagine, this kind of technology veers into some very slippery moral territory. We thought it was important to keep our clients from getting too attached to these machines, despite their near perfection. There are already many ways of communicating after death: wills, books, audio and video recordings. Our technology represents the next step – harnessing innovation for an interactive experience,' her father explained with all the enthusiasm of a well-polished sales pitch. 'In contrast to an arcane sheet of paper or a two-dimensional video, we offer the dying party a more complete medium to express their final wishes, while also giving the mourning family the opportunity to take advantage of a few last days in the company of the dearly departed. But we couldn't risk an emotional transfer of affection for their loved one on to the machine. We learned many valuable lessons from previous attempts. I don't know if you recall, but there was one toy manufacturer whose baby dolls were so convincingly lifelike that their owners ended up treating them like real infants. We don't want to reproduce these sorts of twisted reactions. We are not interested in producing a clone, however tempting that might be.'

Julia rolled her eyes.

'You, however, don't seem especially taken with the concept. At the end of the week my batteries will run out permanently, my memory drives will be deleted and the last signs of life will flicker out and disappear.'

'There's no way of stopping it?'

'No, they covered all the bases. It's irreversible. If some smart aleck tries to tamper with the battery, the memory drives are automatically wiped clean. A bit of a dismal thought, especially for me, but I'm like a disposable flashlight. All I have is six more days of light and then . . . poof! Darkness. Six days, Julia. Six short days to make up for lost time – it's up to you.'

'Only you could come up with something this twisted. Ordinary shareholder? I bet you're a lot more than that. Or *were*.'

'Present tense please. Assuming you do decide to go along with this, and seeing as you haven't yet pressed that button that will put me in the past, I'd prefer you speak to me in the present tense.'

'Six full days? I haven't taken six days off since . . . I don't know when.'

'You're a chip off the old block.'

Julia shot her father a furious look.

'All in jest, dear. You don't have to take everything so seriously,' he said.

'What am I supposed to tell Adam?'

'You seemed to have no trouble lying to him just now.'

51

'I didn't lie to him. I hid certain things. Major things. There's a difference.'

'The nuance escapes me. In that case you can just keep on hiding certain things.'

'And what about Stanley?'

'Your gay friend?'

'My *best* friend.'

'Right . . . him,' responded Anthony. 'If he's really your best friend, you'll just have to tread lightly.'

'And what? You'll just hang out here all day while I'm at work? Plug yourself in and recharge?'

'Weren't you supposed to take a few days off for that honeymoon of yours? Perhaps you don't need to go in at all.'

'How do you know about all that?'

'The floor of your apartment, or the ceiling if you prefer, is not soundproof. Typical for an old rundown building.'

'Anthony!' Julia wailed.

'Now, dear, I may not be flesh and blood, but please. Call me Daddy. I can't stand it when you call me by my first name.'

'For Christ's sake I haven't called you Daddy for twenty years.'

'All the more reason for us to make up for it over the next six days,' her father replied with a broad smile.

'I have no idea what to do,' muttered Julia as she leaned against the window frame.

'Best turn in, sleep on it. You're the first person on earth to face such a decision. It's worth thinking over calmly. Tomorrow morning you'll make your choice. Whatever it is, it'll be for the best. At worst, you decide to turn me off, and all you'll be is just a few hours late for work. That wedding would have meant an entire week off the clock. Doesn't the death of your father warrant at least one morning?'

In silence Julia observed the face of the strange machine standing before her, the thing staring back at her all the while. She thought she read something in its eyes that was almost like affection – a sight unfamiliar to her, considering her father had always been so distant in life. And even though it was just a fabricated copy of her 'loved one', Julia had every instinct to wish it good night before heading to bed, but ultimately she said nothing. She closed her bedroom door and stretched out across her bed.

The minutes crept by. An hour passed and then another. With the curtains open, light spilled in across the shelves. Through the windowpane, the full moon seemed to float above the hardwood floors. Childhood memories came flooding back to Julia as she lay in bed. The countless nights she had spent waiting for her father to come home – that same man sitting on the other side of the wall right now. Throughout her adolescence, many sleepless nights were spent reinventing her father's travels, the wind outside her window carrying her mind to thousands of distant countries. So many evenings spent in a state of being awake yet dreaming, and she had maintained the habit over the years. It had taken a dizzying amount of drawing and erasing to invent characters who would take life, come together and satisfy her need for love, one frame at a time. Deep down, Julia had always known that this artistic escape was a vain attempt to find clarity and comfort. But reality was a blinding light that could cut straight through the most carefully drawn illusion in the blink of an eye. She still felt the pain of the lonely girl she had been.

A little ceramic otter from Mexico was perched beside her bed. She had drawn inspiration from the tiny figurine to create Tilly. Julia rose from her bed and took it in her hands. Her intuition had always been her best ally, and with time her imagination had only grown sharper. Why now, when she needed it most, was she left in doubt?

She put the figurine back, slipped on a dressing gown and opened her bedroom door. Anthony was sitting on the living room sofa watching TV.

'I took the liberty of plugging in your cable. I've always been fond of this show.'

Julia sat down next to him.

'I've never seen this episode. Or at least I can't locate it in my memory drive,' continued her father.

Julia grabbed the remote and put the TV on mute. Anthony rolled his eyes.

'You wanted to talk? Let's talk,' she said.

Neither one of them spoke for at least fifteen minutes.

'Ah, look. I've never seen this episode. Or at least I can't locate it in my memory drive,' her father repeated, turning up the volume again.

This time Julia turned the TV all the way off.

'Sounds like you have a bug – some kind of glitch or something. You just said the same thing twice in a row.'

Another fifteen minutes of silence dragged on. Anthony's eyes stayed riveted on the darkened screen.

'I seem to recall one of your birthdays – your ninth if I'm not mistaken – we celebrated together, just the two of us at a Chinese restaurant you liked. And back home we spent the entire evening in front of the TV, just like this. You were spread out on my bed, and even when the channel turned off, you kept watching nothing but static on the screen. You probably don't remember. You were too young. I wanted to carry you to your room, but your arms were so tightly clenched to the pillow and the headboard, I couldn't pry you off. You slept diagonally across the top of the comforter, taking the whole bed for yourself. So I plopped down in the armchair right across from you and watched you sleep. Just watched, all night long. But you couldn't possibly remember. You were only nine.'

Julia said nothing. He turned the TV back on.

'How do they come up with these scenarios? I've always wondered about that. It must take a great deal of imagination. Funny thing is you end up getting quite attached to the characters . . . invested in their lives.'

Julia and her father stayed that way, sitting side by side without saying a thing. Their hands rested next to each other on the couch without ever moving closer. Not a single word broke the silence of the night. When the first light of dawn crept through the room, Julia rose noiselessly and crossed the room. At her bedroom door she turned back to her father and said just one thing before shutting the door.

'Good night.'

6.

The clock radio on the bedside table read nine o'clock. Julia opened her eyes and leapt out of bed.

'Shit!'

She hurried to the bathroom, stubbing her toe on the doorframe along the way.

'Monday strikes again,' she grumbled. 'God, what a night!' She pulled back the shower curtain and stepped inside, letting the water glide down her skin for what seemed like a long time. A while later, as she was brushing her teeth and looking at her reflection in the mirror above the sink, she was suddenly struck by the giggles. She wrapped a towel around her body and another around her hair, then slipped out to make her morning cup of tea. As she crossed her bedroom, she decided she would call Stanley as soon as she finished her first sip. Sharing her strange dream with him would probably have repercussions: he'd almost certainly try to set her up forget her an appointment with his shrink. Still, there was no way she could keep it from him. She never managed to spend even half a day without calling him or dropping by for an impromptu visit. Such an incredible dream simply had to be shared with her best friend.

She smiled and was about to leave her bedroom when a clatter of dishes made her jump.

Julia waited a moment, heart pounding. She threw the wet towels to the floor, shimmied into a pair of jeans and a shirt and tried to untangle her hair in a rush. Looking at her reflection in the mirror, she threw on a last-minute dab of blusher, then opened the door to the living room a little and whispered worriedly, 'Adam? Stanley? It couldn't be . . .'

'I didn't know whether you took coffee or tea, so I made coffee,' her father called from the kitchen, victoriously brandishing a steaming pot of coffee. 'Good, strong coffee, the way your father likes it!' he added jovially.

Julia looked at the old wooden table. A place was set for her. Two jars of jam had been arranged just so, impeccably aligned with a jar of honey. The butter dish stood at a ninety-degree angle to the cereal box. A carton of milk stood directly across from the sugar bowl.

'You have got to be kidding me.'

'What? What is it now?'

'This ridiculous game. You went your whole life without ever fixing me breakfast, so you're not going to start now that you're—'

'No, we agreed: no past tense. It was my only condition. Present tense at all times . . . After all, the future won't get me very far.'

'I don't recall agreeing to a single thing. And for your information I drink tea in the morning.'

Anthony poured some coffee for Julia.

'Milk?' he asked.

Julia scoffed, then filled the kettle.

'So have you made up your mind then?' asked her father, taking two slices of bread from the toaster.

'If the point of all this is for us to actually talk, last night wasn't much of a start,' replied Julia softly.

'Nonetheless I enjoyed the time we spent together. Didn't you?'

'It was my tenth birthday. Not my ninth. Our first weekend without Mom. It was a Sunday, and she had been taken to the hospital on Thursday. The Chinese restaurant was called Wang's, which closed last year. Anyway, early the next morning you packed your bags and flew off without even saying goodbye.'

'Right. I had an early-afternoon meeting in Seattle. Or was it Boston? Who knows? Then I came back Thursday. Or was it Friday?'

'What's the point of all this?' asked Julia as she sat down at the table.

'Well, in just a few short moments we've already said quite a bit, don't you think? If you want hot tea, I'd advise turning on the stove.'

Julia sniffed at the steaming coffee, taking in the potent aroma.

'You know? I don't think I've ever tasted coffee in my entire life,' she said, taking a sip.

'Then how could you know you don't like it?' asked Anthony, watching his daughter as she took a larger gulp this time.

'Because!' she said, grimacing as she put the mug down.

'If you can get used to the bitterness, then you come to enjoy its rich undertone,' Anthony said.

'I should get to work,' replied Julia as she opened the jar of honey.

'Have you made up your mind then? Your indecision has been quite vexing. At the very least you could let me know.'

'I don't know what you want me to say. What do you expect when you ask the impossible? You and your partners overlooked one small ethical quandary.'

'Please share. I'm curious.'

'The whole thing amounts to barging in uninvited and turning somebody's life upside down.'

'Somebody?' Anthony retorted, his voice tightening.

'Don't take it personally. I don't know what to tell you. Figure it out without me. Call in that code and let them decide.'

'Six days, Julia. Six days so you can mourn the loss of your father, not just some stranger – as you seem to consider me. Don't you want to make that choice yourself?'

'Six days for *you* you mean.'

'I'm not alive any more. What could I possibly get out of it? There's nothing for me in this at all, which is a rather novel concept. Pretty ironic come to think of it,' continued Anthony with a smile. 'That's another thing we didn't anticipate. It's positively unprecedented . . . Before perfecting this incredible invention, never in the history of the world could one discuss the events of one's own death with one's own daughter. And get to witness the reaction! It really is extraordinary. Okay, I can see you don't think it's very amusing. I guess it's not that funny after all.'

'No, it isn't.'

'I do have some bad news for you, though. I can't call in the shutoff order myself. It isn't possible. Only one person has authorization to halt the program, and that's the beneficiary. Besides, I've already forgotten the password I gave you. It was erased from my memory. You did jot it down last night, didn't you?'

'1-800-300-0001. Confirmation pin 654.'

'Oh, so you memorized it. Very good.'

Julia got up and put her mug in the sink. She turned around, took a long, hard look at her father. Then picked up her phone to make a call.

'It's me,' she said to her work colleague Dray. 'I'm going to take your advice, at least sort of. I'm taking today and tomorrow off. Maybe more. We'll have to wait and see. I'll keep in touch. Send me an email update on the project at the end of each day, and don't think twice about calling me if you have any problems.'

Julia put the phone back down without taking her eyes off her father.

'It's good to look after your team,' Anthony stated approvingly. 'I always say that any company worth its weight in gold is held up by three pillars: teamwork, teamwork and teamwork.'

'Two days! You get two days, understand? Take it or leave it. In forty-eight hours, like it or not you give me back my life and—'

'Six days!'

'Two.'

'Six!'

The telephone rang, cutting their negotiations short. Anthony picked it up, only to have Julia grab the receiver and muffle it, signalling to her father to be as quiet as possible. It was Adam, who expressed his concern after trying to get in touch with Julia at work and being unable to reach her there or on her cell phone. He said he was kicking himself about the night before, for his lack of trust and his drastic over-reactions. Julia apologized herself for having been short-tempered and thanked Adam for being thoughtful enough to come over after hearing her voicemail. Even if it hadn't been their finest hour as a couple, Adam showing up unexpectedly outside her window had been very romantic.

Adam offered to pick her up after work as her father started doing the washing up in the background, seemingly making as much noise as he could. Julia explained over the racket that her father's death had affected her more than she had been letting on. She had spent the night tossing and turning, plagued by nightmares. She was exhausted and couldn't handle another night like that. What she needed was a calm afternoon and an early night. They would see each other tomorrow at the very latest. By then she would be herself again, more like the woman he wanted to marry.

'Exactly like I said. A chip off the old block,' repeated Anthony as soon as she had hung up. Julia glared at him.

'What is it now?' he asked.

'You've never washed a single dish in your entire life.'

'How would you know? Besides, dishes are part of my new pro-gramming,' he replied cheerfully.

Julia left him to it and turned away without a word, grabbing the door keys from the hook.

'Where are you off to?' asked her father.

'I'm going upstairs to set up your room. There's no way you're spending the whole night pacing back and forth in my living room. I have to catch up on some sleep.'

'If the TV bothers you, I can turn down the volume.'

'You're sleeping upstairs tonight. Non-negotiable.'

'Come now, you're not really going to force me into the attic!'

'Give me one good reason I shouldn't.'

'Rats! The place is infested. You said so yourself,' Anthony replied, sounding like a chastised child.

As Julia headed out the door, she heard her father calling after her in a firm voice.

'Young lady! We'll never get anywhere staying cooped up in here.'

As Julia closed the door behind her and climbed one flight of stairs up, Anthony Walsh checked the time on the oven clock. He hesitated a moment and then looked for the white remote control, which he found right where Julia had left it on the counter.

He heard his daughter's footsteps in the apartment above . . . the sound of furniture being moved around . . . the opening and closing of a window. When she came back down, he was back inside the packing crate with the remote control in hand.

'What do you think you're doing?' she asked.

'I've elected to turn myself off. Better for both of us this way, most of all you, dear. I can see that I'm in your way.'

'I thought you couldn't do it yourself,' she said, yanking the remote from his hand.

'I said you were the only one who could call the company and give them the pin. I think I'm quite capable of pushing a simple button,' he grumbled, stepping back out of the crate.

'Do what you want,' she responded, handing back the remote. 'But do it soon. You're wearing me out.'

Anthony set the remote down on the coffee table, then returned to face his daughter.

'Might I ask, where were you supposed to go on this honeymoon of yours?'

'Montreal. Why?'

'Your fiancé didn't exactly go all out, did he?'

'What do you have against Canada?'

'Nothing at all! Nothing against Montreal. Lovely city, many cherished memories there. But that's beside the point,' he said with a cough.

'What is the point then?'

'Well, it's just . . .'

'Just what?'

'For a honeymoon . . . a one-hour flight is hardly a change of scenery! Why not rent an RV to save on paying for a hotel while you're at it?'

'What if it was my idea to go? What if I love Montreal? What if it's a special place for both of us, full of cherished memories? What would you know about any of it?'

'No daughter of mine would ever choose that kind of destination. A mere hour from home? Never!' affirmed Anthony emphatically. 'And don't go telling me you're a maple syrup fanatic. One must draw the line somewhere.'

'You'll always be blinded by your preconceived ideas, won't you?'

'I'll grant you it's a little late for me to change now. But please! Spending the most memorable night of your entire life in a place you already know? Au revoir to your sense of discovery. Adieu, flames of romance. Innkeeper, same room as last time! After all, this is just a night like any other. Barkeep, the usual! Wouldn't want to do anything to agitate my fiancé – or should I say, husband – by straying from the precious routine.'

Anthony let loose a deep belly laugh.

'Are you done?' Julia was fuming now.

'Yes,' he said, regaining his composure. 'You know it's not half bad this whole death thing. Suddenly free to say whatever comes running down your circuits!'

'You're right – we're getting nowhere,' said Julia, bringing her father's mood down a notch.

'Not here at least. We need to find some kind of neutral ground.'

Julia looked perplexed.

'How about we stop playing hide and seek in this drab little shoe box? Even with that room upstairs you want me to inhabit, we're crammed like sardines in here. Wasting precious time bickering like spoiled children. Every last minute counts. We can't get them back.'

'What do you suggest?'

'Why not take a little trip together, you and I? No calls from work, no surprise visits from that Adam of yours, no evenings spent glaring at one another like zombies in front of the TV. Just long, lovely strolls where you and I can really talk. After all, that's why I came all this way. To spend time together, just the two of us.'

'You're asking me to give you what you never gave me? Is that what you're saying?'

'Why fight a ghost, Julia? You'll have the rest of your life for that. My side of the argument only exists in your memories now. Six days is all we have left. That's all I'm asking for.'

'And where are we supposed to go on this little trip?'

'Montreal.'

Julia couldn't hold back a smile.

'Montreal?'

'No refunds, no exchanges . . . but that doesn't mean we can't try to have them change the name of one of the passengers.'

Julia pulled back her hair and put on a coat. When Anthony realized she was leaving, he stood in her way, blocking the door.

'Don't be like that. Adam said they were as good as trash!'

'He suggested I keep them as a souvenir. Maybe you were so busy eavesdropping you missed the sarcasm. I don't think he meant I should go with someone else.'

'I'm your father. I'm not just "someone else".'

'Will you please get out of my way?'

'Where are you going?' asked Anthony as he stepped aside.

'To get some fresh air.'

'Are you mad at me?'

He received no response, save his daughter's footsteps heading down the stairs. He headed straight to the window to watch before turning away to make two phone calls.

Julia climbed into a taxi at the corner of Greenwich Street. She didn't need to look up to know that her father would be watching as the cab pulled away towards Ninth Avenue.

She had the driver drop her off in SoHo. Normally she would have gone on foot – it was only a twenty-minute walk, and she knew the neighbourhood like the back of her hand – but she had been so desperate to get away from her apartment she would have stolen a bike if she had found one unattended. She pushed open the door of the quaint little antique shop. Seated in a baroque armchair, Stanley looked up from his book at the sound of the little bell jingling above the door.

'Garbo in *Queen Christina* couldn't have done better!'

'What are you talking about?'

'Your entrance. Majestic and terrifying all at once.'

'Don't make fun of me. Not today.'

'No matter how bad your day is, there's room for a bit of humour. Aren't you supposed to be at work?'

Julia walked over to an old bookcase and admired a delicately gilded clock perched on the top shelf.

'Don't tell me you're playing hooky just to check what time it was in the eighteenth century?' asked Stanley, straightening his glasses.

'It's very pretty.'

'So am I. Something wrong, sweetie?'

'Not a thing. I just stopped by to see you, that's all.'

'Right. And I'm giving up Louis XVI for pop art,' Stanley quipped, putting down his book.

He approached her and took a seat on the corner of a mahogany table.

'Is my baby doll having a bad day?'

'You could say that, yeah.'

Julia rested her head on Stanley's shoulder.

'Yikes. Worse than I thought,' he said, giving her a hug. 'I'll make you some tea a friend sent me from Vietnam. It's a great detox – he needs the strong stuff, and it looks like you could use some, too.'

Stanley took a teapot from a shelf. He put the kettle on a hot plate he kept on the antique desk that served as the shop's counter. After a few minutes' letting it infuse, he poured the miracle tea into a pair of porcelain cups he'd drawn from an old armoire. Julia wafted the aroma towards her nose, taking a deep breath to savour the scent of jasmine before taking a sip.

'So? Talk to me. Don't bother resisting. This divine potion is known to unlock even the most fiercely guarded of secrets.'

'Would you run away with me on a honeymoon?'

'If I had married you, why not? But you'd have to be a Julian instead of a Julia. Otherwise, I fear our honeymoon would be rather dull.'

'Come on, Stanley. Close the store for one week and elope with me.'

'How very romantic. Where would we go?'

'Montreal.'

'Oh no. Never.'

'Why does everyone have something against Quebec all of a sudden?'

'I didn't endure six months on the brink of starvation in order to lose ten pounds just to gain them back in a few days. The restaurants in Montreal are almost as irresistible as the waiters. Plus I hate the thought of being somebody's plan B.'

'What makes you say that?'

'Am I the first person you thought about for this trip?'

'What does that matter? Anyway, you wouldn't believe me even if I told you.'

'How about you begin by explaining what's bothering you?'

'If I told you everything, beginning to end, you wouldn't believe a single word of it.'

'Right. I'm an idiot. When was the last time you took even half a day off at the beginning of the week, huh?'

Julia stayed mute. Stanley ploughed on.

'You show up at my store on a Monday morning with coffee breath when you don't even drink coffee. A rushed make-up job that's barely hiding the fact that your sweet little head didn't spend nearly enough time on your pillow last night. Ten minutes? Less? Then you ask me at the last minute to come on a trip with you instead of your fiancé. Cards on the table, baby doll. Did you sleep with another man last night?'

'God, no!' exclaimed Julia.

'Okay. Then what exactly are you running from?'

'Nothing.'

'All right, honey. I have work to do, so until you trust me enough to talk to me, I'm going to get back to my inventory,' Stanley replied, and made a weak attempt at heading off towards the back of his shop.

'You're a terrible liar. Inventory? You were falling asleep with a book in your hand when I got here,' said Julia, cracking up.

'Ah, she can still smile after all! *Wunderbar!*' Stanley gave Julia an affectionate and knowing grin. 'The grumpy face was getting a little old. How about a walk? The stores open soon, and I'm sure you could use a new pair of shoes.'

'To add to the collection gathering dust in my closet?'

'This isn't about the shoes, darling. It's about your life.'

Julia got up and walked back over to the old bookcase with the little gilded clock. As she picked it up, she noticed the glass face of the clock was missing, and she started exploring the circumference inside with the tip of her finger.

'What a pretty little thing,' she said, nudging the minute hand counterclockwise. The hour hand followed suit, moving in the wrong direction.

'How great would it be if we could go back in time.'

'Turn back time? You wouldn't want to restore that clock to its youth; you'd kill the effect. Look at it this way – it gives us the beauty of its age,' he replied, taking the clock from Julia and putting it back on the shelf. 'I really wish you'd tell me what's up.'

'If you had the chance . . . to take a trip that would let you walk in your parent's footsteps, would you take it?'

'If there was even a chance of learning the tiniest little thing about my mother? I'd already be on a plane hassling the flight attendant instead of wasting my time chatting away with an old queen in an antique shop. You get a chance like that? You take it, honey, no questions asked.'

'What if it's too little, too late?'

'No such thing. He may be gone, but in some ways your father is still right by your side.'

'You have no idea.'

'No matter what you keep telling yourself, you do miss him.'

'How could I? After all these years I got used to him being gone. I learned to live without him.'

'Baby doll, even children who never knew their biological parents feel the need to find their roots sooner or later. Hard as that may be for those who raised them and loved them, it's just human nature. It's hard to move ahead in life when you don't know where you come from. So even if it takes embarking on some vague vision quest or whatever you're thinking, if there's a chance to really know who your father was and finally come to grips with the past . . . you should do it.'

'I barely have any memories of us together.'

'Maybe you have a few more than you think. For once forget that adorable pride of yours and take a chance. And if you can't justify doing all this for yourself, do it for someone near and dear to my heart. I'll introduce you to her someday. She's one hell of a mother, and I'm sure she would understand why you have to do this.'

'And who exactly is that?' Julia asked with a tinge of jealousy.

'You, baby doll. You just a few years down the line.'

'You're the best, Stanley.' Julia planted a kiss on his cheek.

'I had nothing to do with it, darling. It was all the tea.'

'Well, be sure to tell your Vietnamese friend to send more. The stuff is incredible,' added Julia on her way out the door.

'If you like it so much, I can get you some when you come back. I found it at the bodega on the corner.'

7.

Julia went up the stairs two at a time and opened the door to her apartment. The living room was empty. She called out several times but heard nothing in response. After searching the other rooms, she was certain the apartment was empty. She noticed that a photograph of Anthony in a little silver frame now sat right in the middle of her mantelpiece.

Her father's voice gave her a jolt as he asked her where she had been.

'God, you scared me! Where were you?'

'You sound concerned. That's touching. I was just out for a stroll – boring sitting here all alone.'

'What's that all about?' Julia asked, pointing at the picture on the mantelpiece.

'I was settling into my upstairs bedroom – or *dungeon* might be more appropriate – and I found it, covered in dust. I didn't think I'd sleep so well with a dirty photo of myself staring back at me. I thought it looked good here, but feel free to move it somewhere else if you like.'

'Do you still want to go on this trip?' asked Julia, ignoring his comment.

'As a matter of fact I just got back from the travel agency down the street. The Internet can never replace good old-fashioned customer service. There was a lovely young girl working there – in fact, she reminded me of you. But she smiled more . . . What was I saying?'

'Lovely young girl . . .'

'Yes. Well, I managed to convince said girl to make an exception. She spent so long tapping away at her keyboard, I thought she was retyping the collected works of Hemingway, but eventually she confirmed that she could reprint the ticket in my name. While I was at it, I had her issue us an upgrade.'

'You really are something else. All that before I even say yes?'

'Yes or no, if you're really bent on pasting the tickets in your scrapbook as a souvenir, they might as well be first class. It's a question of family honour, my dear.'

As Julia headed towards her bedroom, Anthony asked her what she was doing.

'I'm going to pack a bag for a *two*-night trip,' she responded. 'Isn't that what you wanted?'

'Might be wise to pack a little extra, since the trip is six days. No refunds, no exchanges. I begged and begged, but lovely as she was, the girl was stubborn and couldn't bend on that part.'

'*Two* days!' shouted Julia from the bedroom.

'Oh have it your way. If worst comes to worst, we can buy you a new pair of pants in Montreal. I don't know if you've noticed, but the jeans you're currently wearing are full of holes. I can even see the skin of your knee. They thought ahead and packed everything I might need in order to remain in elegant attire for the duration of my battery life,' he said with a slight air of satisfaction as Julia popped her head out of the bedroom. She noted he held a black leather suitcase, and there was a false bottom revealed in the crate where it must have been stowed. 'In your absence I took the liberty of reclaiming watch,' he added, proudly extending his wrist. 'You don't have any objections, do you? You'll inherit it all over again soon enough if you know what I mean.'

'I'd be very grateful if you'd stop poking around in my things.'

'My dear, poking around in your apartment should be reserved for experienced spelunkers only. I found my things in a manila envelope sitting abandoned in the middle of your messy attic.'

Julia zipped her bag shut and put it near the door, muttering to herself. All that was left was to work out how to justify her upcoming absence to Adam.

'What do you plan on telling him?' Anthony Walsh asked.

'I think that's between the two of us,' Julia responded.

'Sure, sure. Just thought you might want to run it by me.'

'Oh really? Is "listening" also part of your new programming?'

'Whatever you come up with, I highly recommend you don't tell him *where* we're going.'

'I suppose I should take your advice, given your vast experience in secrets.'

'Simply take it for what it is. Now hurry up and go. We have to leave for the airport in two hours.'

The yellow cab dropped Julia off at 1350 Sixth Avenue, and she zipped straight into the towering glass building of the New York publisher where Adam worked. Her phone didn't get reception in the lobby, so she presented herself at the front desk and asked the security officer to connect her to Mr Coverman in the children's books department.

'Is everything okay?' Adam asked when he heard Julia's voice.

'Are you in a meeting?'

'Yes, we're going over a mock-up. We'll be done in fifteen minutes. How about we go to our favourite Italian place after? I can call and book us a table for eight.'

Adam must have glanced down at his phone and noticed the number on his caller ID.

'Wait, are you in the building?'

'Yeah, I'm down at reception.'

'Jeez, I'm really sorry, but we're so busy reviewing these new releases—'

'We have to talk,' Julia said, interrupting him.

'Can't it wait until this evening?'

'I can't make it to dinner this evening, Adam.'

'I'm coming down,' he responded before hanging up.

Julia waited for him near the reception desk.

'There's a cafe on the other side of the lobby,' suggested Adam.

'Why don't we just head over to the park instead? We'll be more comfortable outside.'

'Wow. That bad, huh?' he said as they left the building.

Julia didn't answer. They walked up Sixth Avenue and entered Central Park four blocks later.

The tree-lined paths were shady and deserted, apart from a few joggers wearing headphones, sealed off from the world around them, wholly concentrating on the rhythm of their feet. A grey squirrel came towards Julia and Adam and stood up on its hind legs, hoping they might have some food for him. Julia plunged her hand into the pocket of her trench coat and knelt to offer him a handful of nuts.

The brave little animal scurried a bit closer, then hesitated a moment, greedy eyes still fixed on the unexpected bounty. Hunger eventually trumped fear, and the creature darted forward to snatch a nut, retreating a few feet to gnaw away at it, all the while followed by Julia's wistful gaze.

'Since when do you carry nuts in your jacket?' asked Adam.

'I knew we would be coming here, so I bought some before I got in the taxi,' Julia replied. She offered a second nut to the squirrel, who was now joined by a jumpy little entourage of his fellow creatures.

'I'm guessing you didn't have me bail on a meeting to show off your talents as an animal tamer.'

Julia threw the rest of the nuts on the grass and signalled that they should continue their walk. Adam followed her.

'I'm going away for a little while,' she said, her voice tinged with sadness.

'You're leaving me?' Adam asked with a mix of worry and disbelief.

'Of course not. I'm just going away for a few days.'

'How many days?'

'Two or . . . six. Six at most.'

'Is it two? Or six?'

'I don't know yet.'

'Julia, you show up unannounced at my office, drag me out of the building with a look on your face like your whole world has fallen apart. Then you barely say a word, like pulling teeth, and I have to—'

'Fine. Sorry I wasted your precious time,' Julia said, growing more caustic and defensive.

Adam stopped her short, placing his hands gently on her shoulders. 'You're angry. You have every right to be, but not at me. I'm not the bad guy, Julia. I'm the guy who loves you, good times and bad. Don't punish me for things that aren't my fault.'

Julia's face softened. 'My father's personal assistant called this morning. I have business to take care of. Out of town.'

'Out of town? Where?'

'Vermont, near the Canadian border.'

'Okay, so how about this weekend we head up, the two of us?'

'It's urgent. It can't wait.'

'Does this have something to do with the travel agency that just contacted me?'

'Contacted you . . . about what?' Julia asked, her voice unsteady.

'Somebody came by apparently, and now they've agreed to refund my ticket, but not yours for some reason. Whole thing was pretty baffling. They didn't really go into all the details. I was already in a meeting and didn't have time.'

'It was probably my father's personal assistant. He's very good at his job.'

'You're going to Canada?'

'Near the border. I told you.'

'You really want to go?'

'I think so, yes,' she responded darkly.

Adam took Julia in his arms and held her tightly.

'Go wherever you need to. I won't ask any more questions. I don't want to be the untrusting guy twice in a row. Besides, I know you'd never stay away from work for very long. Walk me back to my office?'

'I think I'll stay here a little while.'

'With your squirrels?'

'Yes, with my squirrels.'

He kissed her on the forehead, took a few steps back and waved goodbye as he turned and made his way back down the tree-lined path.

'Adam?' Julia called after him.

'Yes?'

'It's a shame you have a meeting. I really would have liked to, I don't know . . .'

'Me too, but the two of us haven't had much luck these past few days.'

Adam blew her a kiss. 'Gotta run. Call me when you get to Vermont, okay?'

Julia nodded, her words suddenly stuck in her throat.

◆ ◆ ◆

'Well? How did it go?' asked Anthony, obviously delighted to see his daughter walk back through the door.

'Couldn't have gone much better.'

'Why the long face then? You look like you came straight from a funeral. Better late than never I suppose.'

'God, I wonder. Could it be because I just lied to the man I love for the first time?'

'First time since yesterday. Or, if you'd rather, we can chalk yesterday up as a false start and say it didn't count.'

'No, you're right! That makes two betrayals in two days! And of course he's being extra sensitive and just letting me go, no questions asked. In the taxi on the way back I felt like . . . the kind of woman I always swore I would never become.'

'Let's not exaggerate.'

'Oh no? What could be more revolting than lying to somebody who's being trusting enough not to ask any questions?'

'Being so caught up in your work that you're blind to the other person's life?'

'My God, the nerve! That coming from *you*?'

'Yes, as you note it's coming from somebody who knows what he's talking about. I think the car is downstairs. Let's not dawdle. With all the security checks, we'll spend more time in the airport than we will on the plane.'

While Anthony took their bags downstairs, Julia looked around her apartment. Before leaving, she turned the photo of her father on the mantelpiece to face the wall, then closed the door behind her.

◆ ◆ ◆

An hour later the limo pulled up outside the terminal at JFK.

'We could have just taken a taxi,' said Julia, looking through her window at the planes parked on the runway.

'Why sacrifice comfort? You have to admit how nice this is. Besides, I found my credit cards at your apartment and we may as well use them before they're cancelled. From what I gather you don't have much interest in your inheritance, so allow me to blow the whole thing on your behalf. Believe me, once you kick the bucket it really is a thrill to spend the fortune you worked and slaved your whole life to accumulate . . . just one more perk. This really is an unprecedented opportunity when you think about it. And stop it with all the gloom and doom. You'll see Adam again in a few days, and you'll be even more in love. Until then, why not make the most of your time with your father? How long has it been since we went on vacation together?'

'I was seven. Mom was still alive. She and I ended up spending the whole vacation at the pool, while you were crammed in a phone booth making work calls,' Julia replied, getting out of the limo.

'Well, it wasn't my fault cell phones hadn't been invented yet,' grumbled her father as he opened his own door and stepped out.

The international terminal was packed. Anthony rolled his eyes and went to the end of a long queue of passengers that snaked its way to the ticket counter. Later, with boarding passes in hand as the precious reward for their patience, the waiting began anew at security.

'All this hassle really spoils the pleasure of travelling. Look how irritated everyone is. And who could blame them for being impatient? Standing like this for hours, hauling around kids, chasing down restless toddlers who can't possibly sit still for very long to begin with. And for what? Like anyone really suspects that woman in front of us is hiding explosives in her baby food? Dynamite apple sauce, a Molotov cocktail out of a juice box? I don't think so.'

'Believe me, anything's possible.'

'Oh come on. A bit of common sense is all I'm asking for. Think of the English, sitting down for tea during the Blitz!'

'Under falling bombs?' whispered Julia, embarrassed that Anthony was talking so loudly. 'After all these years you're still such a complainer. And what if I told the security officer that the man I'm travelling with is not *actually* my father? What if I explained the details of our situation? Common sense. Ha! Good luck with that if anyone finds out the deal. I know I lost every last ounce of common sense the moment you stepped out of that box and said hello.'

Anthony shrugged and moved forward in the queue. It was almost his turn to walk through the metal detector. The implications of what Julia had just said hit her all at once. She tugged frantically at his arm.

'Come on,' she whispered with rising panic. 'Let's get out of here. Flying was a dumb idea. We can rent a car. I'll drive, and we'll be in Montreal in six hours. We can talk along the way – I promise. It's easier to talk in a car anyway.'

'What's gotten into you, dear?'

'Don't you get it?' she hissed into his ear. 'You'll get busted in two seconds. You're full of electronics. The metal detectors will start shrieking the moment you step through. Cops will tackle you, cuff you, search you and run you through an X-ray head to toe, then take you apart to understand how you work!'

Anthony just smiled and stepped towards the security officer. He opened his passport and unfolded a letter tucked inside the cover, which he then handed to the guard.

After reading it, the security officer asked Anthony to step aside while he summoned his supervisor, who promptly arrived and read the letter. From that point on he treated Anthony with the utmost respect, letting him bypass the metal detector to be courteously patted down before continuing on his way.

Julia, on the other hand, wasn't spared the extensive security screening imposed on all the other passengers. She was forced to take off her shoes and belt. Her hair clip was confiscated because it was too long and pointy, as were a pair of fingernail clippers she had forgotten in her bag and a matching nail file that exceeded the acceptable length by a few millimetres. The supervisor lectured her for being so careless.

Didn't she see the screens along the way with the lists of prohibited items? Julia scoffed in response and said it would be shorter to list the things that *were* authorized. The officer's tone shifted to that of a drill sergeant. He asked if she had a problem with the regulations. Julia hastily reassured him that she did not. Her flight took off in only forty-five minutes, and she didn't have time for any further delays. She hurried off to claim her bag and join Anthony, who had been observing her from afar. He looked amused.

'Someone's feeling more smug than usual,' she said when she reached him. 'How'd you get through so easily?'

Anthony waved the letter in his hand, then handed it over to his daughter to read.

'What? Since when do you have a pacemaker?'

'I've had it for ten years.'

'Why?'

'I had a small heart attack. I wasn't really given a choice in the matter.'

'When was this?' Julia asked, a bit stunned.

'If I told you it was on the anniversary of your mother's death, it would only give you one more excuse to call me dramatic.'

'Why didn't anybody call me?'

'Maybe because you were too busy living your life. And you had a new phone number. You never shared it with me.'

'Nobody told me anything about this.'

'As I said, we didn't know how to reach you. Anyway, that's all water under the bridge now, isn't it? For the first few months I was infuriated about having to live off a device. The irony of course is that now I'm forced to live *in* a device. Shall we be off then? Don't want to miss that plane,' said Anthony, looking up at the departures board and sighing as he found their flight. 'Of course. A one-hour delay. Just once for a flight to be on time . . . far too much to ask.'

Julia took advantage of the extra time to nose around the airport bookshop. She peered at Anthony from behind a magazine rack, her father fully unaware. He was seated in the waiting area, facing the runways, staring off into the distance. For the first time Julia felt the ache and sting that meant she missed her father. She decided to call Stanley.

'I'm at the airport,' she said in a low voice.

'Are you getting ready for takeoff?' asked her friend, his voice barely audible.

'Are you with somebody? Is this a bad time?'

'I was about to ask you the same question.'

'Of course not. I'm the one who called you!' Julia replied.

'Well, then why are you whispering?'

'I was whispering?' Julia cleared her throat and looked around, feeling a little foolish.

'You know, you should really stop by my store more often. You're a regular good-luck charm. I sold that eighteenth-century clock an hour after you left. It had been gathering dust up there for over two years.'

'If it really was eighteenth century, another couple of months wouldn't have made much of a difference.'

'Goes to show you never can tell,' Stanley said, pausing for a moment before continuing. 'I don't know who you're with, and I don't care. But don't treat me like an idiot who can't tell when some-thing is up. I hate that!'

'It's really not what you think. Have a little faith, will you?'

'You can't begin to imagine what I think.'

'I'm going to miss you.'

Stanley sighed. 'Make the most of the next few days. Travel can do wonders for clearing your mind.'

Stanley hung up before Julia could have the last word. He stared at the lifeless phone and muttered to himself, 'I don't care who he is as long as he's not some Canadian come to sweep you up north. It's horribly dull here without you. I'm already bored out of my mind.'

8.

At 5.30 p.m., American Airlines flight 4742 touched down at Montreal-Trudeau Airport. Julia and Anthony passed through customs without a hitch and found a driver waiting for them outside. Traffic was light, and half an hour later they were already going through the financial district. Anthony gestured towards a glimmering skyscraper across the way.

'I remember watching that come up as it was built,' he said wistfully. 'It's the same age as you.'

'Any particular reason you're telling me this?'

'You said you're fond of this city, so I'm giving you something to remember. Someday you'll be walking around this neighbourhood, and you'll remember that your father spent a few months of his life working in that skyscraper. This street will seem less anonymous.'

'Wonderful,' she said dryly.

'Aren't you going to ask what I did there?'

'Business as usual I suppose.'

'Yes and no. Back then I was the proud owner of a little newsstand. You see, you weren't born with a silver spoon in your mouth. That came later.'

'Wow. Did you work there long?' Julia asked, taken aback.

'Well, one day I had the idea of selling coffee, too. That's when business really started picking up,' Anthony continued with a twinkle in his eye. 'People would stagger into the lobby, frozen stiff from the harsh winter wind. You should have seen them throw themselves at me for coffee, hot chocolate, tea . . . I was charging twice the market price and making money hand over fist. Eventually I added sandwiches to the menu. Your mother would get up at the crack of dawn to make them. The kitchen in our apartment became a regular sandwich factory.'

'You and Mom lived in Montreal?'

'Indeed. Surrounded by lettuce, cold cuts and plastic wrap. When I started offering deliveries both to the offices above and to the building that had just sprung up next door, I had to bring on my first employee.'

'Who was that?'

'Your mother. She tended the newsstand while I made deliveries. She was so striking, people would come by four times a day just to steal a peek at her. God, we really had a ball back then. She had faces and preferences memorized down to the last customer. The accountant from 1407, who had a little crush on her, got extra cheese, but the director of human resources on the eleventh really rubbed her the wrong way, and all he ever got was the dregs of the mustard jar and a sad little wilted leaf of lettuce.'

Their car pulled up in front of the hotel, and they followed the bellboy to the front desk.

'We don't have a reservation,' Julia said, handing her passport to the receptionist.

The man behind the desk nodded but then furled his brow when he saw Julia's name. He started tapping info into his computer.

'Actually you do have a reservation, ma'am. And a very nice one at that.'

Julia just gaped at him. Anthony inched back with a guilty look on his face.

'Mr and Mrs Walsh . . . Coverman,' the receptionist continued. 'And unless I'm mistaken, it looks like you're with us the entire week.'

'You didn't!' Julia whispered to her father, mortified. Anthony did a poor job of feigning innocence until the receptionist came to the rescue.

'You have the, uh . . .' He stumbled over his words, seeming to notice all at once the age difference between the two. 'Honeymoon suite.'

'You could have at least picked a different hotel,' Julia growled at her father under her breath.

'It was one of those package deals!' said Anthony, defending himself. 'All inclusive. Surprise, surprise. Your future husband went the whole hog, airfare plus lodging. We're lucky he didn't choose the hotel meal plan. I promise it won't cost him a thing. We'll put it on my card. Though don't thank me – everything that's mine is now technically yours, so really I should be thanking you!' He chuckled.

'That's not the real problem.'

'What is then?'

'*Honeymoon* suite?'

'Not to worry. I checked with the travel agency about that as well. Two bedrooms linked by a sitting room. In the penthouse. I hope you haven't developed a fear of heights.'

As Julia continued to lecture her father, the concierge gave them their room key and wished them a pleasant stay.

As the bellboy escorted them towards the elevators, Julia turned and marched right back up to the receptionist.

'It's not what you think! He's my father.'

'But I didn't think anything, ma'am,' he replied, embarrassed.

'Oh no, you thought something all right. And it's not true.' Julia's cheeks were pink with embarrassment.

'Mademoiselle, I assure you I've seen it all,' he said, leaning over the counter so nobody would hear. 'Your secret's safe with me,' he said in a tone that was meant to be reassuring.

Julia's embarrassment quickly turned into anger, and she was just about to spit a catty comeback when Anthony took her by the arm and forcefully steered her away from the front desk.

'You worry far too much about what other people think.'

'So what?'

'Come on, the bellboy is holding the elevator doors open. We're not the only guests in this hotel, you know.'

◆ ◆ ◆

The suite fit Anthony's description to a T. The bedrooms were separated by a sitting room, with windows looking out over the old city centre. Julia barely had time to put her things down before there was a knock on the door. A waiter stood outside in the corridor, proudly presenting a room service trolley with the full works: champagne on ice, two crystal flutes and a box of chocolates.

'What on earth is all this?' demanded Julia.

'Compliments of the hotel, ma'am,' he replied. 'It's part of our honeymoon package.'

Julia gave him a withering look and picked up a card which had been delicately placed on the white linen tablecloth. The director of the hotel wished to express his sincere thanks to Mr and Mrs Walsh-Coverman for choosing the establishment to celebrate their union. The entire staff would be at their disposal to make their honeymoon unforgettable. Julia tore the card into little pieces, which she carefully put back on the cart, before slamming the door in the waiter's face.

'But ma'am! It's included in the price of your room!' she heard from the corridor outside.

Julia didn't bother responding. The trolley's wheels creaked as it trundled back towards the elevator. Julia whipped open the door and strode over to the waiter. She snatched the box of chocolates and spun back around. The door of Room 702 slammed a second time.

'What was all that?' asked Anthony, coming out of his bedroom.

'Nothing,' replied Julia, now seated calmly on a window ledge in the main space between the two bedrooms.

'Quite the view, don't you think?' her father said as he gazed out at the Saint Lawrence River in the distance. 'The weather is beautiful today. Would you care for a walk?'

'Anything to get out of here.'

'I'm not the one who chose the hotel,' her father retorted as he wrapped a cardigan around his daughter's shoulders.

With uneven cobblestones and quaint architecture, the streets of Old Montreal had an old-fashioned charm to rival that of many cities in Europe. Anthony and Julia began their walk at the Place d'Armes. Anthony took it upon himself to recount the biography of Montreal's founder in painstaking detail as they stood at the feet of a statue portraying the historical figure above a small fountain. Julia yawned, leaving her father halfway through the tale to check out a sweet seller a few yards away.

She returned with a bagful of sweets, which she offered to share with her father. Anthony rejected the sugary treats, half offended at her insolence and half out of pure disgust. Julia glanced back and forth between the bronze statue of Lord Maisonneuve high on his podium and her father with a mix of amusement and self-satisfaction.

'What?' Anthony asked.

'The resemblance is uncanny. You two make quite the pair. I think you would have gotten along very well.'

She led her father in the direction of rue Notre-Dame. Anthony made her stop at the facade of Number 130, explaining that it was the oldest building in the city. He told her it still housed a few of the priests who were once the island's city leaders.

Julia let out another yawn and pushed onwards in the direction of the Notre-Dame Basilica of Montreal. Fearing what would come next, she begged her father to spare her more of the guided tour.

'You have no idea what you're missing,' he called after her as she tried to speed past the monument. 'The ceiling is painted like a starry night sky . . . It's incredible!'

'Well, now I know,' she answered from a distance.

'Your mother and I baptized you in there!' Anthony had to shout after her.

Julia stopped short, did an about-turn and returned to her father's side.

'Fine, we'll go in and have a look at your starry ceiling,' she said, capitulating.

The painted ceiling was a sight of staggering beauty. Framed by sumptuously carved wooden ornaments, the ceiling seemed to be covered in lapis lazuli. Enthralled, Julia walked towards the altar.

'I never imagined anything could be so beautiful,' she murmured.

'Glad to hear it,' Anthony replied triumphantly.

He led her over to the side chapel of the Sacred Heart.

'You really had me baptized right here?' she asked.

'Of course not. Your mother was an atheist. She never would have allowed it!'

'What? Then why the hell did you say that?'

'Because I didn't want you to miss out on all this beauty,' Anthony responded as they retraced their steps back towards the massive wooden doors at the front of the church.

As they crossed rue Saint-Jacques, Julia almost felt like she was back in downtown Manhattan, with tall buildings like those of Wall Street on both sides. The sky began to dim, and the street lights of rue Sainte-Hélène flickered to life. A little further on they arrived at a small square with tree-lined paths bordered by grass. All of a sudden Anthony lunged for a bench to steady himself, nearly collapsing in the process. Julia hurried to his side.

'It's nothing,' he said. 'Just a glitch. Something wrong with my knee.'

Julia helped him sit down.

'Does it hurt?'

'Oh no. Pain is a thing of the past,' he said with a grimace. 'Dying must have a couple of perks after all.'

'Well, then why are you making that face? You certainly look like you're in pain.'

'It must be part of my programming. If a person got hurt and showed no outward signs of pain, it would seem suspicious, don't you think?'

'Okay, okay. I don't need all the details. Is there . . . anything I can do?'

Anthony took a little black notebook and pencil from his pocket and handed them to Julia.

'Can you note that on the second full day the right leg suffered a malfunction? And be sure to give them this notebook on Sunday. Our observations could help improve future models.'

Julia said nothing. Her hand shook as she struggled to write down her father's words. Anthony noticed and gently took the pencil back.

'On second thought it's really not that important. I can walk fine now, I'm sure of it.' He got up and took a couple of steps. 'A minor anomaly that seems to have corrected itself.'

At the sight of a horse-drawn carriage rolling into the Place d'Youville, Julia declared that she had always dreamed of taking a carriage ride. She had watched them trot by a thousand times in Central Park without ever having dared, and now was the time. She caught the coachman's eye and gave a little wave. Her father gave the carriage a horrified look, but Julia made her way straight towards it, the issue clearly not up for discussion. Anthony rolled his eyes and grunted as he hoisted himself up on to the seat.

'Ridiculous. We look absolutely ridiculous,' he muttered under his breath.

'Whatever happened to not caring what other people think?'

'There are limits.'

'You wanted to travel together, didn't you? Well, this is travelling.'

Clearly uncomfortable, Anthony peered back towards the horse's rear, watching it swing with each step.

'I'm warning you, if the tail of that pachyderm makes even the slightest upward movement, I'm getting out.'

'It's a horse. Not an elephant or a rhino,' Julia replied, correcting him.

'With an ass like that, you could've fooled me!'

◆ ◆ ◆

The carriage pulled up in front of Café des Éclusiers, on the Old Port. Julia and Anthony climbed down for a look, but enormous grain silos blocked the view of the opposite shore. Their colossal curving forms thrust upwards out of the water as though climbing into pure darkness.

'Let's go this way,' said Anthony gloomily, turning away from the river. 'I've never much cared for those ugly concrete monsters. I can't believe they've never gotten around to knocking them down.'

'Maybe they're under some kind of protection,' Julia responded. 'Who knows? They could take on a certain charm as they age.'

'Well, I certainly won't be around to see it. And frankly I doubt you will be either.'

He led his daughter down the Old Port promenade. As they wandered along the green stretches that bordered the Saint Lawrence River, Julia started walking a few paces ahead of her father. A flock of seagulls took flight and caught her eye. As Julia turned her gaze skyward, the evening breeze blew a lock of her hair loose. She tucked it back behind her ear, catching sight of her father out of the corner of her eye.

'What are you looking at?' she asked.

'Only you.'

'And why is that?'

'I was watching and thinking how beautiful you are. How much you look like your mother,' he replied with a faint smile.

Julia looked at him flatly. 'I'm hungry,' was her only response.

'We should be able to find a place you'll like a bit farther ahead. The area is swarming with little restaurants, each more revolting than the last.'

'Ah, and in your humble opinion which is the most horrible?'

'Don't worry, I've got faith in us as a team. If we put our heads together, I'm sure we'll find the worst one, you'll see!'

Along the way Julia and Anthony loitered in front of the shop windows where the promenade crossed the Quai des Evénements, with the former dock extending out into the Saint Lawrence River.

Julia suddenly caught sight of a familiar figure bobbing about in the crowd, a silhouette that was unmistakable. 'Look! Look over there. It's him!' she exclaimed, pointing.

'Who? Where?' Anthony's gaze followed her finger.

'Right there! Black sports jacket, by the ice cream stand.'

'I don't see him.'

She dragged her father ahead, forcing him to walk faster.

Anthony wrenched himself free of her grip. 'What's gotten into you?'

'Hurry up, we're losing him!'

Julia dived straight into the flow of tourists walking out on to the jetty.

'Who on earth are we following?' complained Anthony as he struggled to keep up with her.

'Trust me! Come on!' she called back over her shoulder, leaving her father behind.

Anthony plonked himself straight down on a bench, refusing to take another step. Julia broke into a near full-on sprint after the mysterious man who had caught her attention. A few moments later she returned to her father's side, disappointed.

'I lost him,' she panted, dropping down next to him on the bench.

'Will you tell me what the hell you're going on about?'

'Over there, near those stands . . . I could have sworn I saw Wallace! Your assistant.'

'Wallace is completely ordinary looking. He looks like everyone, and everyone looks like him. Your eyes were playing tricks on you.'

'Well, the least you could do was keep up so I would've known for sure.'

'Yes, well . . . my knee,' Anthony responded plaintively.

'I thought you said it didn't hurt.'

'It's the damned programming again. Cut me some slack – I can't control everything. I'm a very complicated machine. Anyway, let's imagine Wallace is here. Why not? He's a free man now. He has every right. He's retired.'

'I suppose so, but . . . you've got to admit it would be a strange coincidence.'

'It's a small world. Anyway, I'd be willing to bet the man you saw wasn't Wallace. Didn't you say you were hungry?'

Julia helped her father to his feet.

'All better now,' he said, giving his leg a shake. 'Right as rain. Let's stroll around a bit longer and get something to eat.'

With the warm early-summer weather, the Old Port promenade was overflowing with vendors selling souvenirs and trinkets.

'Come on, let's go over there,' said Anthony, leading his daughter out on to the jetty.

'I thought we were going to have dinner.'

Anthony noticed a ravishing young woman sketching ten-dollar portraits.

'Quite the talent,' Anthony said, observing her work.

A few sketches clipped to the fence served as proof, further confirmed by the portrait of a tourist to which she was applying the finishing touches. Julia dismissed the entire scene. When she was hungry, she had little patience for anything else. For her, hunger was an urgent matter. Her appetite had always astounded the men around her, work colleagues and ex-boyfriends alike. Once, Adam had made the mistake of challenging her to a pancake-eating contest. As Julia eagerly attacked her seventh, Adam, who had tapped out after five, was already grappling with the early stages of an unforgettable case of indigestion. And to make matters worse, Julia never put on a pound.

'Can we go already?' she insisted.

'Hold on,' Anthony responded, slipping down into the seat and taking the place of the tourist who had just left.

Julia rolled her eyes.

'What are you doing now?' she asked impatiently.

'What's it look like? I'm getting my portrait done,' Anthony retorted with an uncharacteristically playful lilt. He turned to the artist, who was already sharpening her charcoal pencil. 'Full or profile?'

'How about three-quarter profile?' suggested the young woman.

'Left or right?' he asked, shifting in the folding chair to show both views. 'People always say I'm more distinguished from this angle. What do you think? Julia? What's the verdict?'

'Nothing. No opinion,' she said, turning away.

'Come now. With all the gummy bears you just devoured, there's no way you're still hungry!'

The portrait artist gave Julia a sympathetic smile.

'My father,' Julia said, gesturing down at Anthony. 'We haven't seen each other for years. He was always too busy. Last time we took a walk together, it was around a petting zoo, and he's elected to pick up right where we left off. Whatever you do, don't let him know I'm an adult in my thirties. He'd die of shock.'

The young woman chuckled and set down her pencil. 'It'll ruin his portrait if you keep making me laugh.'

'See?' Anthony interjected. 'You're distracting this young lady from doing her job. Why don't you quit hovering about and go have a look at her other portraits? It won't take long.'

'He couldn't care less about what you draw, you know. Just an excuse to get close to a pretty young girl!' declared Julia.

Anthony beckoned his daughter to lean in closer. Sceptical as she was, she did, and he whispered in her ear, 'How many daughters get to see their father have his portrait done three days after his death?'

At a loss for a clever reply, Julia walked away. Anthony held his pose like a statue, eyes following his daughter as she looked over the older sketches the artist had hung up to attract customers.

Suddenly something she saw stopped Julia's heart. She froze in place, eyes widening and throat constricting. One particular drawing had opened the floodgates of her memory. Clipped to the fence . . . a face with a shaded cleft in the chin, slightly exaggerated lines tracing the cheekbones, a noble, almost insolent brow . . . and a gaze that seemed to lock eyes with her, transcending the limits of the paper. The mere sight of it sent Julia spiralling years into the past, awakening a torrent of forgotten feelings . . .

'Thomas?' she stammered.

9.

Julia had turned eighteen on 1 September 1989. To celebrate her coming of age and her newfound independence, she decided to drop out of the college Anthony had forced her to go to. Her rebellion would be to study abroad in an international exchange programme, with a drastic change of majors. Over the years she had saved up money from tutoring jobs, which she combined with winnings from late-night card games and a generous scholarship. Getting the scholarship, considering her father's fortune, required the help of her father's personal assistant. Despite Wallace's misgivings ('Miss, if your father had any idea what I was doing . . .'), he ultimately signed the paperwork that certified it had been years since Julia had received support from Anthony Walsh. When that paperwork was presented in combination with her payslips, the exchange programme had been convinced, and her scholarship approved.

She was able to get her passport on the sly from her father's Park Avenue townhouse during a brief and stormy visit. Slamming the door behind her, she hopped on a bus to JFK.

Early morning, 6 October 1989: Julia landed in Paris.

In her mind's eye she could still picture her old student apartment. Beside a window with a view of the sagging rooftops of the Left Bank stood a rickety table, a metal folding chair and a lamp – a survivor from another century. She remembered the sweet-smelling but scratchy bed sheets, but she couldn't recall the names of the two girls who had lived across the landing. She could picture each step of the walk from boulevard Saint-Michel to her classes at the École des Beaux-Arts with complete clarity. She could see the facade of the dingy bar on the corner of boulevard Arago, with its clients smoking and drinking cafe cognac, even in the morning. She had been so happy with her newfound independence that her studies flowed by smoothly, uninterrupted by anything, even romance. Julia drew continuously through the days and nights that followed. She sat sketching on nearly every bench in the Jardin du Luxembourg, walked down all of the tree-lined paths and stretched out on all of the 'Keep Off The Grass' lawns to observe the clumsy gait of the birds, the only ones authorized to be there. October flew past and the last days of her first autumn in Paris evaporated into the grey of early November.

She thought back to what started as an ordinary evening at Café Arago, with students from the Sorbonne fervently discussing the latest news from Germany. Since the beginning of September, thousands of East Germans had crossed the border into Hungary in a desperate attempt to reach the West. Just that week a million citizens had been out protesting in the streets of East Berlin.

'It's the end of the world as we know it! History's being made!' one of the students cried out.

His name was Antoine.

The memories flooded back.

'We have to go! Go to the Wall!' another declared.

And that one was Mathias. I remember . . . a chain-smoker. He would fly off the handle at the drop of a dime. He never stopped talking, and on the rare occasion he had nothing to say, he would hum. I've never met anybody so afraid of silence.

A group of interested students had gathered at the cafe and were debating taking a trip straight into the heart of the revolution. They decided to leave for Germany by car that night. If they drove in shifts, they could reach Berlin by noon. Show of hands?

Julia couldn't say what had pushed her to raise her hand in Café Arago that evening. It felt as though some mighty wind was pushing at her, bringing her straight to that table of students from the Sorbonne.

'Can I come along?' she asked as she approached the group.

I remember every word.

'I know how to drive, and I'm well rested. I just slept most of the day.'

That was a total lie.

'I could take the first shift and drive for hours.'

Antoine checked with the others. *Was it Antoine or Mathias?* The group was swept up in the drama of the epic journey ahead, the whole thing becoming more and more concrete with each passing moment. They took a quick vote on Julia coming along for the trip.

'We should have an American representative along with us,' Mathias suggested, seeing Antoine's reservations.

He was finally swayed and raised his hand, along with the others.

'When she returns home, she can testify to France's sympathy for contemporary revolutions.'

They pushed back their chairs to make room, and Julia was suddenly surrounded by new friends. A while later they stood on boulevard Arago and said their goodbyes to the others staying behind. She planted farewell kisses on the cheeks of countless faces – she didn't recognize half of them, but as part of the group she now had to pay her respects to those not coming along for the journey. Those heading to Berlin were divided into different cars, each taking a different route. Julia would join Mathias and Antoine. There was no time to lose; a six-hundred-mile drive lay ahead of them. The night of 7 November, as they drove along the Seine, Julia never imagined she was saying goodbye to Paris forever and that she would never again see that view of the Left Bank rooftops from her studio.

Senlis, Compiègne, Amiens, Cambrai . . . One after another signs with names of mysterious towns she had never heard of appeared as the road stretched on.

Julia took the wheel around midnight, in Valenciennes, just before crossing the border into Belgium. Her American passport aroused curiosity from the border guard, but her student ID from the École des Beaux-Arts allowed the group to continue their road trip without incident.

Mathias was always singing, and it got on Antoine's nerves. Julia spent her time trying to make out the lyrics, which she couldn't always understand. At least it helped her stay awake.

The memories brought a smile to Julia's face . . . and more kept coming back to her. They had stopped at a service station along the highway. *We counted our money and decided to buy some baguettes and ham.* One of them bought a bottle of Coke in honour of Julia's roots. In the end she drank only a sip.

Her travelling companions spoke French too quickly, using many expressions that were completely indecipherable to her. She had mistakenly assumed that the six years of French classes would make her bilingual. *Why did Daddy insist I learn French in the first place? Was it in honour of his days in Montreal?*

They took the wrong exit outside of Mons, at La Louvière, and had to endure a harrowing drive through Brussels. They stopped to ask a local for directions to Liège. Julia couldn't understand a word due to the man's thick Belgian accent, which kept Mathias laughing for a long time. Antoine recalculated their journey time. The detour had cost them an hour. Mathias begged Julia to drive faster. The revolution wasn't going to wait for them! They checked the map and turned around, deciding that the northernmost route would take too long. They decided to go towards Liège, then through Düsseldorf.

First they crossed through Flemish-speaking Belgium. As the French signs thinned out and disappeared, Julia marvelled at the three different languages spoken just a few miles apart. 'A quaint country full of waffles and lace,' concluded Mathias dismissively, urging her to pick up the pace. Just before Liège, Julia's eyelids grew heavy with fatigue and the car swerved, jarring her two passengers.

They stopped on the hard shoulder to gather their wits. Antoine gave her a lecture, and she was banished to the back seat.

Julia didn't mind her punishment all that much. She fell asleep before the border crossing and didn't remember a second of it. Mathias's diplomatic passport – attained through his ambassador father – persuaded the West German border guards to let his 'stepsister' sleep. After all, she was exhausted from the overnight flight to Europe from the States.

The officer had been understanding and waved them on after a cursory glance at the three passports stowed in the glove compartment.

The two boys decided to make a pit stop without consulting Julia. It was clear that everyone could use a proper breakfast at a real cafe. And so, on the morning of 8 November, just as they were driving into Dortmund, Julia woke up to find herself in Germany for the first time in her life. Little did she know that her world would be turned upside down the very next day.

Julia took the wheel once more just past Bielefeld, near Hanover. Antoine protested, but it was clear the two guys were in no shape to drive, and Berlin was still a great distance away. Both French passengers crashed straight away, leaving Julia to enjoy a few moments of silence. As the car approached Helmstedt, the journey took on a more ominous tone. In the distance barbed-wire fences marked the border of East Germany. Mathias woke up and told Julia to pull over on the hard shoulder right away.

They plotted a strategy, deciding what roles they would play when crossing the border. Mathias would take the wheel, Antoine would be in the passenger seat and Julia would stay in the back. All of their hopes rested on Mathias's precious diplomatic passport. Mathias insisted they rehearse their lines. Any mention of their real objective had to be carefully avoided. When they were asked why they wanted to enter the East, Mathias would say he was visiting his father, who was a diplomat in Berlin. Julia would play up the fact that she was American and also claim to have a diplomat father currently in the city. 'What about me?' Antoine asked. 'Just try and keep your mouth shut,' replied Mathias, turning the key in the ignition.

A dense fir-tree forest stretched up to the edge of the road. In a clearing ahead stood the leviathan forms of the checkpoint compound. The buildings were more on the scale of a train station than a border crossing. Their car wove between two articulated lorries. A guard motioned for them to change lanes, and Julia could see Mathias's optimism evaporate.

Two enormous pylons studded with searchlights towered above the treetops of the vast forest. Four watchtowers nearly as high as the searchlights stood across from them. A sign marked 'Marienborn Border Checkpoint' loomed over the metal gates, which opened, then shut behind each vehicle.

At the first inspection point they were told to open the boot. As the officers rifled through Antoine's and Mathias's bags, Julia realized she hadn't brought a single thing of her own. They were told to move their car ahead. A little further on they drove through a corridor flanked by white corrugated-iron buildings, where their passports would be inspected. An officer ordered Mathias to stand away from the others. Antoine began to grumble that the whole trip was utterly insane, just as he had insisted from the beginning. Mathias reminded him about the promise he had made to be silent during the border crossing. Julia threw anxious glances at Mathias, completely lost as to what she was supposed to do next. The guard asked Mathias to follow him.

Mathias took our passports and followed the customs officer. I remember it like it was yesterday. Antoine and I waited. Even though we were all alone in that gloomy tin shed we followed his orders – we didn't utter a word about what we were really doing. Mathias returned with a soldier behind him. We had no way of knowing what would happen next. The young soldier looked us over one at a time. He gave the passports back to Mathias and gestured for us to continue down the road. I had never been so terrified in my entire life. I'd never before experienced that heart-stopping sensation, having my personal space and freedom violated so completely, like something slipping under my skin and chilling me to the bone. Our car slowly rolled towards the next checkpoint, where we came to a stop under the roof of an enormous building. Mathias was taken aside, and we found ourselves alone once more. When he finally came back, his smile told us we had made it. We were free to continue on into Berlin. We were told to stay on the highway until we reached our final destination.

A cool breeze blew across the promenade from the Old Port of Montreal, sending a chill down Julia's spine. Her eyes remained glued to the face on the charcoal drawing. The paper it was drawn on seemed far whiter than the corrugated buildings that had once stood on the border, cutting Germany in two.

I was making my way toward you, Thomas. Neither of us had any idea what was to come. And you . . . you were still alive.

It took at least another hour before Mathias started to sing again. Aside from a few lorries, the only vehicles they encountered were little East German Trabants. It was as though all East Germans owned identical cars to avoid competition with neighbours. In comparison the students' Peugeot 504 made quite an impression. The other drivers gawked in wonder as the car continued on its way.

They drove past Magdeburg, Schermen, Theessen, Köpernitz and finally Potsdam, just twenty miles outside Berlin. When they entered the Berlin suburbs, Antoine insisted that he drive. Julia burst out laughing, reminding him that it was *her* compatriots who had liberated the city forty-five years earlier and not his.

'And they're still there,' Antoine replied with a bitter undertone.

'Alongside the French,' was Julia's icy response.

'Give it a rest. The two of you are wearing me out,' Mathias chimed in.

They fell silent once again until they reached the gates of the Western enclave in the middle of East Germany. Nobody spoke until they had crossed into the city. Then Mathias triumphantly cried, *'Ich bin ein Berliner!'*

10.

They arrived in Berlin much later than planned. The afternoon of 8 November was already drawing to a close, but they ignored the time they had lost and denied the exhaustion wearing away at them. The electricity in the air was palpable; they could feel that something enormous was happening, just as Antoine had predicted. Four days earlier a million East Germans gathered in protest in the streets. The Wall loomed over everything, with thousands of soldiers and guard dogs patrolling it day and night. For twenty-eight years families, friends and neighbours had been separated from one another by twenty-eight miles of concrete, barbed wire and watchtowers. The sudden and brutal growth of these horrific structures came to symbolize the Cold War during that dismal summer. People who had once lived side by side were helpless to do anything but wait, desperately longing to be reunited, without ever daring to hope that day would come.

Seated at a bar, the three friends eavesdropped on the conversations around them. Antoine did his best to translate for Mathias and Julia, putting the whole of his high school German to use. People were saying that the communist regime could not possibly hold out much longer. Some even thought it was just a matter of time before the borders would be opened.

Everything had changed since Gorbachev's visit to East Germany in October. A journalist from *Der Tagesspiegel*, who had dropped in to grab a quick beer, described how his newspaper was buzzing with activity. He even confessed that headlines which normally would have already gone to print were currently on hold. Something important was about to happen, but he could not say more.

At nightfall their long journey finally caught up with them. Julia couldn't stop yawning and got hiccups. Mathias tried everything he could to stop them. First he tried scaring her, but each attempt just made her burst out laughing, intensifying the jolting hiccups, which shook her body each time. Antoine got involved. They contorted their bodies and did gymnastics. They made her drink a glass of water while being held upside down with her arms stretched out. The cure was supposedly foolproof, yet her hiccups returned immediately with a vengeance. A few regulars at the bar proposed other solutions. Downing a pint in one gulp might work. She could try holding her breath as long as possible. Another person suggested she lie on the ground and bring her knees to her chest. Everyone had an idea. Finally a friendly doctor having a beer at the bar told Julia in nearly flawless English that she simply needed to get some rest. The dark circles under her eyes gave away her exhaustion – sleep would be the best medicine. The three friends decided to search for a youth hostel.

Antoine tried to ask the bartender where they could find a place to stay, but he was exhausted as well, and the man couldn't understand a single word he said. They finally found two rooms in a little hotel close by. The boys could share one, and Julia would have the other to herself. They crawled up the stairs to the fourth floor and collapsed in bed. Mathias fell asleep instantly, sprawled across the entire bed before Antoine could protest, so he ended up spending the night on a down duvet on the floor.

◆ ◆ ◆

The portrait artist was having trouble finishing her sketch. She had already asked Anthony three times to hold still, but he took no notice of her. Each time she tried to capture his likeness, he turned his head to look at his daughter. Julia was still staring at the sample portraits. She had an expression on her face like her thoughts were elsewhere. Not once had she taken her eyes from the board since Anthony sat down.

◆ ◆ ◆

It was almost midday on 9 November when the three travellers reunited in the lobby of the little hotel. They took that afternoon to explore Berlin. *A few hours, Thomas . . . I'll meet you for the first time in just a few short hours.*

Their first stop was the Siegessäule Victory Column. Mathias found it far more striking than the one that stood at Place Vendôme, in Paris. Antoine insisted that comparing the two was completely point- less. Julia asked if they always bickered like this. The two were aston- ished at the question – for them it was just a normal conversation, and they didn't understand what she meant. They walked on through the Kurfürstendamm shopping district. They wandered down hundreds of streets, slumping against each other on trams, until Julia insisted she couldn't take another step. In the middle of the afternoon the three stopped to collect their thoughts in front of the memorial church that the locals referred to as *Der hohle Zahn*, or 'the hollow tooth'. After bombs had destroyed most of the building during World War Two, the wrecked tower had been preserved as a memorial. What remained of the church did indeed bear a strong resemblance to a jagged incisor.

At six thirty, Julia and her friends found themselves at the edge of a park, which they decided to cross on foot.

A short while later a spokesman for the East German government made a declaration that would change the course of history, or at least the end of the twentieth century. East Germans would be allowed to come and go as they pleased. They would be free to cross into the West without being shot at by soldiers or torn to pieces by guard dogs. Hundreds of men, women and children had died trying to get to the other side during those bleak Cold War years, only to be cut down by bullets from zealous guardians in their watchtowers, and now the East Berliners were suddenly free to go. A journalist asked the spokesman when the decision would come into effect. The bureaucrat must have misunderstood the question and simply responded, 'Immediately!'

The news received wall-to-wall coverage from all radio and television stations, echoing incessantly throughout the East and the West.

Thousands of West Germans gathered at the checkpoints. Thousands of East Germans did the same. Two French students and an American girl were swept along with them, riding the wave as the mass of humanity made a mad dash for freedom.

At ten thirty, the border crossings on both sides were flooded with thousands of citizens hungry for freedom. The soldiers guarding the checkpoints found themselves at the foot of the Wall. The barriers at Bornheimer Strasse came down, and Germany took one giant step closer to reunification.

You ran through the city, making your way through the streets, rushing toward freedom, and I walked toward you without knowing or understanding the force that pushed me onward. The victory of the Wall coming down was not my own and Germany not my country. The streets of Berlin were entirely foreign to me.

I also started running, trying desperately to escape the crush of the mob. Antoine and Mathias tried to shield me. We ran along the interminable concrete wall that hopeful artists had covered with layer upon layer of paint. Some of your compatriots couldn't bear to wait at the checkpoints and began to climb over the top. We watched from this side of the world. It was as if you and I were already together even though we were still separate. We watched and waited, holding our breath. All around me people stood with open arms, hoping to cushion falls or to hoist one another up on shoulders for a view of the people running toward them, prisoners of the Iron Curtain who would be free in only a few short moments. Our voices rang out and joined together, a cry of encouragement, a cry to chase away the fear, a cry to let you know we were waiting on the other side. All at once I changed. The American girl who had fled New York, the child of a country that had been at war against yours – I was suddenly swept up in the tide of emotion. At that moment I was German, too. In the innocence of my adolescence I also dared to whisper, 'Ich bin ein Berliner,' and I wept. I wept like a child, Thomas . . .

That evening, lost in the middle of a very different crowd of people, among the wandering tourists on a Montreal wharf, Julia cried once more. The tears flowed freely down her cheeks as she stared at the charcoal-sketched portrait.

Anthony Walsh's eyes were fixed on Julia. He called out to her again.

'Julia? Are you all right?'

His daughter was too far away to hear. Twenty years too far away.

The crowd became increasingly agitated. People started to chip away at the Wall with whatever tools they could get their hands on – screwdrivers, rocks, pocketknives – all pathetic in the face of concrete, but the Wall was an obstacle that was destined to crumble. Just twenty feet away something incredible had started to happen. A world-renowned cellist, who had also come from Paris, heard about the events and came to join us, to join you. He sat down and began to play. Was that really the same evening or a day or two after? It doesn't matter. His music helped pull down the Wall as much as the blows against the concrete. Melodies of freedom floated through the air

and over the Wall toward you. I wasn't the only one crying, you know. I saw many tears that night. Those of a mother and daughter holding each other tightly, overwhelmed to be reunited after twenty-eight years of separation. I saw greying fathers recognize their sons among thousands of others. I saw so many Berliners for whom tears were the only release after all the suffering they had endured. And suddenly, in the middle of it all, I saw you. On top of the Wall, the dust on your face serving only to intensify your beautiful eyes. You were the first man I had ever seen from the East, and I was the first girl you had ever seen from the West.

You stayed crouched atop the Wall for a long time. A new world spread itself before you, and you stared at me as though we were connected by an invisible thread. I cried like a fool, and you smiled down at me. You swung your leg over the Wall and jumped. I did what others had done and opened my arms to you. You fell on top of me, and we rolled across the ground – hallowed ground upon which your footsteps had never tread. You apologized in German, and I said hello in English. You stood up and dusted off my shoulders as though you had done it a hundred times before. You continued speaking, but I couldn't understand a word. From time to time you nodded. I laughed at how ridiculous we were. You extended your hand, and you spoke the name that I would come to repeat so many times, a name that I haven't said in such a very long time.

Thomas.

On the docks a woman bumped into Julia without stopping to apologize. Julia didn't even notice. A black-market street seller hawking jewellery waved a string of wooden beads in her face. She slowly shook her head, deaf to his sales pitch. Anthony got up and gave the portrait artist ten dollars. She gave him the sketch. She had captured his expression to a T; the resemblance was striking. Satisfied with the final product, he got another ten dollars out of his pocket, a generous doubling of her fee. He went to Julia's side.

'What on earth have you been staring at over here for the past ten minutes?'

◆　◆　◆

Thomas, Thomas, Thomas. I had forgotten how good it feels to say your name. I'd forgotten your voice, your dimples and your smile, forgotten every-thing until I saw this portrait. I wish you had never left to cover that war. If I had known what would happen the day you told me you wanted to become a reporter, if I'd had even the slightest notion of how things would end, I would have begged you to choose a different path.

You would have insisted that telling the truth about the world is the best job there is, even if the photographer's lens can be a cruel device, even if the truth can haunt one's dreams, turning them into nightmares. You would have continued with your speech, declaring with a serious tone that our leaders would have knocked down that wall much sooner had the press known the truth about what was happening beyond that concrete barrier. But they did know, Thomas. They knew the details of your lives. They spent their time spying on you. Those who governed in the West simply didn't have enough courage. You would have said that only someone like me, who had grown up in a place where people are free to say and think whatever they want without any fear of reprisal, would be so adamantly against taking risks. We would have argued through the night and into the next morning. If you only knew how much I miss arguing with you, Thomas.

Unable to find a winning argument, I would have given up eventu-ally, just like I did the day I left. How could I possibly hold you back, you who had always longed for freedom? You were right, Thomas. You had one of the best jobs in the world. I wonder if you ever met Masoud and if he finally granted you that interview somewhere in the afterlife. Was it worth it, Thomas? He died nearly a decade after I lost you. Thousands of people joined in his funeral procession through the Panjshir Valley, yet no one ever found your remains. What would my life be like now if that mine hadn't destroyed your convoy? If I hadn't been a coward? If I hadn't abandoned you just a short time before?

◆　◆　◆

Anthony placed a soft hand on Julia's shoulder.

'Who are you talking to?'

'Nobody,' she replied, startled.

'Julia, you're trembling.'

'Go away. Leave me alone,' she whispered.

◆　◆　◆

There was an awkward moment, or perhaps we can call it a delicate one. I introduced you to Antoine and Mathias, going so overboard emphasizing the word friends *that I must have said it six times to be understood. It was ridiculous. You could barely speak English back then. Maybe you did understand. You gave them a smile, and Mathias gave you a congratulatory hug. Antoine was content with a handshake, though he was just as overwhelmed as his friend. The four of us set off into town. You were looking for somebody. I thought it was a woman, but it turned out to be your childhood friend. He had managed to make it over the Wall with his family ten years prior, and you hadn't seen him since. How were we supposed to find your friend among the thousands of people hugging, singing, drinking and dancing in the streets? You turned to me and said, 'The world is big, but friendship is bigger.' I don't know if it was your accent or the innocence behind the thought, but Antoine made fun of you. Yet I thought the notion was absolutely wonderful.*

We decided to help you in your search, and together we combed the streets of West Berlin. You walked with a purpose, as though you were going to meet somebody in a specific place. Along the way, examining every face, you pushed through the milling crowd but constantly turned to look behind you. The sun had already set when Antoine at last stopped in the middle of a square and shouted, 'Could you at least tell us the name of the guy we've been hunting for all this time, stumbling around like fools?' You didn't understand what he was asking. In growing frustration Antoine shouted even louder, 'Prénom! Name! Vorname!' You lost your temper and screamed back your friend's name. 'Knapp!' To show you he wasn't angry, Antoine shouted the same name back as reassurance. 'Knapp! Knapp!'

Laughing hysterically at the scene, Mathias started shouting it, too, and I followed suit. 'Knapp! Knapp!' You looked at us like we were crazy, then started to laugh and eventually joined in yourself. 'Knapp! Knapp!' We were practically dancing, chanting our heads off with the name of the friend you hadn't seen for ten years.

Just then someone in the middle of the enormous crowd turned to face us as we shouted. A man your age. When your eyes met, I felt something akin to jealousy.

Like two wolves separated from the pack finding themselves face-to-face in the forest, you stood completely still . . . just staring at one another. Then Knapp said your name. 'Thomas?' The sight was otherworldly and utterly sublime: two long-lost friends coming together in an embrace, your faces full of pure joy. Antoine started crying, and Mathias tried to console him. Mathias swore that had the two French friends been separated just as long, their reunion would be no different. Antoine replied, between ever-intensifying sobs, that it was unfathomable; they hadn't known each other nearly as long as the two Germans had. You laid your head on your best friend's shoulder. You saw that I was watching, and you immediately straightened up. Then you simply repeated the same words from earlier. 'The world is big, but friendship is bigger.' Antoine wept uncontrollably.

We sat at wooden tables outside a bar. The cold nipped at our cheeks, but we didn't mind. Together, you and Knapp sat off to the side. Catching up on ten years of life called for a lot of words exchanged, yet just as much silence. We all stayed together for the rest of the night and into the following day. The next morning you told Knapp that you couldn't stay any longer and had to go back. Your grandmother lived in the East, and you couldn't leave her alone. You were the only family she had.

She would have turned a hundred years old this winter. I hope, wherever you are now, the two of you are together once more. God, how I adored your grandmother! I remember her knocking on our bedroom door, so pretty with her long white hair in braids. You promised Knapp you'd return soon, as long as things didn't move backward, as long as freedom continued to reign. Knapp assured you it would, and you replied, 'Perhaps, but if I had to wait ten more years to see you again, I'd still think about you every day.'

You rose and thanked us for the gift we had given you, which was nothing at all, but Mathias chimed in that it was his pleasure and he was delighted to have been of service. Antoine suggested we accompany you back to the former checkpoint between East and West.

We set off, following the streams of people. All of them, like you, returned to the East because, revolution or not, their families and homes were still on the other side of the city.

Along the way you took my hand in yours. I said nothing, and we walked like that for miles.

◆ ◆ ◆

'Julia, you're shivering. You'll catch your death out here. Let's go. If you like, I'll buy the damn drawing, and you can look at it as long as you like . . . somewhere warm.'

'No. You can't buy it. It's . . . priceless. We have to leave it here. Just a few more minutes, and then we'll go.'

◆ ◆ ◆

Here and there around the former checkpoint, people were still hacking away at the Wall. We almost said goodbye there. You shook hands with Knapp first. 'Call me as soon as you're able,' he urged, handing you his card. Was it because your best friend was a journalist that you decided to follow the same path? Was it some pact the two of you had made during your younger years? I must have asked you a hundred times without ever getting a direct answer. Instead, you would give me one of those cryptic little smiles, the ones you reserved for the moments when I annoyed you. You exchanged handshakes with Antoine and Mathias, and then you turned to me.

If you knew, Thomas, how fearful I was at that moment – fearful that I might never know the touch of your lips. You came into my life out of nowhere. You held my face in your hands with pure tenderness and placed a gentle kiss on each of my eyelids. 'Thank you,' was all you said, and by the time I opened my eyes you were already walking away. Knapp had watched the two of us, and when at last you let me go and I caught Knapp's eye, the expression on his face surprised me. He looked as though he expected me to say something, to find the words that would forever erase the years the two of you had spent apart. Those long years had shaped each of you so differently; your experiences had been as disparate as your destinations that very night – one to a newspaper, the other to the East.

I cried out, 'Take me with you! I want to meet this grandmother of yours.' I didn't wait for a response. I took your hand in mine once more, and nothing in the world could have broken my grip at that moment. Knapp shrugged, and seeing you at a loss for words he said, 'The roads are open now. Come back whenever you like!' Antoine tried to talk me out of it. He said it was madness, and maybe it was, but I had never felt such an intoxicating feeling before. Mathias elbowed Antoine in the ribs: how was this any of his business? He ran up and hugged me. 'Call us when you get back to Paris,' he said, scribbling his phone number on a scrap of paper. In turn I hugged them both, and the two of us set off.

I never went back to Paris, Thomas. I followed you instead. At dawn on 11 November we took advantage of the general state of chaos and crossed the border. At that moment I was possibly the first American girl to ever enter East Berlin . . . If not the first, certainly the happiest.

I kept my promise, you know. Do you remember that day in the gloomy cafe? You made me swear that if ever we were separated by the cruel hand of fate, I should try to be happy no matter the cost. I knew you said it because the weight of my love was suffocating you. The long years you spent without freedom made it unbearable to think of someone else's life being forever bound to yours. Even though I hated the idea of tainting my happiness, I gave you my word.

I'm getting married, Thomas. At least I was going to. This past Saturday. My wedding was postponed. It's a long story, and it brought me here right now. Maybe I was supposed to see your face one last time. Give your grandmother up in heaven a kiss from me.

◆ ◆ ◆

'This is ridiculous, Julia. If you could just see yourself – you're the one experiencing a glitch now. You've been standing there muttering in the same spot for the past fifteen minutes.'

Julia wandered away without responding. Anthony quickened his pace to catch up with her.

'Can't you please just clue me in as to what's going on?' he asked as he arrived by her side.

Julia remained silent.

'Look,' he continued, holding out his portrait to Julia. 'It's really something, don't you think? Here, it's for you,' he added happily.

Julia ignored him and continued making her way back towards the hotel.

'Okay, we'll save it for later. Clearly this isn't a good time.'

And since Julia still said nothing, her father continued: 'That drawing you were staring at . . . does remind me of someone. Of course that can't have anything to do with your behaviour; it's just a drawing. But for some reason the face does seem . . . vaguely . . . familiar.'

'That's because it's the face you punched when you came looking for me in Berlin. It's the face of the man I loved when I was eighteen years old. Remember? The one you tore me away from when you dragged me back to New York.'

11.

The restaurant was nearly full. An attentive waiter brought them two flutes of champagne. Anthony didn't touch his, but Julia downed hers in a single gulp. She chased it with her father's glass and promptly motioned to the waiter for a refill. By the time the menus arrived, she was already feeling tipsy.

'I think you've had enough,' advised Anthony as she ordered a fourth glass.

'Why? It's got bubbles and it tastes good.'

'You're drunk, Julia.'

'Getting there,' she said, giggling.

'Try toning it down a notch. You don't need to make yourself sick just to ruin our first dinner out together. We can go back to the hotel. Just tell me.'

'No way! I'm starving.'

'Then order room service.'

'I think I'm a little too old for you to speak to me in that tone.'

'You're right, Julia. We're both too old for this. You're acting like when you were a little girl and wanted to push all my buttons.'

'When you think about it, it was the first time I ever made a choice for myself.'

'What are you talking about?'

'Thomas!'

'True, it was your first independent choice. But far from your last if my memory serves.'

'You always wanted to control my life.'

'A common condition among fathers. But your accusation doesn't hold water, not for a father you also accuse of being so absent.'

'Oh, I would have preferred that you be fully absent. In fact you were far too present, just never in person!'

'Keep it down. You're drunk and it's unbecoming.'

'Unbecoming? You don't think it was unbecoming when you showed up out of nowhere at our apartment in Berlin? When you scared the daylights out of Thomas's grandmother so she'd tell you where to find us? When you kicked in the door to find us sleeping and struck the man I loved? You broke his jaw! I'd say that was all pretty goddamn unbecoming.'

'Perhaps I did go a touch too far. I admit it.'

'Oh, you admit it, do you? Would you admit it was unbecoming when you dragged me by my hair and stuffed me into that car? Or when you pulled me across the airport by my arm, shaking me like a rag doll? Makes my skin crawl just thinking about it – the way you buckled me into my seat on the plane like you were afraid I was going to jump out mid-flight. And I'd certainly call it unbecoming the way you locked me in my room back in New York like some kind of low-grade criminal!'

'Sometimes I wonder if it wasn't for the best that I died when I did last week . . .'

'Oh, spare me.'

'Don't get me wrong. That wasn't in response to your sparkling little monologue. I was thinking of something else entirely.'

'And what might that be?'

'The way you've been acting since you saw that drawing.'

Julia's eyes widened.

'What could that possibly have to do with you dying last week?'

'It's funny, isn't it? One could say that, well . . . my death did manage to stop you from getting married on Saturday,' Anthony concluded with a broad smile.

'And you're happy about this.'

'I wasn't, not initially. Up until now I was quite sorry you had to call off the wedding, but I'm beginning to have second thoughts.'

The waiter arrived, nervous after their loud exchange, and delicately asked if they were ready to order. Without hesitation Julia ordered a steak.

'And how would you like that cooked?' asked the waiter.

'Bloody I'd imagine,' replied her father.

'And for you, sir?'

'Are there any lithium batteries on the menu this evening?' Julia asked pointedly.

The waiter searched for a response, but none came. Anthony explained that he was fine and wouldn't be having anything to eat.

'Getting married is one thing,' he continued to his daughter, 'but truly sharing your life with someone is a whole other ball game. It takes a lot of love, a lot of space. It's something both people have to be comfortable with . . . Neither party should feel boxed in.'

'Who are you to judge my relationship with Adam? You don't know the first thing about him.'

'I'm not talking about Adam. I'm talking about you. I'm talking about how much of yourself you're truly ready to give him. If your heart is clouded by the memory of another man, it clearly puts your future happiness in peril.'

'You'd know something about that, wouldn't you?'

'Your mother is dead, Julia. I can't do anything about it even if you keep holding it against me.'

'Thomas is dead, too. And even if you can't do anything about that either, I'll still hold it against you. Adam and I have all the space in the world.'

Anthony coughed. A few beads of perspiration gathered on his brow.

'You're sweating,' said Julia with surprise.

'Another malfunction. It'll pass,' he said, dabbing his temples with a napkin. 'You were only eighteen, Julia. For God's sake, you wanted to throw away your life for this communist whom you had only known for a few short weeks!'

'Four months!'

'Fine. Sixteen weeks – what's the difference?'

'And he was from East Germany. That doesn't make him a communist.'

'You're right, that's something else entirely,' retorted Anthony sarcastically.

'If there's one thing – one sole thing – I'll never forget, it's how much I hated you sometimes!'

'We had an agreement: no past tense. Don't be afraid to talk to me in the present. Dead or not, I am still your father, or what's left of him.'

The waiter brought Julia's food. She asked him for a refill, but Anthony covered her glass with his hand.

'I think we still have a few things to say to one another.'

The waiter nodded and left without a word.

'You were living in East Berlin. I hadn't heard anything from you in months. What was next? Moscow?'

'How did you track me down?'

'Somebody was kind enough to send along a copy of the interview you gave in that German newspaper.'

'Who?'

'Wallace. It was his way of making up for going behind my back and enabling you to study abroad.'

'You knew about that?'

'Or maybe he was just as worried as I was and decided it was time to put an end to your rebellion before you actually put yourself in danger.'

'I was never in danger. I was in love with Thomas.'

'When you're young, you think you're being swept off your feet by love for someone else. More often than not it's actually love for yourself. You were supposed to study prelaw in New York. You dropped everything and ran off to study drawing in Paris, then dropped that to go charging into Berlin. Puppy love from day one. Goodbye artist dreams, goodbye law career! Suddenly you wanted to be a journalist. And what do you know? That man of yours wanted to be one, too.'

'How was that any of your business?'

'I was the one who told Wallace to give back your passport the day you asked for it, Julia. I was sitting right in my office when you came to pick it up.'

'Then why not give it to me yourself?'

'We weren't getting along terribly well back then if you recall. If I had given you your passport, your adventure would have lost its edge. Rebelling against your father added a touch of spice to the whole affair.'

'You really thought all that?'

'I even told Wallace where to find your passport, but I was right in the next room. Truth be told the whole situation really hurt my pride.'

'Hurt. You?'

'And Adam?'

'Adam has nothing to do with any of this.'

'I'd like to remind you that, strange as it is, you'd be Mrs Coverman right now if not for my untimely demise. So, let me rephrase my question. But first . . . close your eyes.'

Julia couldn't fathom why her father was asking her to do this, but after some coaxing she gave in and shut her eyes.

'Tightly now. Until you see nothing but complete darkness.'

'Come on. What is this?'

'For once in your life please just do as I ask. It will only take a moment.'

Julia shut her eyes tight, blocking out all the light.

'Now . . . eat.'

Amused by the absurdity of the whole thing, Julia did as she was told. She groped the tablecloth until she found her fork. She made a clumsy attempt at harpooning a piece of something on her plate. With no idea what she was putting in her mouth, she took a bite.

'Did your food taste different because you couldn't see it?'

'I guess. Maybe,' she replied, keeping her eyes closed.

'Now, one other thing. Whatever you do, don't open your eyes.'

'Go ahead, I'm listening,' she said with a hushed voice.

'I'd like you to picture a time when you experienced pure happiness.'

Julia could feel her father's gaze even with her eyes closed.

◆　◆　◆

I remember walking side by side with you on the Museumsinsel. When you introduced me to your grandmother, the first thing she asked was what I did for a living. You tried to translate what she said with your rudimentary English. I told her I was a student at the École des Beaux-Arts, in Paris. She smiled and fished a postcard out of a dresser: a painting by Vladimir Radskin, a Russian artist she liked. Then she told us to go out and get some air – to enjoy the beautiful day. You hadn't told her a thing about your incredible trip to the West or how we had met. When we were saying our goodbyes at the front door, she asked if you had seen Knapp. Your hesitation and the look on your face gave the truth away. With a broad smile she said she was happy for you.

As soon as we were outside, you took me by the hand once more. Each time I asked where we were going, you answered, 'Come on, come on . . .' We went over the little bridge that spanned the Spree and stepped on to the island.

I had never seen so many buildings dedicated solely to art. I had pictured your country only in shades of grey, but here everything was in colour.

You led me to the entrance of the Altes Museum. The building itself was square, with a sort of rotunda inside. I had never before seen architecture like that. It was strange, almost unbelievable. You brought me to the centre of the rotunda and then started to spin me around in circles, faster and faster, until I was dizzy. Our crazy waltz came to a stop, and you held me in your arms. You said it was German romanticism through and through – a circle inside a square, the marriage between two completely different forms. Then you took me to the Pergamon Museum.

◆ ◆ ◆

'Pure happiness,' Anthony repeated softly. 'Did you find it?'

'Yes,' Julia replied, her eyes still shut.

'And who was by your side?'

She opened her eyes.

'Keep it to yourself. That's yours and yours only. I won't live your life for you.'

'Why would you make me do that?'

'When I close my eyes, I see your mother's face. Every time.'

'It was Thomas . . . coming through that portrait, like a ghost or the shadow of some memory. It was meant to tell me I should stop thinking of him and get married without any regrets. It was a sign.'

Anthony coughed. 'Oh for the love of . . . it was just a drawing! If I throw my napkin at that umbrella stand by the door, whether it makes it or not doesn't mean we'll have rain tomorrow or clear skies. If the last drop of that bottle of wine lands in that woman's glass, it doesn't mean she'll marry the ass she's having dinner with – and for her sake I certainly hope she won't. Don't give me that look! If that idiot hadn't been trying to impress his girlfriend so hard, I wouldn't have heard every word of their conversation since we sat down.'

'Of course you'd say all that. You don't believe in signs. You don't believe in anything you can't control.'

'There are no such things as signs, Julia. I used to toss countless crumpled balls of paper into my office trash basket, telling myself if I made ten shots in a row my wish would come true. Then? Nothing happened. So I pushed the idea further, believing that three or four *perfect* shots would make it happen. After two years of relentless practice, I could hurl an entire ream of paper directly into the centre of a wastebasket thirty feet away. It changed nothing.

'Once, I was out to dinner with three important clients from China, and while one of them was going on and on about various branches and global subsidiaries, my mind wandered . . . I thought of the one I loved most and hoped she was thinking of me. I imagined her footsteps along the streets she walked when she left home in the morning. As we stepped out of the restaurant on to the street, one of the clients shared a wonderful legend. He said that if you leaped into a puddle bearing the reflection of the full moon – leaped with both feet – the one you're thinking of would magically appear before you. Once outside my coworker turned white as a sheet when he saw me leap straight into the gutter. The client ended up soaked from head to toe, with water dripping from the brim of his hat. In lieu of an apology, I told him his trick didn't work – the woman on my mind had not appeared.

'So, yes, I've given up on senseless, idiotic signs. They're nothing more than a crutch for people who've lost their faith in God.'

'Don't you say that!' cried Julia. 'When I was little, I would have jumped in a thousand puddles to make you come home at night.'

Anthony's sad eyes pleaded with his daughter, but her anger seemed to only be rising. She pushed back her chair and walked straight out of the restaurant.

'Please excuse my daughter,' Anthony said to the waiter as he left a few bills on the table. 'She must be allergic to your champagne.'

◆　◆　◆

They walked back to the hotel in silence down the narrow, winding streets of Old Montreal. Julia had trouble walking straight and stumbled from time to time on the uneven cobblestones. Anthony held out his arm to steady her, but she shunned him and regained her balance on her own, avoiding contact with him at all costs.

'I'm a happy woman!' she said as she staggered along. 'Happy and perfectly fulfilled . . . I have a job I love. I live in an apartment I love. I have a best friend I love, and guess what? I'm about to get married to the man I love. Life couldn't be better!'

Julia's ankle buckled and she nearly fell, catching hold of a lamp post just in the nick of time and sliding down to the ground in a heap.

'Shit,' she grumbled, sitting on the sidewalk.

She batted away her father's helping hand, so Anthony simply eased himself down and sat next to her. The street was empty. The two of them stayed there, backs against the lamp post, for a whole ten minutes. Then at last Anthony took a little bag from his coat pocket.

'What is that?' she asked.

'Your candy.'

Julia rolled her eyes and turned her head.

'I reckon there are still a few gummy bears tumbling about at the bottom . . .'

Julia showed no reaction, but when Anthony started to put the bag back in his pocket, she promptly yanked it out of his hands.

A carriage being pulled along by a reddish-brown horse was making its way in their direction. Anthony hailed it.

◆ ◆ ◆

It took an hour to get back to the hotel. Julia crossed the lobby and took the elevator on the right. Anthony took the one on the left. They crossed paths again in the corridor on the top floor and walked side by side to the door of the honeymoon suite. Anthony stepped aside and let his daughter pass. She went directly to her bedroom, and he went to his.

Julia threw herself on to her bed and rummaged around in her purse for her cell phone. She glanced at the time before calling Adam but only got his voicemail. She listened to the prerecorded message but hung up before the ominous beep. Instead she called Stanley.

'Well look who it is.'

'I miss you, you know that?'

'Do tell. So how's your trip going?'

'I think I'm coming back tomorrow.'

'So soon? Did you find what you were looking for?'

'More . . . or . . . less.'

'Adam just left my place,' announced Stanley abruptly.

'Really? He was at your place?'

'That's what I just said. Have you been drinking, baby doll?'

'Maybe just a teensy bit.'

'Feeling okay?'

'I'm fine! Why do you all think I'm such a mess?'

'Who's "you all"? I'm solo here, honey.'

'What did Adam want?'

'To talk about you I imagine. I highly doubt he was here for me, and anyway, it'd be a waste of time. Not my type.'

'Adam came to talk to you about me?'

'No, he came hoping that *I* would talk to *him* about you. It's the sort of thing people do when they miss somebody they love.'

Julia sighed softly into the mouthpiece.

'He's feeling pretty sad, baby doll. Even if I'm not exactly Adam's biggest fan, I never like to see a man suffer.'

'What's he so sad about?' she asked, sincerely concerned.

'Should be plain to see, unless you're totally drunk or you've lost your senses. Imagine: two days after he was supposed to marry his lovely little fiancée, she up and disappears without a trace, no explanation and no forwarding address. Do you understand now? Or do I need to FedEx you a cup of detox tea and some aspirin?'

'First of all, I didn't disappear without a trace. I came by to see him at work, and I told him where I was going.'

'Vermont, darling. You told him you were going to Vermont. Your cover story was flimsy at best.'

'What's so flimsy about Vermont?' asked Julia.

'Nothing. At least . . . not any more.'

'Stanley. What did you do?' asked Julia, holding her breath.

'I sort of kind of maybe – okay, more than maybe – told him you were in Montreal. It just slipped out! How was I supposed to know you told him Vermont? Next time take some advice from the master before you start crafting your alibi. Or at least give me a heads-up so our stories match!'

'Shit, Stanley!'

'You got that right.'

'Did he come for drinks? Dinner?'

'Oh, it was nothing. I just whipped up a little something . . .'

'Stanley!'

'I couldn't let the poor bastard starve to death. I don't know who you're with or what you're up to – and hey, I'm the first to say it's none of my business – but please call him. It's the least you could do.'

'I know you're thinking the worst, Stanley. It's not like that.'

'How should you know what I think? If it helps at all, I told Adam that you taking off had nothing to do with him. I said you were on a vision quest to learn more about your father. See what I did there? Now that's a proper cover story.'

'Because it's the truth!'

'I told him you were really shaken by your father's death and you needed to sort it out in order to move on with your life. After all, you can't start a marriage on the right foot if you've got ghosts hanging around.'

The words stung. Julia said nothing.

'So, how is the investigation into Papa Walsh's past coming along?' continued Stanley.

'Found lots of reminders of all the things I hated about him.'

'Perfect. What else?'

'And maybe . . . one or two things I loved.'

'So why come home so soon?'

'I don't know. I feel like I have to be with Adam.'

'Right. "Have to".'

'Earlier tonight, Stanley . . . there was this portrait artist . . .'

Julia recounted her experience at the Old Port of Montreal. For once there were no witty interjections. Stanley just gasped.

'So you understand why I feel like I have to come home. It's weird being away from New York. Don't you miss your favourite good-luck charm?'

'Do you really want my advice? Get out a piece of paper and write down the first thing that comes to mind about tomorrow. Then do the exact opposite. Good night, baby doll.'

Stanley hung up. When Julia got up to go to the bathroom, she was too exhausted to hear the sound of her father retreating from her door and back into his room.

12.

The sky was a blush of pink as dawn broke over Montreal. Sunlight gently flooded into the sitting room between the two bedrooms in the suite. A knock came at the door, and Anthony greeted the waiter, who wheeled in breakfast on a tea trolley. The young man offered to set up the meal himself, but Anthony slipped him a few dollars and took over instead, leaving the waiter to quietly leave the room. Anthony couldn't decide whether to set up breakfast on the coffee table or on a side table with a sweeping view of the city. He opted for the view and set about preparing breakfast with the utmost care: tablecloth, a single plate, silverware, a small jug of orange juice, a bowl of cereal, a basket of pastries, with the final touch of a single rose standing proudly in a vase. He stood back, adjusted the flower until it was just perfect, then moved the milk jug a millimetre so it was perfectly aligned with the bread basket. He carefully placed a rolled-up piece of paper tied with a red ribbon on Julia's plate, then covered it with a napkin. Anthony moved back a few feet to assess the arrangement. Then he straightened his tie and knocked on his daughter's bedroom door, announcing that madame's breakfast was served. Julia groaned and asked what time it was.

'Rise and shine! Time to wake up. The school bus will be here in fifteen minutes, and you don't want to miss it again!'

Buried up to her nose in blankets, Julia opened one eye and stretched. She ran her fingers through her hair and kept her eyes shut tight until they had adjusted to the daylight. At last Julia got up, but the movement was a bit too quick for her hangover, and she had to sit for a moment as she grappled with a brutal head rush. The alarm clock on the bedside table read six o'clock.

'Why so early?' she moaned as she stumbled into the bathroom.

While Julia took a shower, Anthony sat waiting in an armchair in the small sitting room. He contemplated the red ribbon peeking out over the edge of the plate with a heavy sigh.

◆ ◆ ◆

The Air Canada flight had taken off from Newark at 7.10 a.m. Not long afterwards the captain's voice crackled over the loudspeakers, announcing the plane was starting its descent into Montreal. They would be arriving at the gate right on schedule. The head flight attendant took over and directed the passengers to prepare for landing. Adam stretched as much as the cramped confines would allow and put his tray table in the upright position. He glanced out the window. The plane was drifting over the Saint Lawrence River. The suburbs of Montreal loomed ahead, and the outline of Mont Royal could be seen in the distance. The MD-80 banked, and Adam tightened his seat belt. The lights along the runway were already visible.

◆ ◆ ◆

Julia tied the sash of her dressing gown in a knot and walked into the sitting room. She looked at the impressive breakfast laid out on the table and smiled at Anthony, who pulled out a chair for his daughter.

'I asked for Earl Grey,' he said, standing over her and filling her cup. 'The waiter gave me the choice of breakfast tea, black tea, green tea, white tea, Lapsang souchong, jasmine and about forty others before I threatened to jump out the window if he listed one more.'

'Earl Grey is perfect,' replied Julia, unfolding her napkin.

She caught sight of the paper tied with the red ribbon and peered up at her father suspiciously.

Anthony took it straight from her plate and held it behind his back.

'Best wait until after breakfast.'

'What is it?' asked Julia.

'Those?' he said, pointing to the pastries. 'Those long twisty things are known locally as "croissants". That one there with the brown stuff sticking out is a *pain au chocolat*, and the spiral-shaped one with the dry fruit on top is a *pain aux raisins*.'

'Very funny. And how about the thing you're holding behind your back?'

'Like I said – after breakfast.'

'Why put it in my plate in the first place?'

'I changed my mind. It'll be better on a full stomach.'

Julia shrugged, then waited until Anthony turned his back to her. In one fell swoop she deftly snatched the paper out of his hands.

She untied the ribbon and rolled out the paper to see Thomas's portrait, his smile beaming straight back at her.

'When did you . . . ?' she asked.

'Yesterday, as we were leaving the wharf. You were walking ahead, not paying me any mind. The artist must have been so pleased with my generous tip, she gave it to me free of charge.'

'Why would you do that?'

'I thought it might make you happy. You spent such a long time gazing at it.'

'No, seriously: tell me why.'

Anthony took a seat on the sofa and at last met his daughter's eyes.

'We need to talk. I hoped this day would never come, and what I'm about to tell you I truly wish could be left unsaid, especially during our time here together, since it's bound to ruin everything. I can just imagine your reaction. And yet all your little "signs" seem to be saying one thing and one thing only: the time has come—'

'Cut the theatrics,' she said abruptly.

'I have reason to believe that Thomas – *your* Thomas – is not exactly dead after all.'

◆ ◆ ◆

Adam was livid. He had made a point of travelling without luggage so he could make a quick getaway from the airport, but the passengers exiting a 747 from Japan were causing a bottleneck in customs. He glanced at his watch. The queue stretching before him would mean another twenty minutes of waiting before he could jump in a taxi.

Suddenly a word sprang up from the depths of his memory: '*Sumimasen!*' His work contact at a Japanese publishing house had used the word so often Adam thought apologizing must be a national pastime in Japan. '*Sumimasen!* Excuse me!' he repeated over and over, weaving and cutting a path through the line of people. Ten *sumimasen*s later, Adam finally reached the front of the queue and presented his passport to the Canadian customs officer, who promptly stamped it and gave it back. Ignoring the rule against using cell phones in the baggage claim area, he took out his phone, turned it on and dialled Julia's number.

◆ ◆ ◆

'Is that your phone ringing? Sounds like it's coming from your room,' said Anthony, once more avoiding Julia's eyes.

'Don't you dare try to change the subject! I'm asking again, what does that mean, "not exactly dead"?'

'Well . . . you could even say he's . . . *alive*. Yes, I suppose that's the appropriate choice of words.'

'Thomas is alive?' said Julia, growing visibly unsteady by the moment.

Anthony nodded.

'How do you know this?'

'From the letter. The one he wrote. Typically speaking, the dearly departed aren't in the habit of composing letters. Myself being the exception of course.'

'*What letter?*' asked Julia, the ground shifting beneath her feet.

'The one that arrived, addressed to you, six months after his accident. The postmark said Berlin. His name was on the envelope.'

'That's impossible. Because I never received any letter from Thomas!'

'You couldn't have, because you'd left home and were living on your own, and I couldn't forward it to you because I didn't have your address.' Anthony deflated, his shoulders slumping. 'There, it's done. You can add another one to the list.'

'What list?'

'The list of reasons why you hated me.'

Julia stood up and shoved back the entire table, glaring at her father.

'Whatever happened to no past tense? Because I can tell you that one is very much in the present!' she shouted, storming out of the room.

Her bedroom door slammed behind her. Anthony, alone in the middle of the room, sat down in her chair with the spread of pastries sitting untouched right in front of him.

'What a waste,' he sighed.

◆ ◆ ◆

It was impossible to jump to the front of the queue for taxis. A uniformed woman stood guard, directing each person to a cab. Adam was forced to wait for his turn. He dialled Julia's number again.

◆ ◆ ◆

'Will you answer the phone already? The ringing is driving me up the wall,' said Anthony as he came into Julia's bedroom.

'Get out.'

'For God's sake, Julia, it was almost twenty years ago.'

'Right. Twenty years! And you never found an opportunity to tell me?' she screamed.

'It was twenty years in which opportunities for us to really talk were few and far between,' he replied firmly. 'And it may have been for the best at that time anyway. What good would it have done? You were just getting back on your feet, and I didn't want to see you throw that away for one small letter. You had just landed your first job in New York, living in a studio on Forty-Second Street. You had a new boyfriend, a theatre type if I remember correctly. Or maybe it was the chap with the dreadful paintings at that gallery in Queens, the one you dumped right after you got a new job and a new hairdo. Or was it the other way around?'

'How do you know all this?'

'Just because my life never piqued your interest doesn't mean I didn't find ways of keeping up with yours.'

Anthony looked at his daughter for a long moment and then turned to go. She called him back.

'Did you open it? The letter?'

'I would never read your mail,' he said, turning back to her.

'Where is it now?'

'It's in your old room, right where it's been since the days when you called that place home. It's in your desk drawer. I thought that was the best place for it.'

'Why didn't you say anything about it before?'

'As you may recall, you never wanted to see me again. The one time you called was because I had caught sight of you through the window of that shop in SoHo, not because you had actually started to miss your father after all that time. You make it sound like you were my own personal punching bag, but you threw a fair deal of jabs yourself.'

'That's our relationship to you? A boxing match?'

'I should hope not. I've seen your uppercut.'

Anthony placed an envelope on her bed.

'I'll leave this with you,' he added. 'I should have said something earlier but . . . I never had the chance.'

'What is it?'

'Return tickets to New York. I had the concierge book them early this morning while you were sleeping. I had a hunch our father–daughter time would come to an end after this conversation. Get dressed, pack your bag and meet me in the lobby. I'll go settle the bill.'

Anthony closed the door gently behind him.

The highway was clogged with bumper-to-bumper traffic, so the taxi driver opted for rue Saint-Patrick, but the gridlock was just as dense there. The driver suggested they get back on the 720 up ahead and cut across boulevard René Lévesque. Adam didn't give a damn about the route, as long as it was fast. The driver sighed and insisted there was nothing he could do and that being impatient wasn't going to help matters. They'd get there in half an hour, maybe less if the traffic cleared up within the city. After a sarcastic quip about people saying taxi drivers were the crabby ones, the driver turned up the radio and cut off the possibility of further conversation.

The tip of a skyscraper in Montreal's financial district was already appearing on the horizon as the car continued on towards the hotel.

With her bag hanging from her shoulder, Julia crossed the lobby and marched confidently towards the front desk. The concierge left the counter and strode out to meet her.

'Mrs Walsh!' he exclaimed in an apologetic tone, arms spread wide. 'Mr Walsh is waiting outside. Your car is running late. Traffic is very heavy out there today.'

'Thank you,' Julia replied.

'We're very sorry to hear that you're cutting short your stay, Mrs Walsh. I hope there was nothing about our service that caused the early departure,' he enquired.

'No, best croissants in town!' fired back Julia. 'But once and for all: it's *Ms* Walsh, not *Mrs*!'

She walked out of the hotel and found Anthony waiting for her on the sidewalk.

'Our car should be along any moment now,' he said. 'Ah, there it is.'

A black Lincoln pulled up in front of them. The driver popped open the boot before getting out to welcome them. Julia settled in the back while the bellboy dealt with their luggage. Anthony walked around the back of the car. A taxi honked and missed hitting him by mere centimetres.

'Why don't these people watch where they're going?' Adam's taxi driver lamented as he double-parked in front of Hôtel Saint Paul.

Adam shoved a handful of dollars at him. Without waiting for change, he bolted out and made a dash for the revolving door. At the front desk he introduced himself and asked for Ms Walsh's room.

Outside, the black town car was boxed in by the taxi. The taxi's driver was casually counting his money and seemed in no hurry.

'Unfortunately Mr and Mrs Walsh have already checked out,' the woman at reception replied.

'*Mr* and Mrs Walsh?' Adam repeated with shock.

From his desk next to the receptionist, the concierge overheard the exchange. He rolled his eyes, before introducing himself.

'May I be of any help to you, sir?' he asked, twitching slightly.

'Did my fiancée stay at your hotel last night?'

'Fiancée?' the concierge asked, looking over Adam's shoulder at the street outside.

The town car was still sitting there, blocked in.

'Ms Walsh?' Adam asked.

'Ms Walsh did indeed stay with us last night, but I'm afraid she has already left.'

'Okay. She left alone?'

'I really couldn't say, sir,' replied the concierge, his anxiety growing stronger by the moment.

A chorus of honking horns came from outside, and Adam turned to look towards the source.

'Sir?' the concierge intervened, trying to distract Adam and keep him from looking at the town car. 'Perhaps we could offer you something to eat? Compliments of the—'

'Your receptionist said "Mr and Mrs Walsh". Sure sounds like she meant two people. So was she alone or wasn't she?' Adam persisted firmly.

'My colleague must have been mistaken,' the concierge replied, shooting daggers out of his eyes at the young woman. 'We have many clients. Can I offer you a coffee? Some tea?'

'How long ago did she leave?'

The concierge took a stealthy glance outside. The black car finally pulled away from the kerb, and he sighed with relief as it disappeared down the street.

'Quite some time ago I'd say,' he replied. 'Let me show you to the dining room. Our fruit juices are second to none, and breakfast is of course on the house.'

13.

Julia kept her nose glued to the airplane window the whole way home. She and her father didn't exchange a word during the whole flight.

◆ ◆ ◆

Every time I was on a plane, I'd watch for your face in the clouds, imagining your features among the forms stretching across the sky. I wrote you twice a week, maybe a hundred letters, and got as many in response. We promised we'd be together again as soon as I'd saved enough money. When I wasn't studying, I worked every chance I got so that one day I could come back to you. I waited tables, ushered at theatres, handed out flyers. I spent every moment on the job imagining the morning when I would finally land in Berlin to find you waiting for me at the airport.

I spent countless nights falling asleep just picturing your face, remembering the laughter that overcame us as we walked the streets of that grey city. When I was alone with your grandmother, she used to tell me not to grow too attached to you. She said our relationship couldn't last, that there were too many differences between us – a girl from the West and a boy from the East. It would never work. I thought it was sweet how she tried to protect us. But every time you came home and took me in your arms, I looked over your shoulder and smiled at her, just waiting to prove her wrong. When my father forced me into that car waiting out on the street, I screamed your name up at your window, wanting with all my heart for you to hear.

I was working at a restaurant when the evening news spoke of an 'incident' in Kabul that had killed four journalists, one of them German. I knew right away that it was you. The TV anchor said your car had hit a landmine left behind by Soviet troops. My blood ran cold, and I fainted behind the wooden counter where I'd been drying glasses. It was as though fate wanted to snuff out your light, to keep you from living with the freedom so lacking in your youth. The newspapers didn't provide any details, just four deaths. That was enough for their viewers. What did their names matter, let alone their lives and those they left behind? Deep inside I knew you were the German journalist they were talking about. It took me two days to contact Knapp. During those two days I couldn't eat a thing.

When Knapp finally called me back, I knew from his voice that he had lost his best friend and that I had lost the only man I had ever loved. My best friend, he repeated over and over again. He felt guilty for having helped you become a reporter. I tried to console him, even though my soul had been shredded to pieces. He had offered you a chance to become the person you wanted to be. I told him how frustrated you had been that you were never able to find the right words to thank him. Knapp and I kept talking about you, as though it would make your presence linger a while longer. He said your remains would never be identified. An eyewitness had reported that the truck you were riding in had been blown to pieces when it hit the mine. Chunks of sheet metal were scattered across the ground, stretching out in a hundred-foot perimeter. In the spot where you died, all that remained was a gaping crater and a twisted metal carcass – a testament to the absurdity of men and their cruelty.

Knapp would never forgive himself for having sent you to Afghanistan. Between sobs he told me about how you had only gone as a last-minute replacement. How different things could have been . . . if you hadn't been nearby to answer that call. I later realized that Knapp had given you the most beautiful gift imaginable. 'I'm sorry, I'm sorry,' your best friend repeated as he wept. I was incapable of shedding a single tear. Crying would have taken a little more of you away from me. I couldn't even bring myself to hang up after the call. I set the receiver on the counter and wandered out into the street. I walked without knowing where I was headed. Around me, the hustle and bustle continued, business as usual in the city, as though nothing had happened.

None of the passers-by that morning knew that somewhere on the outskirts of Kabul a thirty-year-old man named Thomas had died. Who would have even suspected? Who would have cared? Who could comprehend that I would never see you again and that my world would never be the same?

I didn't eat for two days. Did I mention that already? It doesn't matter. Just remembering what it's like to talk to you is worth repeating everything twice. Eventually I collapsed on a street corner.

Thanks to you I met Stanley. We were friends from the moment we met. He came out of the room next to mine and began walking down the hospital corridor. He looked like he was lost. My door was open, and he stopped, looked down at me lying in my bed and smiled with sadness. His lips trembled as he struggled to say the words I could not bring myself to utter. 'He's dead,' said the man I would later know as Stanley. And I echoed the words right back at him. 'Yes, he's dead.'

Perhaps I was able to open up to him because I didn't know him. It's never the same with someone you know. Somehow when you confide in a stranger the truth still seems reversible. He talked to me about his friend, and I talked to him about you. That's how we met, Stanley and I, on a day when we both lost the one we loved. Edward died from AIDS, and you from another pandemic ravaging the human race. Stanley sat at the foot of my bed and asked if I'd been able to cry yet. I told him the truth, and he admitted he hadn't either. He extended his hand, and I took it in *mine. Together we shed our first tears, the tears that at last carried you far away from me and Edward from him.*

◆ ◆ ◆

Anthony Walsh refused the drink the flight attendant offered him. He glanced behind him. The cabin was nearly empty, but Julia had preferred to sit ten rows back, next to the window. Her gaze remained lost in the sky.

◆ ◆ ◆

When I got out of the hospital, I decided to leave home. I tied a red ribbon around your hundred letters and left them in the desk drawer of my childhood bedroom. I didn't need to reread them to remember. I packed a suitcase and left without saying goodbye to my father. I was incapable of forgiving him for separating us. I used the money I had saved to start a new life far away from him. A few months later I began my career as an artist and my new life without you.

Stanley and I spent all of our time together. That's how our friendship grew. He was working at a Brooklyn flea market at the time. We had a routine of meeting in the middle of the Brooklyn Bridge, where we would sometimes stay for hours, leaning against the guardrail and watching the boats drift up and down the river. Sometimes we'd walk along the promenade on the Brooklyn side. He'd talk to me about Edward, and I'd tell him about you. When we both went our separate ways, he'd have a little piece of you to take with him.

In the morning I would search for your shadow among those of the trees extending out across the sidewalk. I looked for the lines of your face in the glimmering reflections on the Hudson. I listened in vain for your voice in the sound of the wind blowing through the city. For two years

I relived every moment we had spent together in Berlin. Sometimes I'd laugh about the way we had been. I never stopped thinking about you.

I never got your letter, Thomas, the letter that would have told me you were still alive. I don't know what you wrote. That was almost twenty years ago, but I have the strangest sensation – as though you sent it yesterday. Maybe after all those months without hearing from me you wrote to say you weren't waiting around any more. Maybe you wrote to tell me that too much time had passed and I had been gone too long. Or that we had come to a point where your passion for me had started to wither. Love can fade into autumn when feelings grow distant, when emotion is merely a memory . . . Maybe you stopped believing in our love. Maybe I lost you some other way. And now . . . nearly twenty years is a long time to wait for a response to a letter.

We're not the same people we were then. Would I still take the same trip from Paris to Berlin today? What would happen if our eyes were to meet again, you on one side of a wall and I on the other? Would you open your arms to me, like you did for Knapp that November evening in 1989? Would we run off through the streets of a town that has grown younger while we have grown older? Would your lips still feel as soft? Perhaps that letter was meant to stay sealed in that drawer. Maybe it's better that way.

◆ ◆ ◆

The flight attendant tapped Julia on the shoulder. It was time to fasten her seat belt. The plane was beginning its descent into New York.

◆ ◆ ◆

Adam had to resign himself to spending part of his day in Montreal. The Air Canada reps had done everything they could, but the only seat back to New York was on a flight that took off at 4 p.m. He kept trying to reach Julia but only got her voicemail.

◆ ◆ ◆

Along a highway on the outskirts of another city far away, the skyscrapers of New York appeared on the horizon. The Lincoln entered the tunnel that shared its name.

'I have a funny feeling I'm no longer welcome in my own daughter's home. So I think I'll forego the dusty attic and retreat to my townhouse, spend my final days in the comfort of my own home. I'll be back Saturday to step back into my crate before it gets picked up. I think it would be wise if you'd call ahead and make sure Wallace isn't home,' said Anthony, handing Julia a piece of paper with a telephone number on it.

'Your personal assistant still lives at your house?'

'I don't really know what he's doing. I haven't had much time to touch base with him since I died. If you want to avoid giving the poor fellow a heart attack, please do make sure he's not there when I arrive. And as long as you have him on the line, it would be lovely if you could find a good reason for him to go to the other side of the world until the end of the week.'

Julia dialled Wallace's number. A recording explained that he was taking a month's holiday following the untimely death of his employer. It wasn't possible to leave a message. For urgent business matters concerning Mr Walsh, the caller was instructed to contact the late Mr Walsh's lawyer.

'The coast is clear. You can stop worrying,' said Julia, putting her phone back in her pocket.

Half an hour later their car parked at the kerb outside Anthony Walsh's townhouse. Looking up at the building, Julia was immediately drawn to a window on the third floor. One afternoon, coming home

from school, Julia had looked up to see her mother leaning dangerously over the railing of the balcony. What would she have done if
Julia hadn't shouted her name? When she spotted her daughter, Julia's
mother gave her a little wave, as though the gesture might wipe away
any trace of the fatal act she had been on the verge of committing.

Anthony opened his briefcase and handed her a set of keys.

'How did you manage to get ahold of those?'

'Let's just say we anticipated a scenario in which you wouldn't
allow me to stay at your place but you also hadn't elected to pull the
plug either. Could you go ahead and open the door? We can't risk any
neighbours recognizing me.'

'You know your neighbours? That's new.'

'Julia!'

'Fine, I get it,' she snapped, getting out the car and approaching
the door.

Julia turned the knob of the heavy iron door and stepped inside,
casting light across the empty hallway. Nothing had changed; the
inside was just as she remembered from her very earliest memories.
The black-and-white tiles of the hall floor still spread before her like
an enormous chessboard. To the right a flight of dark wooden stairs
traced a gentle curve up to the second floor. The burled walnut banister of the staircase had been carved by a renowned carpenter, as her
father used to enjoy telling guests when he gave them a tour of the
house. Further on stood the door to the kitchen and the butler's pantry. Together the two rooms were larger than any of the apartments
Julia had lived in since leaving home.

To the left was the office, where her father had balanced his personal chequebook on the rare nights he was home. Signs of wealth
were everywhere, a reminder of the vast distance between the father
Julia knew and the man serving coffee in a Montreal skyscraper. A
portrait of Julia as a child hung on the wall. She wondered if any
of the glimmer the painter captured in that five-year-old's eyes still

remained. She looked up at the carved wooden ceiling, which would have seemed Gothic and spooky had there been even a single spider-web in the corners of the woodwork, but Anthony Walsh's home was impeccably well kept.

'Remember the way to your old bedroom?' asked Anthony as he entered his office. 'I'll let you go up alone. If you're hungry, there's probably something to eat in the kitchen cupboards . . . pasta or some canned food. After all, I haven't been dead that long.'

Julia climbed the stairs two at a time, sliding her hand along the banister, just as she always did in her youth. Then, arriving at the top, she turned around to see if anyone was following her, the same way she used to as a little girl.

'What?' she asked, looking down at her father from the top of the stairs.

'Nothing,' replied Anthony, trying to conceal a smile.

He went into his office.

The corridor extended before her. The first door led to her mother's bedroom. Julia put her hand on the knob. The latch opened slowly and softly . . . then closed once more just as softly as she decided against going in.

A strange, opalescent light filtered in through the sheer curtains. They had been pulled shut and floated above the carpet, whose colours hadn't faded a bit over the years. She went over to her bed, sat down on the edge and pressed her face against her pillow, taking in its scent. Memories flooded back – nights spent reading under the covers with a flashlight, evenings with imaginary characters coming to life and moving across the curtains, or nights when the window was left open and familiar shadows fuelled her insomnia. She stretched her legs and had a look around. The ceiling light looked like a mobile, but it didn't move, not even when she would stand on a chair and blow on its black wings. Near the dresser sat the wooden box where she kept her old notebooks, a few photos and a set of cards printed with the names of magical countries – odds and ends bought at the corner store or traded with friends by exchanging cards she already had in her collection. Why go to the same place twice with so many new places to discover? Her gaze wandered to the bookshelf where her schoolbooks were neatly propped up between two old toys, a red dog and a blue cat. The couple had never come together from the opposite ends of the shelf. Catching sight of the dark red cover of a history book she hadn't opened since junior high, Julia was reminded of the place where she had spent so much time doing homework. She got up from the bed and went over to her desk.

Countless and hours spent doodling aimlessly at this wooden desk, with its compass point scratches, then masking her inactivity by writing interminable nonsense every time Wallace knocked at her door to check on her progress. She had filled entire pages with:

I'm bored, I'm bored, I'm bored.

The porcelain knob was shaped like a star. All it took was a gentle tug for the drawer to slide out, but she opened it just a tiny bit. A red marker pen rolled around at the bottom of the drawer. Julia squeezed her hand in through the narrow opening and patted around but couldn't reach it. She turned the blind search into a game and kept exploring the inside of the drawer with her hand.

Her thumb made out the shape of a ruler, and her little finger brushed over a necklace won at a carnival, too ugly to ever actually wear. Her ring finger hesitated a moment. Was that her frog-shaped pencil sharpener? Her turtle-shaped tape dispenser? Her index finger brushed against some kind of paper. In the upper-right-hand corner she felt what was undoubtedly the perforation of a stamp. Over the years it had peeled back around the edges. Within the darkened shelter of the drawer, she caressed the surface of the envelope and traced over the lines of ink made by a fountain pen. She felt her way blindly, like playing a guessing game by tracing words on the skin of a lover's back. Without even looking at it, Julia recognized Thomas's handwriting.

She pulled the envelope out of the drawer, carefully opened it and read the letter.

September 1991

Julia,

I was the only one to escape from this expedition. As I wrote to you in my last letter, we had finally set off in search of Masoud. But in the thunder of the explosion that still resonates inside me, I forgot why I ever wanted to meet him in the first place. I forgot about the fervour that possessed me, filling me with the desire to document his side of the story. After the blast the only thing I could see was the force of the hatred that I narrowly escaped . . . and that had taken the lives of my companions. The villagers fished me out of the wreckage a full twenty metres from the spot where I should have died. I'll never know exactly why the blast sent me hurtling through the air while it tore the others to shreds. Thinking I was dead, they laid my body on a little cart. If an opportunistic young boy hadn't tried to steal my watch, and if my arm hadn't twitched just then and made the child cry out, I would have most likely been buried alive. But . . . somehow I have survived the folly of men.

People say that when death reaches out a cold hand to pull you into its embrace, your whole life passes before your eyes. But I can tell you when death curls its arms around you, what you see is unlike anything you've ever seen before. In my feverish delirium all I saw was your face. I wish I could make you jealous, tell you that the nurse who took care of me was a beautiful young woman, but the truth is it was a man with a long beard, and the only thing beautiful about him was his devotion. I have spent the last four months in a hospital bed in Kabul. My body is severely burned, but I'm not writing to you to complain.

It's been five months since I've sent you a letter. Five months is a long time after writing to each other twice a week. Five months of silence, almost half a year – it seems far longer because it's been so long since I saw you. Since I touched you. It's funny how hard it is to love from a distance, which brings up the question that haunts me each day.

Knapp flew to Kabul as soon as he heard the news. You should have seen him cry when he came into the ward. I have to admit I cried a little, too. Luckily my neighbour in the next bed was sound asleep. Otherwise I don't know what he would have thought of the two of us sobbing that way amid such fearless soldiers. Knapp didn't call you right away to tell you I was alive, because I asked him not to. I knew he was the one who told you I was dead, and I decided it was up to me to tell you I'd survived. Maybe there's another reason. Perhaps in choosing to write you this letter I wanted to leave you free to continue mourning our relationship – that is, if that's what you've been doing.

Our love was born out of our differences, Julia. Our shared thirst for discovery filled every morning that we woke up in each other's arms. When I think of you in the morning, I think of all the hours I spent watching you sleep, watching you smile, blissfully unaware. The way you smile when you sleep, even if you don't know you're doing it, is something I'll never forget. You can't know the number of times you curled up against me, saying things I didn't understand, but I do. One hundred times exactly. Not one more, not one less.

I know that building a life together is another matter entirely. My hatred for your father made me long to understand him. Would I have done what he did under the same circumstances? If we had a daughter together, and if I was left alone to care for her and she ran off with a foreigner from a world where everything appeared strange and terrifying to me, maybe I would have acted like he did. I never wanted to tell you about all of those years I lived behind the Wall. I didn't want to taint a single second of our time together with memories from that absurd time. You deserved more than sad memories about the darkest corners of human nature. But your father must have known about those things, and they probably didn't have a place in the future he had planned for you.

I hated your father for taking you away from me, for leaving me standing with a bloody face in our bedroom, powerless, having you torn from my arms. I punched the walls where your voice still echoed, and yet I still wanted to understand the man. How could I tell you that I loved you without having at least tried to understand?

Forces beyond your control pulled you out of my world and back to your own. Do you remember how you always talked about the signs fate sends us? I never believed in such things before, but I've learned to see things your way. Tonight, as I write this letter, the signs seem to be mounting against me.

I loved you so much just for being you. I never wanted you to be someone else. A love so strong and so pure, without any real understanding, had me convinced time would make everything clear. Maybe, lost in the grip of all that love, I didn't try hard enough to find out if your love for me was strong enough to overcome our differences. Maybe you never gave me the opportunity to find out the answer – maybe because you had never really asked yourself that vital question. But the time has come now, whether we like it or not.

I'm going back to Berlin tomorrow. I'll put this letter in the first letterbox I see. It will take a few days to get to you, as it always does. By the time you read this it should be the 16th or the 17th.

You'll find in this envelope a secret I've kept from you. I'd have liked to send you a photo of me, but I can't say it would make a very pretty picture, and in any case I wouldn't want to be vain. So instead I'm sending a plane ticket. You don't have to work for months saving to come back here – that is, if you still want to come back. I had the ticket with me in Kabul, and I meant to send it to you . . . But luckily it's an open ticket.

I'll wait for you at the Berlin airport on the last day of each month until the year's end.

If we are reunited and if we ever have a daughter together, I solemnly swear to never rip her away from the man she loves. Julia, I will respect your choice whatever it is, and I won't hold it against you if you choose not to come back to me. If that happens, if on the last day of the month I have to leave the airport without you, please know that I'll understand. It is the very reason I'm writing you this letter – to tell you that I will understand.

I'll never forget the sight of that face, a gift life handed me on a November evening at the moment when hope finally returned and I scaled a wall and fell into your arms, me from the East, and you from the West.

I will cherish you always if even just as a memory. It will be the memory of the most beautiful thing that ever happened to me. As I write these words, it dawns on me once more just how much I love you.

See you soon . . . maybe. Whether in my arms or in my heart you will still be with me. I know you are breathing somewhere out there, and that means so much. More than you could know.

I love you,
Thomas

Inside the envelope Julia found a plastic sleeve, yellowed with age. She opened it. *Fräulein Julia Walsh, New York–Paris–Berlin, 29 April 1991* had been typed on the red carbon paper of a plane ticket.

Julia slipped everything back into the drawer. She opened the window a little and lay down on her bed. With her arms behind her head, she stayed that way for a long time, staring in silence at her bedroom curtains. Upon the two panels of cloth, shadows of her old friends re-emerged, the ghosts and relics of bygone moments of solitude.

◆ ◆ ◆

As morning faded into afternoon, Julia left her room and went downstairs to the pantry. She opened the cupboard where they kept the jam, grabbed a pack of Melba toast and a jar of honey and sat down at the kitchen table. She saw the mark of a spoon left behind in the thick honey. It was a strange indentation, probably made during Anthony's last breakfast in this house. She imagined him sitting in the place where she was sitting now, alone in that enormous kitchen with his coffee mug in front of him, reading his newspaper. She wondered what thoughts had filled his head that day. The mark was a curious echo of a past that was gone forever, never to return. This harmless detail struck Julia – for reasons she could not understand, she suddenly came to the full realization that her father was dead. At times all it takes is a little something, a trinket or a familiar smell, to bring back the memory of someone who is gone. For the first time, in the middle of that huge room Julia felt the sting of her lost childhood, miserable as it had been. She heard her father clear his throat and looked up to see him standing in the doorway, smiling at her.

'May I come in?' he said, sitting down across from her.

'Make yourself at home.'

'I had that sent over from France. It's made from lavender blossoms. Do you still have the same passion for honey?'

'Guilty as charged. Some things never change.'

'What did the letter say?'

'That's really none of your business.'

'Have you come to a decision?'

'A decision? About what?'

'Oh, I think you know. Are you going to write back to him, Julia?'

'Twenty years later? Don't you think it's just . . . too late?'

'It seems that's a question you must answer for yourself.'

'What right do I have just barging in on his life? Thomas is probably married with children.'

'A boy and a girl? Twins maybe?'

'What?'

'Well, with your newfound psychic powers, maybe you can also tell me just what his charming family looks like. So what is it, a girl or a boy?'

'Okay, okay. What's your point?'

'This very morning you thought him dead. Best not to jump to conclusions about what he's done with his life.'

'Twenty years! For Christ's sake it's not six months.'

'Eighteen years to be exact. Enough to get married, divorced, married again – unless your Thomas has switched teams like your antique dealer friend. What was his name again? Ah yes. Stanley. Maybe he ended up like Stanley.'

'You have a lot of nerve making jokes.'

'Humour can be like a coat of armour when reality takes a stab at you. I don't know who said that, but I know it's the truth. Let me ask you again. Have you come to a decision?'

'I'm not making any decisions. It's just too late. Probably comes as a relief to you.'

'Too late only happens when things become definitive. It's too late for me to tell your mother all I wanted her to know before she passed. There is no letter I can read to tell me all I needed to hear before she slipped away. As far as you and I are concerned, too late is Saturday, after which I'll be shut off for good. But if Thomas is still alive and breathing, I must politely contend that it is anything but too late! Julia, think – a mere drawing of him had you incapacitated for hours.

It's what brought us here today. Don't try hiding behind the pretext that it's too late. Find another excuse if you must, but don't delude yourself with that.'

'I don't understand why you're doing this.'

'There's nothing to understand. I just think you should be out there trying to find him, unless . . .'

'Unless what?'

'Never mind. There I go again. Talk, talk, talk . . . but you're right.'

'That's the first time I've ever heard you say I'm right about a single thing. So just what am I right about?'

'Forget about it like I said. It's far easier to just keep whining and complaining about what *could have* been. I can already hear the usual nonsense: "Destiny simply had other things in store for us. That's just the way it is." Or better yet: "It was my father. He ruined my entire life. It's all his fault." Just go on wallowing in your drama. It's certainly one way of living.'

'God, you scared me. For a minute there I thought you were actually taking me seriously.'

'Given the way you've been acting, the risk of that happening is minimal.'

'Even if I felt completely compelled to write to Thomas, and even if I somehow managed to find his address and send him a letter this many years after the fact, I would never do a thing like that to Adam. It would be horrible. He's had enough lies to last him a lifetime.'

'Oh yes, spare him the dishonesty,' responded Anthony, his voice heavy with sarcasm.

'What's that supposed to mean?'

'As if lying through omission were any less deplorable. Go ahead then. Just know he's not the only person you'd be lying to.'

'Who else then?'

'Yourself. Every night falling asleep by his side with even the tini-est memory of your long-lost love from the East popping up in your head. There you go! One little lie. Every tiny pang of regret, another little lie. Every time you ask yourself if you should have gone back to Berlin to clear your conscience – there, one more lie. Let's break it down by numbers. I always was a natural at math. Julia tells herself, let's say, three little lies a week, along with two memories from her past and three comparisons between Thomas and Adam . . . That's three plus two plus three, which makes eight, multiplied by fifty-two weeks, multiplied by thirty years of marriage – perhaps that's a bit optimistic I know – for a grand total of twelve thousand four hundred and eighty lies. Not altogether bad for the course of one marriage come to think of it!'

'Bravo. Impressive talent,' retorted Julia, feigning applause.

'Sharing your life with someone for whom your feelings are shaky at best – how can that be anything but a lie, a betrayal? Do you have even the faintest notion of what life looks like when the person you're with treats you like a stranger?'

'Because you do – is that what you're saying?'

'Your mother called me *sir* for the last three years of her life. When I entered the bedroom, she'd show me where the toilet was, mistaking me for the plumber. Is that evidence enough, or do I need to spell it out for you?'

'Mom really called you *sir*?'

'On the good days, yes. On the bad ones she'd call the police and tell them a stranger had broken into her house.'

'And . . . there were things she never told you before she . . . ?'

'Lost her mind? No need to beat around the bush, dear. And yes, there are things like that. But we're not here to talk about her.'

For a long moment Anthony fixed his penetrating gaze on his daughter.

'How's the honey?'

'Tasty,' she said, biting into a piece of toast.

'A little firmer than usual, wouldn't you say?'

'Yes, a bit firmer.'

'The bees got lazy after you left home.'

'Maybe,' she said, smiling. 'So, you want to talk bees?'

'Well, why the hell not?'

'Do you miss her?'

'Of course I do! What a question.'

'Was Mom why you jumped into a gutter full of water?'

Anthony fished around in his jacket and pulled out an envelope, which he promptly slid across the table to Julia.

'What's this?'

'Two tickets for Berlin, with a layover in Paris. There was nothing direct. Flight leaves at five p.m. You can go alone or I can come along with you. Or you can throw in the towel and forget the whole thing. Your call.'

'Why? Why would you—?'

'Do you still carry around that piece of paper?'

'What paper?'

'That note from Thomas that you brought everywhere. It always appeared like magic whenever you emptied your pockets. A little piece of crumpled paper, the constant reminder of how badly I'd hurt you.'

'I lost it.'

'Lost it? Those kinds of things never really disappear. They come back one day, rising from the bottom of your heart. Go on, dear, get your suitcase.'

Anthony got up to leave. On his way out the door, he turned round.

'Hurry up! You don't need to go back to your place. If you need something, we'll buy it over there. We don't have much time. I'll be waiting outside. I've already called the car. Now, doesn't that feel like déjà vu all over again?'

Julia heard his footsteps trailing out into the hall.

She held her head and sighed, peeping between her fingers at the jar of honey sitting on the table. She knew she should go to Berlin, not to find Thomas, but to take one last trip with her father. In her head she swore to herself – with great sincerity – that it wasn't a pretext or an excuse. Adam would certainly understand one day.

Back in her room, as she was picking up her bag from the foot of the bed she glanced towards her bookshelf. The history book with the red cover was pulled out a bit more than the others, catching Julia's eye. She hesitated a moment, then picked up the book and pulled out a blue envelope hidden inside its cover. She slipped the envelope in her bag, shut the window and left the room.

Anthony and Julia arrived at the airport just as check-in for their flight was closing. The woman behind the counter gave them their boarding passes and urged them to hurry. This late there was no way she could guarantee they'd make it before the final boarding call.

'With this pathetic leg of mine it's a lost cause!' Anthony exclaimed glumly.

'Do you have trouble walking, sir?' the young woman asked.

'You get to be my age, you get quite the list of ailments,' he replied proudly, presenting the certificate for his pacemaker.

'Wait right here,' she said, picking up her phone.

A few moments later an electric golf cart drove them to the boarding gate for their flight to Paris. With an escort from the airline, getting through security was easy.

'Was it another glitch?' Julia asked, shouting to be heard as they sped down the long corridors of the airport terminal.

'Keep it down for God's sake! Don't give us away!' hissed Anthony. 'Don't worry about the leg.'

With that he picked up his conversation with the driver, acting truly fascinated by the minutiae of the airport employee's life. Barely ten minutes later Anthony and his daughter were the first to board.

While two flight attendants helped Anthony get comfortable – one placing pillows behind his back, the other offering him a blanket – Julia went back to the door of the plane. She told the flight attendant she had one last phone call to make. Her father was already on board and she'd be back in a few moments. She ran back up the air bridge and took out her cell phone.

'So, how's the mysterious Canadian quest coming along?' Stanley asked from the other end of the line.

'I'm at the airport.'

'So you did come home after all.'

'Yes. And no. I'm leaving again.'

'Sorry, baby doll, I seem to be a couple steps behind.'

'I came back to the city this morning. I wanted to see you – really *needed* to – but there wasn't a minute to spare.'

'And where might we be headed on the next leg of the adventure? Oklahoma? Exotic Nebraska?'

'Stanley, if you found an unopened letter from Edward written just before he died . . . would you read it?'

'Like I told you, Julia, he used his dying breath to say he loved me. What more could I need to know? Excuses? Regrets? Those three words meant more than all of the things we ever forgot to tell each other.'

'So what, you would just put the letter back where you found it?'

'I think I would, yes. But I've never found anything like that. Edward wasn't much of a letter writer – he barely even wrote a grocery list! I always had to do it for him. You can't imagine how huffy I used to get about that. And now, almost twenty years later, I still buy his favourite kind of yoghurt every time I go to the supermarket. Pretty idiotic the kind of things you remember so long after the fact, don't you think?'

'Not necessarily.'

'Don't tell me you found a letter from Thomas. Any time you bring up Edward, I know he's been on your mind. If that's the case, don't wait – open it!'

'You just said that you wouldn't!'

'Wow. You're telling me after twenty years of friendship you still haven't gotten it through your head that I'm not always the best example to follow? Open the letter! Today. Tomorrow even, but don't you dare destroy it. And you know what? I lied. If Edward had left me a letter, I'd have read it a hundred times, spent hours reading and rereading it just to be sure I understood every last word. Even though I know full well he never would have taken the time to write me one. Can you at least give me a hint about where you're going? How about, say, area code?'

'More like country code.'

'Whoa. You're going abroad? Europe?'

'Germany. Berlin.'

There was a moment of silence. Stanley took a deep breath.

'Okay. I'm starting to connect the dots. Baby doll, forget the letter. Tell me you don't mean that somehow he's—'

'Yes. Yes, he is. He's alive, Stanley!'

'Of course he is,' sighed Stanley. 'And now you're calling me from the airport to ask if you're right to go hunt him down.'

'I'm actually calling from the gateway to the plane . . . and I think you just answered my question.'

'Well, then get your ass in gear, silly! Don't miss that flight!'

'Stanley?'

'What now?'

'Are you mad at me?'

'No, of course not. I just hate thinking of you being so far away, that's all. Any more stupid questions?'

'Yeah, how do you keep on—?'

'Answering your questions before you ask them? Maybe it's my keenly honed feminine instincts. Or it could be because I'm your best friend. Now get out of here before I get all mushy about missing you.'

'I'll call you when we land. I promise.'

'Sure, sure. Bon voyage.'

The flight attendant motioned frantically to Julia that if she wanted to get on board it was now or never. The crew were moments away from closing the cabin door. By the time Stanley remembered to ask what to say if Adam called, Julia was already long gone.

14.

After the trays had been cleared, the flight attendant dimmed the lights and plunged the cabin into near darkness. From the beginning of their time together, Julia had never once seen her father touch any food or get a minute's sleep. She hadn't even seen him rest. It was probably normal for a machine, but it was a strange notion that took some getting used to, especially since these details reminded her that she and her father were on borrowed time, with mere days to make up for a whole lifetime. Most of the passengers slept. A few watched movies on the little seat-back screens. In the last row a man did paperwork by the glow of his overhead light. Anthony spent the flight leafing through a newspaper, and Julia looked out her window at the silvery reflection of the moon on the wing of the plane, with the surface of the ocean below rippling blue in the night.

◆ ◆ ◆

That winter I decided to leave art school and Paris behind. You did everything you could to dissuade me, but my decision was made. I would become a journalist like you. And like you I set out the next morning in search of work, even though it was a lost cause for an American girl. A few days before the tramlines had been restored to what they once were, linking both sides of the city. Everything around us was changing. People talked about the reunification of your country, with hopes it would soon be whole again, back to the past, before the Cold War became the central focus of all. Those who had worked for the secret police seemed to have vanished into thin air from one night to the next, taking their archives with them. A few months earlier they had tried to destroy all of the compromising paperwork, the files that had been created about you and millions of those like you. You were among the first to protest, in an attempt to stop it.

I have to wonder . . . were you also a number on a file? Is it somewhere out there right now in a secret archive, with secret photos of you on the street or at work, including the names of your friends and your grandmother? Could your childhood years really have aroused the authorities' suspicion? I wonder how we could have let all that happen after all of the painful lessons from the last war. Was it the only way for our world to exact its revenge? You and I were born far too late to harbour any hatred for each other. We had too much to discover together.

In the evening, when we walked around your neighbourhood, I saw that you were often still afraid . . . gripped with fear every time you saw a uniform or a car that drove by a little too slowly. 'Come on, let's not stay here,' you'd say, and you'd lead me along until we could duck down the first side street or down a set of stone steps, anything to throw the invisible enemy off our scent. When I made fun of you, you'd become angry and tell me that I didn't understand anything, that I had no idea what they were capable of. It makes me think of all the times we went out to eat and I would catch you searching the faces of people around us. You would suddenly announce that we had to leave – a sombre face at a nearby table had reopened old wounds from your past. Forgive me, Thomas. You were right. I never knew what it was to be afraid. Forgive me for giggling when you forced me to hide under the pilings of that bridge with you because a military truck was crossing the river. I never knew, could never understand. No one in my life could before you.

When you'd point at somebody in the tram, I could tell from the look in your eyes that he was once a member of the secret police.

Stripped of their uniforms, without their authority and arrogance, the former Stasi members melted into the city and became accustomed to the banal lives of those they had once followed, spied on, judged and even tortured – sometimes for years. After the Wall came down, most of them invented a past for themselves to mask their true identities. Others quietly returned to their former careers. For many, any sense of remorse they might have once felt evaporated over the passing months, the memory of their crimes fading away as time marched on.

I remember an evening when we went to see Knapp. The three of us took a walk in the park, and Knapp wouldn't stop asking you questions, without realizing how difficult it was for you to answer. He believed the Wall had cast its shadow on the West, where he had been, but you cried out that the shadow fell on the East, where you had been a prisoner of the concrete. 'How could you get used to living like that?' he kept asking. You smiled and asked him if he had really forgotten what it was like at the start. Knapp persisted, and you finally capitulated, answering his questions. You patiently walked him through a time when everything was organized, secure, when nobody had to take responsibility, and when the risk of doing something wrong was still very remote. 'We had zero per cent unemployment, and the state was omnipresent,' you said with a shrug. 'That's how a dictatorship works,' Knapp concluded.

It was convenient for a lot of people. Freedom is a huge risk, and while most people aspire to attain it, they don't know how to put it to use. I can still picture you at that cafe in West Berlin, describing how everyone behind the Wall in the East found a way of reinventing their lives within the confines of their cozy apartments. The mood soured when Knapp asked how many people you thought had collaborated with the secret police during the dark years. The two of you could never agree on a number. Knapp's guess was 30 per cent at most. You said you had no idea, justifying your ignorance by the fact that you yourself had never worked for the Stasi.

Forgive me, Thomas. You were right. It has taken me this long, until this journey back to you, for me to finally understand fear.

◆ ◆ ◆

'Why didn't you invite me to your wedding?' asked Anthony, lowering his newspaper.

Julia jumped, startled.

'My apologies. I didn't mean to scare you. Were you lost in thought?'

'No, I was just looking outside, that's all.'

'Nothing much to see out there except darkness,' replied Anthony after leaning over to peer through the little window.

'There's a full moon.'

'Perhaps we're a bit high up for jumping into that big puddle down there, legend or no legend.'

'You know, I did invite you to my wedding.'

'You sent me an invitation, the same as you sent to two hundred other people. Not exactly what I'd call inviting your father. I'm the one who was supposed to walk you down the aisle. We might have needed to talk about it in person beforehand.'

'What have you and I talked about during the past twenty years? Not much. If you want to know, I was waiting for you to call me. I thought you might want to meet my future husband.'

'But I did meet him.'

'A chance encounter on an escalator at Bloomingdale's is not what I'd call an official introduction. It was barely enough to show that you had even the slightest interest in him, or in my life at all to be honest.'

'The three of us went and had tea together, did we not?'

'Because I suggested it, and because he wanted to get to know you. It lasted all of twenty minutes, and neither of us could get a word in edgewise.'

'He wasn't the most talkative chap. Seemed borderline autistic. I thought he might have been mute.'

'Well, if you had bothered asking him a single question . . .'

'And you, Julia, since when do you ask loads of questions? God forbid you ask anything, least of all for my advice.'

'What good would that do? All you'd do is tell me what you did at my age, and what I should be doing with myself. I would take a vow of eternal silence if it helped you get the message through your head: I *never* wanted to be like you.'

'Maybe you should try to get some sleep,' Anthony said. 'Long day ahead tomorrow. As soon as we touch ground in Paris, we'll have to hop on another flight to Berlin.'

He tucked Julia's blanket around her shoulders and returned to his newspaper.

◆ ◆ ◆

Moments after they landed on the runway at Charles de Gaulle Airport, Anthony set his watch to Paris time and got down to business.

'We have two hours to catch our connecting flight. That should be plenty.'

Anthony was not aware that their plane, which was supposed to arrive in Terminal E, had been redirected to a gate in Terminal F, which did not have an air bridge compatible with their particular jet. For that reason, the flight attendant explained, a bus would be coming to pick them up to take them to Terminal B.

Anthony raised his hand and motioned to the head of the cabin crew to come and see him.

'Terminal *E*,' he corrected.

Marc Levy

'Excuse me?' the flight attendant replied.

'In the announcement you just said we'd be taken by bus to Terminal B, but from what I understood we were supposed to end up at Terminal E.'

'It's entirely possible,' he responded. 'We get lost ourselves sometimes.'

'Well, I hope at a minimum you did bring us to de Gaulle.'

'Three different gates, no jetway and the bus still hasn't arrived – where else could we be?'

Forty-five minutes after touching down, they finally left the airplane. They still had to pass through immigration and find the gate for their flight to Berlin.

A total of two immigration officers were responsible for checking passports for a whole horde of passengers arriving on three different flights. Anthony looked at the time on the departures board.

'With two hundred people shuffling around like cattle ahead of us, we're never going to make it.'

'Then we'll take the next flight,' replied Julia.

With passport control behind them, they ran through an interminable series of hallways and on to a long travelator.

'We could have made it by foot from New York by now,' groaned Anthony.

No sooner had the words left his mouth than Anthony collapsed.

Julia tried to catch him, but the fall was too sudden and the space too narrow. The travelator continued on, dragging her father along with it.

'Daddy, Daddy! Wake up!' she screamed with sheer fright as she tried to shake her father awake.

Another traveller hurried over to help. Together with Julia, the two were able to lift Anthony's body up, carry him off the walkway and set him down a small distance away. The man took off his coat and slid it under Anthony's head. He still wasn't moving. The man suggested they call a doctor.

'No! There's no need,' insisted Julia. 'It's nothing. He just got dizzy. It happens. I'm used to it.'

'Lady, are you sure? Your husband doesn't look so hot.'

'He's not my . . . he's my father! He's diabetic,' Julia lied. 'Daddy, wake up,' she said, shaking him again.

'Here, let me take his pulse and—'

'Don't! Don't you touch him!' shouted Julia in panic.

Anthony opened his eyes.

'Where are we?' he asked, trying to sit up.

The man who had come to their rescue helped him to his feet. Anthony propped himself against the wall, struggling to regain his balance.

'What time is it?'

'Are you sure he's okay? The guy seems really out of it.'

'I beg your pardon!' retorted Anthony, suddenly regaining his strength.

The Good Samaritan picked up his coat and left.

'You could have at least thanked him,' Julia scolded him.

'For what? Dragging me a few miserable feet?'

'You're impossible, you know that? You scared me half to death.'

'Oh come now, it was nothing. What's the worst that could happen? I'm already dead!' Anthony chided.

'Do you have any idea what went wrong?'

'Blew a fuse in one of my switchboards I'd say, or some sort of interference. I'll have to pass that along to the manufacturer. It's going to get very old very fast if my system starts crashing every time somebody tinkers with their iPhone.'

'I'll never be able to explain this. Not to anyone ever.'

'Maybe my ears are malfunctioning, too. Because I could have sworn I heard you call me Daddy back there.'

'It's your ears,' she replied, leading him towards their gate.

A glance at the time confirmed they only had fifteen minutes to get through security.

'Damn it!' said Anthony after glancing in his passport.

'What? What now?'

'The letter proving I have a pacemaker is gone. I can't find it any more.'

'It must be in one of your pockets.'

'I've checked them all! It's not there.'

He glanced warily at the metal detectors looming ahead.

'If I walk through those, the officers will swoop down on me like flies on—'

'So keep looking for that letter,' Julia said impatiently.

'I told you: it's lost. It must have fallen out in the plane when I gave my suit jacket to the flight attendant. I'm sorry to say it, dear, but we're out of options here.'

'We did *not* come all this way just to turn around and go back to New York. Which we couldn't do even if we wanted to.'

Anthony suggested they get a hotel room for the night. 'We'll rent a car and drive straight into Paris. I'll have it figured out in no time, before we even get there. Two hours from now New York will be awake. You can call my doctor, have him fax a copy.'

'He might find that weird, you being dead and all.'

'Oh, how utterly foolish! I forgot to tell him!'

'Can't we grab a taxi?' she asked.

'A taxi? In Paris? You really don't know this town, do you?'

'And you have to have an opinion on every last little thing.'

'Now's not the time for squabbling. I can see the rental counters from here. A little car will be fine. Perhaps we could bump up to a sedan. It's a question of comfort after all.'

Julia gave in and accepted her father's plan. Just past midday she found herself speeding down a slip road on to the A1, headed into Paris. Anthony leaned forward, reading street signs.

'Take a right up here,' he ordered.

'Paris is to the left. See, there? In all capital letters?'

'I see it, I can still read. Just do as I tell you!' railed Anthony, reaching over and forcing her to turn the steering wheel.

'Are you out of your mind? What the hell are you doing?' she screamed as their car swerved dangerously.

It was now too late for them to change lanes – Julia was forced to merge with traffic on the right, away from Paris. With a cacophony of angry honking hitting them from all sides, Julia found herself driving north.

'Great. Now we're headed to Brussels. Paris is back that way.'

'I am well aware of that. And four hundred seventy miles past Brussels is Berlin. If you're not too exhausted to drive straight through, it'll take us nine hours all told, assuming my calculations are correct. At worst we can take a break along the way so you can rest up. There aren't any metal detectors to get through on the highway, so that particular problem is solved. But we don't have a lot of time left. Only four days before we return – that is, assuming I make it that far.'

'You had all this planned before we even rented the car! That's why you insisted on the sedan. Admit it.'

'Do you want to see Thomas again or not? In that case focus on the damn road. I'd offer to navigate, but I assume you know the way!'

Julia cranked the volume on the radio all the way up and put her foot down.

◆ ◆ ◆

After twenty years the highway route had changed a lot, as had the scenery along the way. They reached Brussels in less than three hours.

Anthony wasn't especially talkative. From time to time he would grumble under his breath while gazing out at the landscape passing by. Julia took advantage of his distracted state to tilt the rear-view mirror towards him so she could watch him unnoticed. Anthony abruptly turned down the radio.

'Were you happy in art school?' he asked, breaking the silence.

'I didn't stay very long, but I loved the place where I was living. The view from my bedroom window was incredible. My office looked out on the roof of the observatory.'

'I love Paris myself. Some of my most cherished memories are there. I'd dare say it's the place where I would choose to die.'

Julia cleared her throat.

'Yes?' asked Anthony. 'What's behind that strange look? Have I said something I shouldn't have again?'

'No, no. It's nothing.'

'Out with it, girl. I can see you're perturbed.'

'It's just that . . . It's kind of hard to say. Just feels *wrong* . . .'

'Come now. Don't make an old man beg.'

'Well . . . you *did* die in Paris, Daddy.'

'Did I?' exclaimed Anthony in surprise. 'I had no idea.'

'You don't remember any of that?'

'The program that uploaded my memory cuts short at my departure for Europe. After that it's all blank. I suppose it's better that way. It's probably not especially fun to remember one's own death. I'm beginning to realize the limited lifespan of this machine might be best for all parties involved, not just the mourners.'

'I can imagine,' replied Julia uncomfortably.

'Oh, I highly doubt that. However strange the situation is for you, it's utterly out-of-body for me. More unnerving by the moment. What day did you say it was today?'

'Wednesday.'

'Three days . . . Do you know how loud the ticking can get when the second hand is literally turning inside your head? And to think I was bad before . . .'

'It was a heart attack at a stoplight.'

'Dead at a red light. Fitting. At least I didn't cause an accident.'

'Well, actually it was green.'

'Shit. I suppose that's even more fitting.'

'You didn't cause an accident if that's any comfort.'

'To be completely frank it doesn't comfort me in the least. Did they say if I suffered?'

'Not one bit. They said you died instantly.'

'Well, that's just something they tell the family either way. Not that any of it really matters all that much in the end. It's over and done with. The details of a death are seldom worth remembering. Best to be remembered for how you lived.'

'Can we maybe change the subject?' Julia asked, a touch of pleading in her voice.

'As you like. I'd be lying if I said I don't get a bit of a kick out of talking with somebody about my own demise.'

'The "somebody" in question here is your daughter. And you can joke all you want but I can see it bothers you, too.'

'It's no time for you to suddenly start being right about things, my dear.'

An hour later the car crossed over into the Netherlands. Germany was only forty-five miles away.

'It's amazing how it works between the countries here now,' Anthony continued. 'No more borders . . . You'd almost think you were free to go anywhere you please. If you were so happy in Paris, why did you decide to up and leave?'

'It was a spur-of-the-moment thing in the middle of the night. I thought I'd only be gone a couple of days. In the beginning it was just a road trip with some friends.'

'Close friends?'

'I met them ten minutes before.'

'I might have known. And what did these old friends of yours do when they weren't running off to Germany?'

'They were students like me. At the Sorbonne.'

'Okay. And what made you decide to go to Germany? I imagine Spain or Italy would have been a little more . . . fun.'

'We wanted to see the revolution. Antoine and Mathias had this hunch that the Wall was going to come down. We knew something important was taking place, though maybe not the full extent of it, and we wanted to be there when it happened.'

'Good Lord. Go find me a time machine so I can fix whatever error I made in your upbringing that could have given you an idea like that,' Anthony grumbled, tapping his knee.

'Go back and change the one thing you did right?'

'Ha! That's one way of looking at it,' muttered Anthony, turning back to look out his window.

'Why are you asking me all this now?'

'Somebody's got to ask questions! You haven't asked me a single one. For example I love Paris so much because that was where I had my first kiss with your mother. Which was no small feat, let me tell you.'

'Spare me the details. I'm all set on—'

'If you only knew how pretty she was back then. We were just twenty-three years old.'

'How did you manage to get to Paris? I thought you were completely broke when you were young.'

'It was 1965. I was drafted and served on a military base in Europe.'

'Really? Where?'

'Actually Berlin. You're not the only one with mixed emotions about that place.'

Anthony turned his gaze back to the passing landscape.

'You don't have to keep watching me in the reflection. I'm right here, you know,' said Julia.

'Well, then you can also put your rear-view mirror back where it belongs. Perhaps so the next time you change lanes you can actually see what's behind you.'

'You met Mom when you were in Berlin?'

'No. It wasn't until I got to France. As soon as I finished serving overseas, I hopped on a train to Paris. It was still cheap back in those days.'

'And it was love at first sight?'

'It wasn't bad . . . the food, the wine, the Eiffel Tower . . . though it's not as tall as the Empire State Building.'

'I was talking about Mom.'

'She was a dancer at a nightclub – one of those big burlesque-style cabarets.'

'Hold up. Mom was a dancer?'

'Yes indeed, one of the Bluebell Girls. The Lido was hosting her troupe's show for a one-month stint.'

'She never said a word of that to me.'

'Well, our family isn't known for being the biggest talkers. A trait you seem to have inherited.'

'So. How did you two meet?'

'I thought you didn't want to hear the details. If you slow down a bit, I'll tell you the whole saga.'

'I'm not driving that fast,' Julia replied, with the needle on the speedometer flirting ever closer to eighty-five miles per hour.

'That's a matter of opinion. I'm more accustomed to American highways, with ample time to watch the scenery. You keep driving that fast, you'll need a monkey wrench to pry my fingers off the door handle.'

Julia slowed down a bit and Anthony breathed a sigh of relief.

'I had a table right next to the stage. The show played ten nights in a row, and I didn't miss a single one, the extra Sunday matinee included.

I managed to bribe an usher with a generous tip so I'd always have the exact same spot.'

Julia turned off the radio completely.

'For the last time, straighten out that mirror and watch the highway!' commanded Anthony.

Julia did so without protesting.

'By the sixth day your mother had figured out what was happening, though in later years she'd insist it was the fourth. Anyway, I caught her eye several times during the show. I don't mean to brag, but I nearly made her miss a step. Of course, to hear your mother tell it the near stumble had nothing to do with me; it was some other distraction. Your mother's version of the truth was just one more way of flirting with me and making me crazy. So, I had flowers sent to her dressing room, where she'd find them after the show. Every evening the same little bouquet of old-fashioned roses, but never a note or a card.'

'Why is that?'

'I was just getting to that if you would let me finish. After the last performance I went to wait for her at the stage door. I wore a boutonniere – a simple rose, the same kind as the ones I'd sent her.'

'No, you didn't!' Julia blurted out, seized by an uncontrollable giggling fit.

Anthony turned away and abruptly fell silent.

'And then?' Julia insisted.

'That's it. End of story.'

'What do you mean, "end of story"?'

'If all you're going to do is make fun of me, then I'm done.'

'I wasn't making fun of you!'

'Then what was that idiotic giggling I just heard?'

'It wasn't meant to make fun of you at all. I just never could have imagined you as a young, hopeless romantic.'

'Pull into the next rest stop. I'd rather walk the rest of the way,' Anthony pouted, crossing his arms in stubborn protest.

'You thought I was driving fast before? See what happens if you don't finish your story.'

Anthony scoffed but gave in. 'For your mother, having admirers waiting after the show was nothing new. There was a guard in place to escort the dancers to the bus that would take them back to the hotel. So, like I said, after the last show I waited for her, standing right in their path. The guard made the mistake of shoving me aside – a bit too roughly – which set me off. And . . . I punched him.'

This was too much. Julia burst out laughing once again.

'Fine! If that's how it's going to be, you're not getting another word.'

'Come on, Daddy! I'm sorry, I am,' she said breathlessly. 'I couldn't help myself.'

Anthony turned and looked at his daughter carefully.

'That time I wasn't hearing things. You just called me Daddy.'

'So what if I did?' said Julia, drying her eyes. 'Please. Go on.'

'I'm warning you, Julia, if you so much as crack a smile, you get left with a cliffhanger and that's that.'

'I solemnly swear,' she said, lifting her right hand.

'First, the punch. Then your mother interceded. She told the bus driver to wait and took me aside. She asked why I had shown up every night, sitting at the same table for every performance. At that point she had yet to notice the old-fashioned white rose on my lapel, so I offered it to her. It hit her all at once and left her speechless: I was the one who had been sending the same flowers every night. So, I took advantage of the pause. And asked her a question.'

'What was it?'

'I asked her to marry me.'

Julia turned to her father in shock. Anthony told her to concentrate on the road.

'Your mother broke into the same sort of cackling giggle you did just now when you were making fun of me. As soon as she realized I was serious, she turned and told the driver he could leave without her.

Then she looked at me and said I could start by taking her out to dinner. We walked to a brasserie on the Champs-Élysées. I can't tell you how proud I was to be by her side, walking down the most beautiful avenue in the world. You should have seen the way everyone's eyes were glued to her. We talked the whole dinner through, but at the end of the meal I found myself in a tight spot . . . and I feared that our romance had come to a screeching halt.'

'So you started out by proposing to her. How could things possibly get *worse*?'

'I didn't have the money to pay for dinner. I was positively mortified. I checked my pockets inside and out as discreetly as possible, but I didn't have a cent. All my service pay had gone to those Lido tickets and the old-fashioned roses.'

'What did you do?'

'I ordered what must have been my seventh espresso. The brasserie was closing, and your mother left to go powder her nose. I called over the waiter with the plan of telling him the truth, offering to give him my watch and passport as security so long as he didn't make a scene, promising up and down that I'd pay the bill as soon as humanly possible, end of the week at the latest. Before I could begin, he simply showed me a tray with a piece of paper where the bill should be. It was a note from your mother.'

'What did it say?'

Anthony opened his wallet and took out a scrap of paper, well worn and yellowed with age, which he unfolded and read in a subdued voice.

'"I've never been good at goodbyes, and I gather you're not either. Thank you for a wonderful evening. Old-fashioned roses are my favourite. We'll be performing in Manchester at the end of February, and I'd love to look out into the audience and see you looking back at me. If you make it, I'll let you treat me to dinner then."'

'See?' Anthony showed the precious note to Julia. 'Signed with your mother's name.'

'That's impressive!' Julia said with a whistle. 'But why would she—?'

'Well, your mother always was adept at connecting the dots.'

'How so?'

'Watching a poor fool gulp down seven espressos at two in the morning, at a total loss for words, with the restaurant practically shutting off the lights around us? She put two and two together.'

'Did you make it to Manchester?'

'Well, first I had to buckle down and work to save up to get there. I had three jobs, back-to-back shifts. At five in the morning I unloaded trucks at the market. From there I scurried over to a cafe in the neighbourhood and waited tables. Come noon I took off my apron and put on a clerk's uniform, worked the rest of the day at a grocery store. I lost ten pounds, but I saved enough to go to England and buy a ticket to the show your mother was performing in and, most of all, to take her out to a proper meal afterward. Against all odds I managed to get a seat in the front row again. As soon as the curtains rose, her eyes locked on to mine with a warm smile.

'After the show we met in an old pub. I was beyond exhausted, really bled dry. Ashamed as I am to admit it, I even dozed off at one point. Of course your mother noticed. We hardly talked at all that evening. We exchanged silences, not conversation. When I asked the waiter to bring the cheque, your mother looked at me and simply said, "Yes." Mind you I hadn't asked a question, so you can imagine the look on my face. But then she repeated herself – "Yes" with a voice that rang so clear I can still hear it in my ears today. "Yes, I'll marry you," she said.

'The troupe was supposed to stay in Manchester for two months, but your mother simply said au revoir to her friends and we hopped on a boat back stateside. Got married the moment we dropped anchor. There was just the priest and two witnesses we'd grabbed in the waiting room. No one from either of our families was in attendance. My father never forgave me for marrying a dancer.'

Anthony folded the cherished scrap of paper with the utmost care and put it back in its place. 'Look here! My pacemaker letter. I can't believe it. Imbecile! I had simply slipped it in my wallet instead of my passport.'

Julia nodded absent-mindedly. 'Going to Berlin was just a way of guaranteeing we'd spend more time together. Am I right?'

'Frankly I thought you'd have asked me sooner.'

'The rental car, the lost pacemaker certificate. All by design, all part of the plan.'

'Let's say it was. Not such a terrible thing, now is it?'

A sign up ahead announced they were entering Germany. Julia looked sombre. She readjusted the rear-view mirror, no longer watching her father.

'What's wrong? You've gotten awfully quiet,' said Anthony.

'The day before you busted into our room in Berlin and knocked Thomas out, we had decided to get married. But it never happened. Because my father couldn't accept me marrying someone who didn't come from his world.'

Anthony turned to look back out the window.

15.

They hadn't spoken a word since they entered Germany. From time to time Julia would turn up the radio, only to have Anthony turn it down just as quickly. A pine forest appeared on the horizon. At the forest's edge a wall of concrete blocks cut off access to a road that was once for diverted traffic. Julia could make out the gloomy, hulking forms of the former Marienborn border inspection buildings, long since converted into a memorial.

'How exactly did you and your friends get across the border?' asked Anthony, gazing at the abandoned watchtowers rolling past on their right.

'By the seat of our pants. One of the guys I was travelling with was the son of a diplomat, and we said we were going to visit his father and mine, who were both posted in West Berlin.'

Anthony laughed.

'Particularly ironic, isn't it? You run away from your real father to visit an imaginary one in Berlin.'

He rested his hands on his knees.

'I'm sorry I didn't give you that letter sooner,' he continued.

'Do you really mean that?'

'I don't really know. I do feel better having said it, though. How about a break soon?'

'What for?'

'It would be wise for you to get some rest. And I'd like to stretch my legs.'

A sign ahead indicated the next service station was ten miles away. Julia said she would stop there.

'Why did you and Mom move to Montreal?'

'We didn't have much money, especially me . . . Your mother had some savings to begin with, but we burned through that pretty quickly. Life in New York kept getting more and more difficult. And we were . . . happy in Montreal. We really were. I think those were our best years.'

'It makes you proud, doesn't it?' asked Julia, her voice bittersweet.

'What does?'

'Coming from nothing and making it so big.'

'And you? Don't you get that same feeling? You did something quite daring. It must fill you with a sense of satisfaction to see a child playing with a stuffed animal that came straight from your imagination. It must make you feel proud when you see a poster outside a movie theatre for a film with a story that you came up with.'

'I'm just grateful to be happy. That's enough for me.'

Julia turned into the service station and pulled up to the kerb at the edge of a broad lawn. Anthony opened his door and ruffled his daughter's hair before leaping out of the car.

'You drive me crazy, Julia!' he said as he walked away.

She turned off the engine and rested her head on the steering wheel.

'What on earth am I doing here?'

Anthony crossed the playground, going straight past the sign that read 'For Children Only,' and entered the petrol station shop. A few moments later he came out with a bag of snacks and drinks, opened the rear door and put his purchases on the seat.

'Go get some air. I bought everything you'll need to recharge. I can keep an eye on the car.'

Julia left without a word. She walked around the children's swing, avoiding the sandpit, and went in the petrol station shop. When she returned, she found Anthony stretched out at the bottom of the playground slide, eyes to the sky.

'Are you okay?' she asked her father warily.

'Do you reckon I'm up there somewhere?'

Thrown off by the question, Julia sat down on the grass by his side. Her eyes also wandered skyward.

'I don't know. I searched for Thomas up there in the clouds for years. I was sure I'd even seen him a couple of times. Yet he's still alive.'

'Your mother didn't believe in God. But I do. Do you think your old man made it up to heaven?'

'I'm sorry, I cannot answer that question. I just can't.'

'You can't believe in God?'

'I'm saying I can't even begin to think about that when I'm sitting here talking to you, even though you're . . .'

'Dead. It's just a word, nothing to be afraid of, like I've been telling you. Finding the right words is important. For example, if you had told me earlier, "Daddy, you're a bastard and an idiot who has never understood a single thing about me. You're a self-centred father, and all you've ever wanted is to shape me in your own image; you hurt me and told me that it was for my own good when it was for *your* own good," maybe I would have heard you. Maybe we wouldn't have lost all those years and we could have been friends. Admit it. It would have been nice to be friends.'

Julia remained silent.

'See, that's what I meant about choosing the right words. Instead of having been a good father or bad, I dare say I would've preferred to call myself your *friend*.'

'We should get back on the road,' Julia said, trying to hide the slight tremble in her voice.

'Just a little while longer. I think my energy reserve isn't quite as robust as the manufacturers forecasted. If I keep on this way, our time together might not be as long as we planned.'

'Take as long as you need. Berlin isn't that far. After twenty years, what's a few more hours?'

'Eighteen years, Julia.'

'Close enough.'

'Two years, two whole years of life? Not even close. Believe me, I know what I'm talking about.'

Father and daughter lay motionless, hands behind their heads, her stretched out on the grass and his legs hanging off the slide, both of them scanning the sky.

An hour went by. Julia had dozed off, and Anthony had turned to watch her sleep. Peaceful dreams, or so it seemed. From time to time she frowned, tickled by the wind dancing across her face. Anthony cautiously pushed back a lock of her hair.

When Julia finally opened her eyes, the sky was already tinged with shadows of dusk, and she found herself alone. She sat up and caught sight of her father's silhouette in the passenger seat of their car. She slipped her shoes back on, though she couldn't remember taking them off, and walked back across the car park.

'Did I sleep long?' she asked as she started the car.

'Two hours, maybe a little longer. I wasn't paying attention.'

'What were you doing?'

'I was waiting.'

Julia drove out of the service station and back on to the highway. Potsdam was only fifty miles away.

'It'll be dark by the time we get to Berlin,' she said. 'I have no idea how to find Thomas. I don't even know if he still lives there. So, you basically dragged me all the way here on a whim. What makes you think we can find him at all?'

'Well, anything is possible. Between the skyrocketing cost of real estate, putting food on the table for the triplets and his in-laws moving in, they certainly could have relocated to a cozy little house in the country.'

Julia glared at her father, who once again motioned for her to watch the road.

'It's fascinating how fear can thrive within the mind,' he continued.

'What's that supposed to mean?'

'Nothing, just thinking out loud. By the way, not that it's any of my business, but don't you think you should check in and let Adam know you're still alive? If not for him then for me. I never want to hear Gloria Gaynor again. She was caterwauling in your purse the entire time you were asleep.'

With that, Anthony broke into a frenzied rendition of 'I Will Survive'. Julia swallowed back her laughter at first, but the louder he sang, the more uncontrollable her giggling became. By the time they were rolling through the outskirts of Berlin, the two of them were roaring with laughter.

Anthony gave Julia directions to the Brandenburger Hof Hotel. When they arrived a bellboy welcomed them as they stepped out of the car. 'Good evening, Mr Walsh,' said the doorman, giving the revolving door a shove to get it spinning. Anthony crossed the lobby to the front desk, where the concierge also greeted him by name. At this time of the year the hotel was fully booked, but even without a reservation the concierge assured Anthony that two of their very best rooms would be at his disposal. The concierge added, with his sincere regrets, that the two rooms would not be on the same floor. Anthony thanked him and said it wasn't important. Handing their keys to the bellboy, the concierge asked Anthony if he wanted to make a reservation at the hotel restaurant that evening.

'How does that strike you, dear?' asked Anthony, turning towards Julia. 'Alternatively I do know a great place just a few minutes from here. Do you still like Chinese food as much as you used to?'

Julia said nothing. Anthony shrugged and asked the concierge to reserve a table for two on the terrace at China Garden.

After freshening up, Julia and her father walked to the restaurant together.

'Something bothering you, dear? Are you in a bad mood?'

'I just can't believe how much everything here has changed,' Julia responded distractedly.

'Did you speak to your fiancé?'

'Yes, I called him from my room.'

'And what did he have to say?'

'He said he missed me. He said he still doesn't understand why I left like I did, or what I'm chasing. He said he came for me in Montreal – he only missed us by an hour.'

'That's a shame. Just imagine the look on his face if he had seen us together.'

'Yeah, well . . . he made me promise that I was alone. Four times.'

'And . . . ?'

'And I lied. Four times!'

Anthony opened the restaurant door for his daughter.

'Ha! Careful you don't start enjoying it,' he said with a chuckle.

'I don't see what's so funny about it.'

'What's funny is that we're in Berlin to track down your long-lost love, and you feel guilty about lying to your fiancé that you were in Montreal with your father. I for one think that's ballsy.'

Anthony used the time they spent at dinner to come up with a plan. First thing in the morning they would pay a visit to the press syndicate offices to find out if a certain Thomas Meyer still had a press pass.

On the way back from dinner, Julia led her father along the gates lining the Tiergarten.

'I used to take naps under that tree,' she said, pointing out a huge linden tree in the distance. 'Crazy. Feels like it was just yesterday.'

Anthony flashed a mischievous look at Julia and crouched down, lacing together ten fingers and offering his daughter a boost over the fence.

'What are you doing?'

'Making you a stepladder. Hurry up. Nobody's watching. Don't think. Just take the leap.'

He didn't have to ask twice. She stepped up and hoisted herself over the fence.

'What about you?' she asked, rising to her feet on the other side and dusting herself off.

'I think I'll just head through that open gate right there,' he said, pointing to an entrance a bit further on. 'The park doesn't close until midnight. I may be a bit too old for that sort of thing.'

As soon as he rejoined Julia, he led her across the lawn, and they sat at the foot of the enormous tree she had shown him.

'Want to hear something funny? I myself took a nap or two under this tree during my time in Germany. It was my favourite spot. Every time I got even a few hours of leave, I came here with a book and watched the girls pass by, one after the next. You and I were both in the same place around the same age, only separated by a few small decades. Along with the skyscraper in Montreal, that makes two places where we now have shared memories. I'm glad.'

'This is where Thomas and I always came,' said Julia.

'I'm beginning to like this guy more and more.'

An elephant could be heard trumpeting in the distance. Berlin Zoo was at the edge of the park, just a few yards behind them.

Anthony got up and gestured for his daughter to join him.

'When you were a little girl, you hated the zoo. You didn't like that the animals were in cages. Back then you dreamed of becoming a veterinarian. You've probably forgotten, but for your sixth birthday I gave you a big stuffed otter if I remember correctly. I must have picked the wrong one off the shelf, because she was always sick. You spent all of your time trying to make her better.'

'Are you trying to say I have you to thank for creating Tilly?'

'Of course not! Childhood experiences don't mean a thing once you're an adult. At least I sure hope not, given all the things you accuse me of.'

Anthony admitted that he felt his strength fading at an alarming rate. The time had come to return to the hotel. They took a taxi.

Back at the hotel Julia stepped out of the lift, and Anthony bid her good night, then continued on to the top floor.

Julia lay in bed for a long time, scrolling through the numbers on the screen of her cell phone. She decided to call Adam again, but when it went straight to voicemail, she hung up and called Stanley.

'So? Have you got news for me?' asked her friend.

'Not yet. I just got here.'

'What, did you travel by rickshaw?'

'We drove from Paris. It's a long story.'

'You miss me?' he asked.

'No, not at all. Why do you think I'm calling, dummy?'

Stanley told Julia he had walked past her apartment on his way home from work. It wasn't really on his way, but his feet had unconsciously led him to the corner of Horatio and Greenwich.

'It's a sad place when you're not around.'

'You're just saying that to make me feel better.'

'By the way I ran into your neighbour with the shoe store.'

'Mr Zimoure? Did you talk to him?'

'In fact I did. He was standing outside and waved at me. I waved back.'

'I leave you alone for a few days and already you're associating with the most unsavoury characters.'

'You know, he's really not all that bad.'

'Stanley, are you trying to tell me something?'

'And what might that be, baby doll?'

'I know you, Stanley. You meeting somebody and not immediately disliking them is enough to make me suspicious. A "not all that bad" rating for Zimoure makes me think I should take the first flight home.'

'Do it! But you need a better excuse than that. We said hello to each other and that was all. Oh, also? Adam stopped by to see me.'

'The two of you are becoming inseparable.'

'He's just lonely. It's not my fault he lives two blocks from my store. And in case you're still interested, he isn't holding up very well. Dropping by my place is not the most promising sign. He misses you, Julia. He's worried, and I think you've given him good reason to be.'

'Honestly, Stanley, it's not like that at all. I swear. In fact it's the total opposite.'

'You don't have to swear to me, just listen to what I'm trying to say.'

'Of course, I'm listening,' she replied, unfazed.

'You're driving me crazy is what you're doing. Do you even know where this mysterious journey is supposed to end?'

'No,' Julia murmured.

'Well, then how can you possibly expect Adam to not be losing it? I have to go now. It's seven, and I have a dinner to get ready for.'

'With whom?'

'And might I ask: with whom did you dine tonight, young lady?'

'I ate alone.'

'Every time you lie? I get a rash. I'm going to hang up now. Call me tomorrow. Kisses.'

Julia didn't have time to respond before she heard a click and knew the conversation was over. She could just picture Stanley walking off, probably towards his walk-in closet.

◆ ◆ ◆

A ringing sound awoke Julia from her slumber. She stretched to pick up the phone but heard only a dialling tone. She got up and made it halfway across the room before realizing she was naked. She picked up the dressing gown she had abandoned at the foot of her bed the night before and scrambled to slip into it on her way to the door.

A waiter was hovering patiently outside in the corridor. When Julia opened the door, he pushed in a trolley with a hefty continental breakfast and two soft-boiled eggs.

'I didn't order anything,' she said as the young man began setting up her breakfast on the coffee table.

'Three-and-a-half-minute eggs. Isn't that you?'

'Well . . . yes,' replied Julia, ruffling her hair.

'That's what Mr Walsh told us.'

'But I'm not hungry,' she added, watching the waiter cut the tops off the eggs with surgical precision.

'Mr Walsh also told us you would say you weren't hungry. One last thing – he says to meet him in the lobby at eight o'clock. That's in roughly thirty-seven minutes,' he said, consulting his watch. 'Have a lovely day, Miss Walsh. You certainly got very lucky with this weather. You should have a very pleasant stay in Berlin.'

The waiter left Julia staring in disbelief.

She looked at the spread of orange juice, cereal and fresh bread laid out on the table. Nothing was missing. She made up her mind to skip breakfast nonetheless and started to walk to the bathroom, then turned, plopped herself down on the sofa and dipped a finger in an egg for a taste. Within moments she had eaten nearly everything.

After a quick shower she hurried to get dressed. She put on a pair of shoes while blow-drying her hair at the same time, hopping around on one foot. She left her room at precisely eight o'clock.

Anthony was waiting for her near reception.

'You're late!' he said as she stepped out of the lift.

'Barely,' she said, throwing him a sceptical look.

'Three and a half minutes late. You like your arrivals the same way you like your eggs I see. Well, let's get a move on. We have a meeting in half an hour, and with the traffic we'll barely make it.'

'Where and with whom do we have a meeting?'

'At the headquarters of the German press syndicate. I thought we covered that. Have to start somewhere!'

Anthony walked through the revolving door and hailed a taxi.

'And just how did we get this appointment?' she asked, taking a seat next to him in the back of the tan Mercedes.

'I called first thing this morning while you were still asleep.'

'You speak German?'

'One of my many technological miracles. Fifteen languages wired in, and that's just on the prototype! However, the German could also be from the years I spent stationed here, unless you've already forgotten that. I still remember enough of the basics to be understood at the very least, when needed. And how rusty is your German?'

'I can't remember a single word.'

The taxi made its way down Stülerstrasse, then took a left across the park. The giant linden tree cast a long shadow across the lush grass.

The car hugged the banks of the Spree. On both sides of the river the recently built area was brimming with showy buildings, each more modern than the last, in a contest for most transparent edifice. Architecture for architecture's sake – just one more sign of changing times. The sinister Wall had once stood on the edge of the area they were driving through, and yet not a trace had been left behind. Before them now was an enormous structure that housed a conference centre under an impressive glass frame. A little further on an even bigger complex sprawled over both sides of the river. Access to the building was through an airy white footbridge.

◆ ◆ ◆

They entered and followed the signs to the offices of the press syndicate. A representative received them at the front desk. In more-than-adequate German, Anthony explained he was trying to get in contact with a certain Thomas Meyer.

'Regarding what subject?' asked the employee without looking up from his book.

'I have some very important information for Mr Meyer, information which is only authorized to be communicated directly to the man himself,' replied Anthony in an even tone.

Since he seemed to have got the receptionist's attention, Anthony added that he would be indebted to the syndicate if they provided an address where he could reach Mr Meyer. Not his personal information of course, just his work address.

The receptionist asked him to wait a moment and went to get his supervisor.

The assistant director arrived and led Anthony and Julia into his office. Comfortably installed on a couch below a wall-size photograph of their host holding a massive trophy fish, Anthony repeated the same speech word for word. The man sized Anthony up with a steady gaze.

'And what kind of information is this that you plan on passing along to Thomas Meyer?' he asked, stroking his moustache.

'I'm not at liberty to say, but rest assured that it's essential he receive it directly from me,' Anthony promised sincerely.

'I don't recall any major articles written by a person of that name,' the assistant director said, his voice full of doubt.

'Well, what if I told you all that was about to change? That is if you help us find him.'

'And what role does your companion play in this scenario?' asked the assistant director, pivoting his desk chair to face the window.

Anthony turned to Julia, who had not uttered a word since their arrival.

'None whatsoever. Miss Julia is my assistant.'

'I'm afraid I'm not authorized to provide any information about the members of our association,' said the assistant director as he rose to his feet.

Anthony stood, approached him and placed a hand on the man's shoulder.

'I have information for Thomas Meyer and for him alone,' he insisted, his voice full of authority. 'What I have to say could change his life for the better. I refuse to believe that a competent administrator such as yourself would want to obstruct the spectacular career advancement of one of the very members he claims to serve. If that's the case, that's just the type of scandalous behaviour I wouldn't think twice about exposing to the public.'

Again the man rubbed his moustache and sat back down. He tapped away at his keyboard and then turned his computer screen towards Anthony.

'See for yourself. There's no one by the name of Thomas Meyer in our database. I'm very sorry. I'm afraid that if he's not listed here, it means he doesn't have a press card, and you won't find him in the directory of affiliated journalists either. But feel free to check for yourself. Now, if you'll excuse me I must return to my work. If there's nobody besides this "Mr Meyer" who can receive your precious information, I'll kindly ask that you leave me to my duties.'

Anthony rose and motioned for Julia to follow him. He warmly thanked the administrator for his valuable time and they left the building.

'You were probably right,' he grumbled, walking back along the pavement. He then summarized the exchange for her.

'Your *assistant*?' asked Julia with a smirk.

'Don't give me that look. I had to come up with something.'

'"Miss Julia." What next?'

Anthony hailed a taxi coming down the other side of the street.

'As I was saying, maybe you were right. Perhaps your Thomas has found a new line of work.'

'I doubt it. Being a journalist was more than a job for Thomas – it was his calling. I can't imagine him doing anything else.'

'You'd be surprised! Remind me again of the name of that depressing street where the two of you lived,' he said to his daughter.

'Comeniusplatz. It's behind Karl Marx Avenue.'

'Of course it is!'

'What does that mean, "of course"?'

'Oh, nothing. It just brings back so many fond memories, doesn't it?'

Anthony gave the taxi driver the address.

They crossed the city. There were no more checkpoints, no traces of the Wall, nothing to serve as a reminder of where the West had ended and the East had begun. They drove past the Television Tower, a sculptural ball at the top of an arrow that pointed skyward. The further they drove, the more they could tell how much the city around them had changed. When they arrived at their destination, Julia recognized nothing of the area where she had once lived. Everything looked so different, her memories could have been from another lifetime.

'It was in these magnificent surroundings that you experienced the most beautiful moments of your young life?' Anthony asked sarcastically. 'I must admit, it does have a *certain* charm . . .'

'That's enough!' shouted Julia.

Anthony looked surprised by his daughter's sudden outburst.

'Easy now, dear, I'm only—'

'Just be quiet. Please.'

The old buildings and houses that once stood on the street were gone, replaced by recently constructed apartment blocks. Nothing from Julia's memories remained, apart from the main square.

She walked to the building marked Number 2, where a fragile house with a green door used to stand, with an old wooden staircase inside that led to the second floor. Julia used to help Thomas's grandmother make it up the last few steps. She closed her eyes and remembered the house. The smell of wax when she went near the dresser. The drapes that were always pulled, allowing a few shafts of light through but protecting the interior from prying eyes. The table in the dining room covered with an ancient oilcloth and surrounded by three chairs. The threadbare sofa stretched out across from an old black-and-white television. Thomas's grandmother did not turn it on once after it began broadcasting only news that the government wanted people to hear. And just behind, the thin screen that separated the living room from their bedroom, before they'd found their own apartment. How many times had Thomas nearly suffocated her with a pillow in an attempt to muffle her laughter at his clumsy groping hands?

'Your hair was much longer back then,' said Anthony, jerking Julia from her daydream.

'What?' she asked, turning around.

'When you were eighteen, your hair was much longer.'

Anthony's gaze swept across the city's horizon. 'There's not much left, is there?'

'There's nothing. Absolutely nothing,' she stammered.

'Come on, let's sit down. You're pale. Take a moment, regain your strength.'

They took a seat on a bench just beside a patch of grass that had been yellowed by the repeated passage of children's feet.

Julia was silent. Anthony lifted his arm as though he meant to put it around her, but he only made it as far as the back of the bench, where he awkwardly rested his hand.

'There used to be other houses here, you know. They needed paint, and they were falling down, but they were cozy on the inside. It was, well—'

'Better in your mind's eye? That's often the way it is with memories,' said Anthony soothingly. 'It's like a strange artist, memory. It alters colours, erases the dull bits and leaves only the pretty lines, the most enchanting curves of one's life.'

'At the end of the street, where that godawful library is now, there was a little cafe. It was the seediest place I've ever been to in my life. The room was painted a muddy grey, lit with fluorescent lights, and the Formica tables and booths were shoved up against the walls. But we had such good times there. We were so happy. All you could get was vodka and watered-down beer. I used to help out the owner when the place got busy. I'd put on an apron and wait tables. It was there, just right over there.' Julia pointed to the library that had replaced the cafe.

Anthony cleared his throat.

'One question. Are you sure it wasn't on the other side of the street? Because I see a little hellhole that seems to match your description to a T.'

Julia turned to look, and sure enough, on the corner of the street opposite the modern library, a neon sign flickered on and off in front of an old rundown bar.

Julia stood up abruptly, and Anthony followed her. She started down the street, moving faster and faster, before finally breaking into a run. By the end of the seemingly endless stretch, she was racing at top speed. Gasping for breath, she pushed open the bar door and went inside.

The room had been repainted, and two ceiling lights had replaced the fluorescent tubes, but the Formica tables were still there, actually giving the place a pleasant retro vibe. A white-haired man stood behind the unchanged bar. He seemed to recognize Julia.

A single customer sat reading a newspaper at the end of the bar, with his back turned. Julia walked up to him, barely breathing, her heart pounding faster with each step.

'Thomas?'

16.

Rome.

The embattled head of the Italian government had just handed in his resignation. The press conference over, he submitted to the demands of the photographers one last time. Hundreds of camera flashes went off, lighting up the stage. At the back of the conference room a man leaned against a radiator and packed up his equipment.

'You're not going to capture the scene?' asked the young woman at his side.

'No, Marina, it's pointless to take the same photo as fifty other people. It's not exactly my idea of journalism.'

'With such a bad attitude it's a good thing you have a pretty face to balance things out.'

'That's one way of admitting I was right. How about I take you to lunch instead of listening to you lecture me?'

'What did you have in mind?' she asked.

'I didn't. But I'm sure you do.'

A journalist from one of the radio stations walked past and kissed Marina's hand before slipping away.

'Who was that?'

'Just some arsehole,' replied Marina.

'He's an arsehole who wants to kiss more than just your hand.'

'Exactly that type of arsehole. Shall we?'

'Let's grab our passports and get out of here.'

Arm in arm they left the large hall where the press conference had taken place and walked down a corridor towards the exit.

'What are your plans?' Marina asked as she presented her press pass to the security guard stationed near the door.

'Just waiting for news from my editors. I've been working dinky little jobs like this for three weeks, waiting for the green light to go to Somalia.'

'"Dinky little jobs"? Even with me here?'

Ignoring this, he followed Marina's lead and flashed his press pass in order to recover his ID, which every visitor to the Palazzo di Montecitorio was obliged to hand over before entering the building.

'Mr Ullmann?' asked the puzzled officer.

'Right. My pen name as a journalist is different from the name on my passport. Same first name, though, and the photo matches my press card if you need to make sure I'm me.'

The officer verified the faces were indeed the same and handed back the passport without any further questions.

'Where did you get the idea to write under a pseudonym? Some sort of celebrity ego trip?'

'It's more complicated than that,' replied the reporter, wrapping his arm around Marina's waist.

They crossed the Piazza Colonna under a blazing sun, dodging hordes of tourists clutching ice creams.

'Luckily you kept your first name.'

'What difference does that make?'

'I like that name. It suits you. You look like a Thomas.'

'Oh really? Names have faces now? What a strange idea.'

'Are you joking? Of course they do. You couldn't have any other name. I can't imagine you as a Massimo or an Alfredo. Not even a Karl. Thomas is exactly the name you were meant to have.'

'You're mad. Where are we going?'

'All the tourists with ice creams have given me a huge craving for a granita. Let's go to the Tazza d'Oro, by the Pantheon. It's not very far from here.'

Thomas stopped at the foot of the column of Marcus Aurelius. As Marina looked over the bas-reliefs sculpted to glorify the column's namesake, he opened his bag, chose a camera, attached a lens and snapped a picture.

'Hasn't that photo already been taken by fifty other people?' she asked, laughing.

'Fifty? Really, I had no idea I had so much competition,' Thomas said with a smile, clicking the shutter again for a shot with a narrower frame.

'I'm talking about the column! Was that of me?'

'Well, as far as I'm concerned this old thing is just like the Victory Column in Berlin. But there's only one Marina.'

'Like I said, you'd get nowhere without your pretty face – you're a pathetic flirt, Thomas. You wouldn't stand a chance here in Italy. Come on, let's get out of here. This heat is killing me.'

Marina took Thomas's hand, and they left the column behind them.

◆ ◆ ◆

Julia ran her eyes up and down the Victory Column, shooting up into the sky over Berlin. Sitting at its base, Anthony shrugged at her.

'It's not like we really expected to find him on the first day,' he said with a sigh. 'You realize how strange it would have been if that guy at the dive bar had turned out to be your Thomas.'

'I know. I got it wrong, that's all.'

'Maybe you were blinded by how badly you wanted it to be him.'

'He looked similar from the back. Same haircut, reading the newspaper the way Thomas used to, from back to front.'

'Why did the owner of the bar make that face when we asked about Thomas? He seemed pleasant enough when you were taking your little stroll down memory lane together.'

'Well, it was nice of him to say I haven't changed at all. I can't believe he even recognized me.'

'Who could forget you, my dear Julia?'

Julia gave her father a friendly jab in the ribs with her elbow.

'I'm sure he was just lying and remembered your Thomas perfectly. Why else would he clam up like that upon hearing the name?'

'Stop calling him "my Thomas". I don't even know what we're doing here. What's the point of all this?'

'Yes, rather pointless, matters of life and death, my own recent demise and whatnot.'

'Will you give it a rest already? If you really think I'm going to leave Adam for a . . . a ghost, then you're sadly mistaken.'

'My dear sweet girl, not to nitpick and risk kicking a hornet's nest, but technically speaking I'm the only ghost in your life, as you've reminded me so very often. You wouldn't deprive a father of that exclusive privilege, considering the circumstances.'

'You're not funny at all.'

'Very well. I'm not funny. Perhaps that's why you cut me off every time I open my mouth. I may be humourless and you may not want to hear what I have to say, but judging by your reaction back there when you thought you'd seen Thomas . . . I wouldn't like to be in Adam's place. Now go ahead, tell me I've got it all wrong, that it's not like—'

'Yes. You've got it all wrong!'

'Well, that's one bad habit I'm not quite ready to kick,' Anthony retorted, crossing his arms.

Julia smiled.

'What? What is it now?'

'Nothing, nothing,' said Julia.

'Come on already. Tell me.'

'You've just got this side of you . . . that's a lot more old-fashioned than I ever realized.'

'Don't be so hard on your old man,' replied Anthony as he got up. 'Come on, let's get you some lunch. It's nearly three p.m., and you haven't had a thing to eat since breakfast.'

◆ ◆ ◆

Adam stopped by at the liquor store on his way to work. The specialist suggested a California wine, an exemplary vintage with elaborate tannins, a nice body and a slightly high alcohol content. It sounded enticing to Adam, but he was looking for something a little more refined and elegant – something that more closely resembled the intended recipient. Immediately catching his drift, the salesman went to the back of the store and came back with an excellent Bordeaux. It was a highly coveted year, and not at all in the same price range as the California bottle, but could you really put a price tag on quality?

Julia once told Adam that her best friend couldn't resist the lure of a good vintage. If the bottle was good enough, Julia had explained, Stanley completely forgot his limits. Two bottles should be enough to get him drunk; then whether he liked it or not, Stanley would let slip wherever it was Julia had run off to.

◆ ◆ ◆

'Let's review our strategy from the beginning,' said Anthony, seated on the outdoor terrace of a sandwich shop. 'We tried the press syndicate, and his name wasn't on the list. You're convinced he's still a journalist. We'll trust your instincts, despite all evidence to the contrary. We paid a visit to where he used to live, and the building is long gone. That, my dear Julia, is what I would call making a clean break with one's past. I can't help but wonder if it isn't all intentional.'

'What exactly are you getting at? That Thomas has gone off the grid intentionally to put our relationship behind him? Fine, okay. Then let's wrap this up and go home,' said Julia, her frustration getting the better of her. She gestured impatiently for the waiter to take away the cappuccino he had served her just moments before.

Anthony shook his head as though to say, *Leave it.*

'I know you don't like my coffee, but give this one a try.'

'What do you care if I just want to drink tea the rest of my life?'

'Do what you like with the rest of your life. But while I'm still here please . . . humour me.'

Julia grimaced as she took a sip.

'Stop acting like it grosses you out. I get it. But I'm telling you, one day you'll get past the bitter exterior and come to appreciate the inner flavour of things. And if you really believe that Thomas has intentionally cut all ties because of you, you're overreacting. Maybe he just wanted to have a fresh start, not necessarily a break from the past you shared, but a break from his life in general. I don't know if you realize how great of a struggle it must have been to adjust to a world so completely different from what he knew growing up. Every new liberty had to be acquired at the price of his childhood values.'

'That's rich. Now you're taking his side?'

'Only idiots never admit they're wrong. The airport is just a half-hour drive from here. We could drop by the hotel, grab our things and be on the next flight. You could sleep at your stunning New York apartment this very evening if you like. At the risk of repeating myself, only idiots never admit they're wrong, and you'd do well to think about that before it's too late. Now, do you want to go home, or would you rather we carry on our search?'

Julia stood up. She drank her cappuccino in one smooth go and wiped her mouth with the back of her hand.

'Okay, Detective. Any new leads?'

Anthony left a few coins on the table and rose to his feet.

'Didn't you once tell me about a close friend of Thomas's who spent a lot of time with the two of you?'

'Knapp? He was his best friend, but I don't remember ever saying a thing about him to you.'

'Let's just say my memory is keener than yours. Tell me about this Knapp. He was a journalist as well, was he not?'

'Yes, of course.'

'Perhaps it would have been a good idea to mention his name when we had that enormous list of journalists in front of us this morning.'

'I hadn't thought of that.'

'See? Like I was saying. This whole thing is clouding your mind. Let's go then!'

'Back to the syndicate?'

'No,' said Anthony, rolling his eyes. 'I somehow doubt we'd get a warm reception the second time around.'

'So where?'

'Leave it to the old man to explain the wonders of the Internet to a girl your age. Laughable! And this from someone who spends her life glued to a computer screen. There's got to be an Internet cafe nearby. And pull back your hair, will you? In this wind I can barely see your face.'

❖ ❖ ❖

Marina insisted on paying for Thomas. Ever since they met on an assignment in Berlin, Thomas had always paid the bill, but now that they were in her country it only seemed fair. Thomas didn't see the need to put up much of a fight over two iced coffees.

'Do you have to work today?' he asked her.

'Perhaps you haven't noticed this, but the afternoon is almost over. Besides, you're my work right now. No photos, no articles.'

'So what should we do?'

'Too early for dinner. How about a walk? It's finally cooling down, and we're in the middle of the city. Let's make the most of it.'

'I have to call Knapp before he leaves the office.'

Marina grazed her hand across Thomas's cheek.

'I know you'd do anything to get away from me as soon as possible, but don't be so anxious. You'll make it to Somalia. Knapp needs you there. You explained it to me a hundred times; I know the story off by heart. He's got his sights set on becoming the editorial director, you're his best reporter and the work you do is essential for his promotion. Give him the time he needs to get things sorted out.'

'He's been sorting things out for three damn weeks!'

'He's just being thorough. Because you're his friend. Don't hold it against him! Come on, go for a walk with me.'

'All of a sudden it's like we're switching roles.'

'I thought you were going to say switching *positions*.'

'You just couldn't resist, could you?'

'Never!' replied Marina, and she burst out laughing.

She led him towards the Piazza di Spagna and the Spanish Steps, pointing out the twin bell towers of Trinità dei Monti.

'Is there any place on earth more beautiful than this?' asked Marina.

'Berlin?' Thomas replied without the slightest hesitation.

'Blasphemy! If you promise to behave and stop that nonsense, I'll take you to Caffè Greco. You have one sip of their cappuccino and then tell me if you can find them like that in Berlin.'

Eyes glued to the computer, Anthony tried to decode the text that unfolded before his eyes.

'I thought you spoke fluent German,' said Julia.

'Spoken, yes. Reading and writing is another story. But this is a technological problem, not a linguistic one. I can't make heads or tails of this damn machine.'

'Let me give it a shot,' said Julia, taking command of the keyboard.

She started tapping away, and a search engine appeared on the screen. She began to enter the word *Knapp*, then stopped.

'What is it?'

'To tell you the truth, I can't even remember his full name. I don't even know if Knapp was his first or last . . . We just always called him Knapp.'

'Let me try,' said Anthony. He added the search term *journalist*.

A list of eleven results appeared – seven men and four women with the name Knapp, and all of them in the same profession.

'That's the one,' exclaimed Anthony, pointing to a Jürgen Knapp on the third line.

'How can you be so sure?'

'Just a hunch. It says he's managing editor, and if I recall the way you talked about him as a young man, he seemed to be of sound enough intelligence to have advanced at least a bit in his chosen profession by the age of fifty. If not, he would have surely switched career paths, just like your Thomas. You should be praising my analytical mind instead of questioning my judgment.'

'I have no memory of telling you about him at all, and certainly not enough for you to complete an in-depth personality profile,' replied Julia, stupefied.

'Please. Are we really still testing the accuracy of your memory? If we had relied solely on that, we would have spent our evening reminiscing about a library instead of finding the bar right across the street. The Knapp we are seeking works as an editor at *Der Tagesspiegel*.

International news desk. Shall we go pay him a visit, or would you rather we keep shooting the breeze over another cappuccino?'

◆　◆　◆

It was rush hour, and the streets were clogged with cars. It took them ages to cross Berlin, until the taxi at last dropped them off at the Brandenburg Gate. After having endured the gruelling traffic, they now had to blaze a trail through the dense crowd of locals returning home from work – not to mention the swarms of tourists gawking in front of famous monuments. It was here that Reagan had once called upon Gorbachev to "tear down this wall" and help bring peace to the world. In those days the concrete borderline was still visible behind the columns of the huge gate. For once two world leaders had actually listened to each other and worked together to reunite East and West.

Julia picked up the pace, and Anthony had trouble keeping up with her. He called out her name several times, sure he'd lost track of her in the crowd, but always managed to spot her outline eventually somewhere in the flood of people streaming into the Pariser Platz.

She waited for him at the front door of the building. They entered together and presented themselves at reception. Anthony asked in English if he could see Jürgen Knapp. The receptionist dialled a number but then put the call on hold and asked if they had an appointment.

'Trust me. He's going to be delighted to see us,' promised Anthony, throwing a grin towards his daughter, who leaned against the desk.

'And who may I ask is here to see Mr Knapp?' asked the receptionist.

'Julia Walsh,' she replied.

◆　◆　◆

Seated behind his desk on the third floor, Jürgen Knapp had to politely ask the receptionist to repeat the name again. He asked her to hold a moment, muffled the receiver with the palm of his hand and crept over to the sloping glass facade that overlooked the glass ceiling of the lobby below.

From that vantage point he had a clear view of the entire front hall and reception. The woman waiting there removed the scarf from her head and ran her fingers through her hair. The hair was different. The years had been long, but there was no doubt in his mind: the elegant woman pacing across the lobby a few storeys down was the very same woman he met in Berlin twenty years before.

He spoke back into the phone.

'Tell her I'm out of town, travelling all week. In fact, say I won't be back until the end of the month. And please . . . make it convincing!'

'Very well, sir,' the receptionist replied with cool professionalism, deftly avoiding the use of his first name. 'I also have a call for you. Shall I put him through?'

'Who is it?'

'I didn't have time to ask.'

'All right, go ahead and put the call through.'

The receptionist hung up.

◆　◆　◆

'Jürgen?'

'Yes. Who's this?'

'Thomas! You really couldn't tell it was me?'

'Sorry, you know – my head's all over the place.'

'They kept me on hold for at least five minutes, and I'm calling from abroad. Did you have a prime minister on the line or something? Hell of a long time to make a man wait.'

'My apologies. Anyway, it wasn't anything important. I have good news for you, though. I was going to call you tonight to tell you: pack your bags for Somalia. I got the green light.'

'Oh, that's fantastic!' exclaimed Thomas. 'I'll come back to Berlin and get a move on ASAP.'

'There's no need. Stay in Rome. I'll take care of the flight, and I can send you all the other documents express. I'll get them to you by the morning.'

'Why don't I just come over so we can talk in person before I—?'

'No, no, no. Trust me. We've waited long enough to get the necessary authorization. There's no time to lose. Your flight for Africa leaves Fiumicino Airport late tomorrow afternoon. I'll call you tomorrow morning with the details.'

'Everything okay?' asked Thomas. 'You sound a bit odd.'

'Everything's fine. You know me. I'm just excited for you and annoyed I can't be with you for a celebratory drink.'

'Well, I don't know how to thank you, Jürgen. I suppose I'll just have to win a Pulitzer and help you land that editorial director job!'

Thomas hung up. Knapp peered out the window just as Julia crossed the lobby and left, trailed by the older man with her. He turned around behind his desk and put the receiver back in its cradle.

17.

Thomas joined Marina, who sat waiting for him at the top of the Spanish Steps. The Piazza di Spagna was crowded with tourists.

'So did you manage to get through to him?' Marina asked.

Thomas avoided making eye contact. 'Come on, there are too many people here. I can barely breathe. Let's do a little window shopping. Maybe we can get you that shawl you liked with all the colours.'

Marina slid her sunglasses down to the tip of her nose and rose to her feet without a word.

'Hey! Wrong way. The shop's back over there,' Thomas shouted after her as she abruptly headed down the steps towards the fountain.

'I'm not going to any shop. You can forget that scarf.'

Thomas ran after her and managed to catch up with her at the bottom of the steps.

'You were in love with it yesterday!'

'That was yesterday. Today I don't want it any more. Women are fickle you know. And men are idiots.'

'What is your problem?' asked Thomas.

'My problem is that if you really want to give me a present, you should have chosen it yourself, wrapped it up nicely and hidden it as a surprise. That's called being attentive. A rare quality, one that women are very fond of, although it takes a lot more than that to get a woman to marry you.'

'All right, slow down, I'm sorry. I thought it would make you happy.'

'Well, it backfired. Any gift meant as a bribe, hoping I'd say "fine" and forgive you—'

'Hold on! What do I need to be forgiven for?'

'As though you don't know! Careful, Pinocchio, or your nose will start growing. Let's celebrate your departure for Somalia instead of arguing. That's what he told you just now on the phone, isn't it? Well, you'd better take me someplace very nice tonight, mister, I can tell you that much.'

Marina started walking again, ending any discussion of the matter.

◆ ◆ ◆

Julia got out of the taxi and followed Anthony through the hotel's revolving door.

'There's got to be some sort of solution here. That Thomas of yours didn't vanish into thin air. He's out there somewhere. We just have to find him. It's simply a matter of patience.'

'We can't wait that long. Twenty-four hours by my count. We have tomorrow, then Saturday we fly back. Or did you forget?'

'I'm the one whose days are numbered, Julia. You have your whole life ahead of you. If you want to see this thing through to the end, you might need to take a trip back to Berlin on your own. But at least this trip of ours got you closer to making peace with the city. Not half bad I'd say.'

'Not half bad? That's why you dragged me all the way here? For a clear conscience?'

'Look at it any way you want to. Given the chance, I'd probably do it all the same, so I can't really make much of an apology. But let's make an effort this time and not fight about it. You'd be surprised by just how much you can accomplish in a single day.'

Julia looked away. She brushed her hand against Anthony's. He seemed to hesitate a moment, then turned away and crossed the lobby.

'I'm afraid I can't join you this evening,' he told his daughter as they stood waiting for the lift. 'I hope you're not mad, but I'm feeling pretty tired. Perhaps best to recharge my batteries, conserve energy for tomorrow. Strange, but in this case I do mean that quite *literally*.'

'Sure, rest up. I'm exhausted, too. I think I'll just order room service. We can meet up for breakfast. I'll come have it in your room if you like.'

'That sounds wonderful,' said Anthony with a smile.

The lift took them upstairs. Julia got out first and waved to her father as the doors slid shut. Hovering out in the hallway, she watched as the red numbers on the screen continued upwards, signalling Anthony's ascent.

As soon as she got back to her room, Julia ran a steaming-hot bath and emptied two little bottles of bath oils into it. She returned to the bedroom and ordered a fruit salad and a bowl of cereal from room service. After the call she turned on the TV hanging on the wall across from the bed. She left her clothes in the bedroom and slipped into the warmth of her bath.

◆ ◆ ◆

Knapp inspected himself in the mirror one last time, adjusted his tie and left the bathroom. At eight o'clock sharp the photo exhibition he had organized under the direction of the cultural ministry would open at Berlin's Museum of Photography. The project had required a considerable amount of extra work, but the investment of time had been well worth it: the exhibition would help him get promoted and advance his career. Assuming the evening was a success, and his colleagues gave the exhibition glowing reviews in print the next day, it wouldn't be long before he moved into the large glass office at the entrance of the news-room. Knapp glanced up at the clock in the front hall of the building. He had fifteen minutes, more than enough time to cross Pariser Platz on foot and be in place at the bottom of the steps to welcome the minister and the television cameras on the red carpet.

Adam screwed up the plastic sandwich wrapper into a ball and aimed for a trash can under one of the lamp posts in the park. His shot went wide, and he rose with a sigh to recover the greasy ball of cellophane. As he neared the lawn, a squirrel lifted its head and stood on its hind legs.

'Sorry, pal,' said Adam, 'I don't have any peanuts in my pockets, and Julia's out of town. Looks like we both got dumped.'

The little animal peered at him, bobbing its head along with each word Adam spoke.

'I don't think squirrels are big fans of cold cuts, but what the hell,' he said, flicking a morsel of ham that had slipped out from between the slices of bread.

The rodent snubbed Adam's offering and scampered up a tree. A woman jogging past stopped to observe the scene.

'Wow. You talk to the squirrels, too? Isn't it amazing how they come up and just wiggle their sweet little faces at you.'

'Yeah . . . it's really something,' Adam mumbled, at a loss for more to say on the subject of the ratlike creatures.

With that, he threw his sandwich in the trash and shuffled off with his hands shoved in his pockets.

A knock sounded at the door. Julia grabbed a facecloth and wiped off her face mask. She stepped out of the bath, grabbed a robe from the hook on the back of the bathroom door and slipped it on. She crossed the bedroom and let the waiter in, asking him to leave the tray on the bed. She took out some notes from her purse and slipped them next to the bill, signing the receipt and handing it back to the waiter. As soon as he had gone, she got under the covers and started picking at the cereal. Remote control in hand, she flicked through the channels in search of any programme not in German.

She flicked through three Spanish shows, a Swiss channel and then two French ones. The war coverage on CNN was a no-go (too violent), the stock market report on Bloomberg was boring and incomprehensible (she was terrible at maths) and a game show on the local station really rubbed her up the wrong way (the female host seemed vulgar). She started again from the beginning.

Knapp stood on his tiptoes for a view of the motorcade as it pulled up. A man nearby tried to step in front of him, but Knapp defended his position and put him back in his place with a firm elbow. If the guy wanted a better spot, he should have arrived earlier. A bodyguard opened the car door, and the minister stepped out into a swarm of cameras. Side by side with the exhibition's curator, Knapp stepped forward and bowed to welcome the high-ranking government official, then escorted him straight on to the red carpet.

Julia browsed through the rest of the room service menu. After devouring her meal down to a single raisin and a couple of seeds, she was torn between a slice of chocolate cake, a strudel, pancakes or the club sandwich. She twisted to get a better view of her stomach and hips, and what she saw made her throw the menu right across the room. The news report playing in the background showed footage of a glamorous art opening. Celebrities in evening wear walked down a red carpet, with the ever-constant glint of camera flashes lighting their way. A long, elegant gown worn by a famous actress or singer, probably from Berlin, attracted Julia's attention. The screen was overflowing with luxury, every face picture-perfect and wholly unfamiliar to her eyes. All but one . . .

Julia leapt to her feet with a jolt, knocking over the room service tray in the process, and stepped closer to the TV. As the man walked down the carpet, Julia was sure she knew his face, certain she recognized that telltale grin as the camera zoomed in on him, only to pan away towards the columns of the Brandenburg Gate.

'That handsome son of a bitch!' exclaimed Julia as she ran to the bathroom.

The concierge assured her that the art opening in question could be nowhere other than at the Stiftung Brandenburger. Even among Berlin's recent architectural wonders, the building stood out as one of the very newest. The front steps had a perfect view of the Brandenburg Gate. *Der Tagesspiegel* had undoubtedly organized the gala Julia had seen on television. He assured Miss Walsh there was no need to hurry, however. The major photojournalism exhibition would run till the anniversary of the fall of the Berlin Wall, still a good five months away. If she wished, he could easily procure two invitations for her tomorrow, once the exhibition was open to the public. But Julia insisted – what she needed was an evening dress right here, right now.

'It's nearly nine o'clock at night, Miss Walsh!'

Julia emptied her purse on the counter and started frantically sorting through its contents. There were dollars, euros, spare coins, even an old Deutschmark she had carried around with her for ages. She took off her watch, threw it in and pushed the whole pile forward with both hands like a gambling addict desperate to stay in the game.

'Find me a dress. It can be red, purple, yellow, anything as long as it's long! Don't make me beg.'

The concierge arched an eyebrow, perplexed. But he was a slave to his sense of duty. This was Mr Walsh's daughter, and she needed his help. Then he got an idea . . .

'Sweep that lot back into your purse and follow me,' he said, leading Julia to a storage room.

Even under the dim light, the gown looked magnificent. Julia's eyes widened as he handed it to her, explaining that it belonged to a client staying in Suite 1206. It had arrived a little earlier, straight from the designer, but luckily for Julia it was already too late to disturb the countess. Of course even slight damage to the dress was an absolute impossibility. And like Cinderella, Julia would have to bring the dress back before the stroke of midnight.

He left her alone to get changed, suggesting she leave her clothes on the hanger.

Julia undressed and slid into the delicate fabric with the utmost care. There was no mirror for her to check how she looked. The best she could do was squint at her reflection in a metal support column, but the cylinder left her so distorted that it defeated the purpose. She let down her hair and blindly applied her make-up. She left behind her purse, pants and sweater, then scurried back down the shadowy corridor towards the lobby.

The concierge motioned for her to take a look at herself in a mirror hanging on the wall behind him. She glided towards it without making a sound, only to be blocked by the concierge before she could even get a view.

'No, no, no,' he said as Julia ducked and bobbed to get a look. 'Hold still, will you?'

He plucked a tissue from a drawer and dabbed softly at a spot with smudged lipstick.

'There. Now you're ready for your close-up,' he concluded, standing aside.

Julia had never seen such a magnificent dress. Suddenly the haute couture she had lusted after in New York's shop windows lost all its allure. This was something else entirely.

'I don't know how to thank you!' she murmured, dumbstruck.

'Too bad the designer can't see you in it. I'm sure you put the countess to shame,' he said, smiling. 'I've called you a car, which will accompany you to the exhibition and then wait nearby until you're ready to come back here.'

'I could have hailed a taxi.'

'In a gown like that? I hope you're joking. Think of the car as both your carriage and my insurance. Don't forget: *midnight*, Cinderella! And of course do enjoy yourself, Miss Walsh,' said the concierge as he led her towards the limousine.

When they were outside, Julia stood on her toes to plant a kiss on his cheek.

'Just one last thing, Miss Walsh.'

'Sure.'

'Don't lift up the bottom of the dress like that again. Luckily it's long enough that this can be our little secret, but I wouldn't recommend letting anyone else get a look at those espadrilles.'

◆ ◆ ◆

The waiter set down a shared plate of antipasti on the table. Thomas served Marina a few grilled vegetables.

'Mind telling me why you're wearing sunglasses in a restaurant with barely enough light to read the menu?'

'Because,' answered Marina.

'Thank you for the detailed explanation,' replied Thomas mockingly.

'It's because I don't want you to see the look in my eyes.'

'What do you mean? What look?'

'*The* look.'

'Sorry. I'm trying here, but I have to tell you: I don't understand a word you're saying.'

'I'm talking about the look that a man can see in a woman's eyes when she feels comfortable around him.'

'I wasn't aware that was a specific look. And what's wrong with me seeing it?'

'Soon as you see it, you'll start thinking about the best way to dump me.'

'What are you talking about?'

'Thomas, a man who tries to cure his loneliness with a simple no-strings-attached relationship – the type who's always ready to sweet-talk a woman but would never make a real declaration of love – a man like that lives in fear of the day she starts giving him *the* look.'

'But what exactly is the look?'

'It's the look that makes you think she has fallen madly in love with you and now wants more. Stupid things: planning holidays together, or making any plans at all, really! And if she makes the mistake of even smiling anywhere near a pram, the whole thing is dead on arrival.'

'And that's the look you're hiding behind those sunglasses?'

'Don't be so full of yourself. My eyes hurt, that's all. Did you really think I was saying I—?'

'Well, there has to be some reason you brought all of this up, Marina.'

'When are you planning to tell me you're leaving for Somalia? After your tiramisu?'

'Who said I was going to order tiramisu?'

'In the two years we've worked together, I've learned your habits.'

Marina pushed her sunglasses down to the tip of her nose, then let them simply fall on her plate.

'Fine. I'm leaving tomorrow. But I just found out about it.'

'Leaving tomorrow for Berlin?'

'No, Knapp's sending me straight to Mogadishu from here.'

'He's kept you waiting for three months. And now, after all that time, he just snaps his fingers and you jump on a flight?'

'It saves a whole day. We've already lost enough time as it is.'

'He's the one who made you lose time, and you're the one doing him a favour. He needs you for his precious promotion, but you don't need him to do top-notch journalism. With your talent, you could win a prize for a shot of a dog peeing on a lamp post.'

'What's your point?'

'Stand up for yourself, Thomas. Stop spending your life running away from the people who love you and actually confront them. Take me for instance. Tell me that I'm boring you with my ranting, that we're lovers and nothing more, and that it's not my place to lecture you. And Knapp – tell him you're not running to Somalia until you've gone home, packed a suitcase and given your friends a hug goodbye. After all, you don't even know when you'll be back!'

'You know? Maybe you're right.'

Thomas picked up his mobile.

'What are you doing?'

'I'm sending a text to Knapp telling him to buy me a ticket that leaves from Berlin on Saturday.'

'I'll believe it when I see it.'

'Fine. Then do I finally get to see *the* look?'

'Maybe . . . if you're lucky.'

◆ ◆ ◆

The limousine pulled up at the end of the red carpet. Julia contorted herself to keep her shoes hidden as she stepped out of the car and approached the steps. No sooner had she reached the top than a group of photographers started snapping away at her.

'I'm nobody,' she insisted to a cameraman, but he didn't speak a word of English. At the entrance the doorman nodded in approval at Julia's incredible gown before being blinded by the bright lights of the TV crew swarming around Julia to get footage of her going in. He didn't even bother to ask for her invitation.

The hall was immense. Julia scanned the faces of the crowd. Cocktails in hand, the guests mingled beneath gigantic photos lining the walls. Julia smiled as she was greeted warmly by complete strangers at every turn. Further on, a harpist was playing Mozart on a slightly elevated platform. Weaving her way through the surreal ballet, Julia stalked closer to her prey.

A ten-foot-high photo caught her eye. The shot could have easily been taken in the mountains of Kandahar or Tajikistan, or even in the border region of Pakistan. The uniform of the soldier lying face down in a ditch gave nothing away. The barefoot child at his side looked like all of the lost children of the world.

Julia jumped as a hand landed on her shoulder.

'Why, you haven't changed a bit,' Knapp declared. 'What in the world are you doing here? I don't recall seeing your name on the list of invitations. Are you in town for long? I certainly didn't expect to see you.'

'I could say the same for you. I thought you were travelling until the end of the month. At least that's what I was told when I came to your office today. Didn't you get my message?'

'I came back from my trip early. Came straight here from the airport.'

'Well, you haven't changed either, Knapp. Still a terrible liar. And I know from experience. I've gained a certain amount of expertise these past few days.'

'Come on, you can't really expect me to have guessed that was you who came today. It's been twenty years!'

'Eighteen. Do you know another Julia Walsh?'

'I barely knew your last name, Julia. Trust me, I just didn't put two and two together. An endless stream of people come to pitch useless stories to me, so I'm in the habit of screening my calls for crazies.'

'Well, isn't that sweet.'

'You still haven't told me what brings you to Berlin.'

Her eyes returned to the photograph. It was signed *T. Ullmann*.

'That's exactly the type of photo Thomas would take. It reminds me of his work,' said Julia sadly.

'Except for the fact that Thomas hasn't touched a camera in years. He doesn't even live in Germany any more. He left all that behind him.'

The news hit Julia like a slap in the face, but she forced herself to keep her reaction under control.

'Where did he go?'

'He moved to Italy, with his wife. We don't talk very often. Once a year maybe, and that's in a good year.'

'Did the two of you have a falling-out?'

'No, nothing like that. Our lives just went in different directions. I did my best to help him live his dream of becoming a journalist, but after Afghanistan he was a changed man. He decided to move on, do something else with his life. I'm sure you of all people can understand that.'

'No. I can't say I do,' retorted Julia, her jaw tightening.

'The last I heard, he was in Rome running a restaurant with his wife. Now, if you'll excuse me, I really should attend to some of the other guests. It's been nice seeing you, and hopefully next time it can be for a bit longer. How long are you here for?'

'Until Saturday morning,' replied Julia.

'You still haven't told me why you're here. Business?'

'Goodbye, Knapp.'

Julia left without looking back. As soon as she made it past the glass doors, she quickened her pace and ended up breaking into a full-on sprint down the red carpet towards the waiting car.

◆　◆　◆

Back at the hotel, Julia made a beeline for the unmarked door across the lobby and the storage room. She slipped out of the gown, put it back on its hanger and put on her jeans and sweater. She heard the concierge clear his throat from the shadows behind her.

'Are you decent?' he asked, covering his eyes with one hand and holding out a box of Kleenex with the other.

'No,' sobbed Julia.

The concierge pulled out a tissue and waved it blindly.

'Thank you,' Julia said as she took the Kleenex.

'I thought your mascara looked a bit runny when you flew past me just now. So the evening didn't quite live up to your expectations.'

'That's one way of putting it,' Julia replied between sniffles.

'It happens to the best of us. Some nights just take an unexpected turn for the worse.'

'My God, my whole life has become one big unexpected turn for the worse. This trip, this hotel, this city and all this useless running around. Everything was perfect before. I wouldn't have changed a thing. And now . . .'

The concierge took a step closer, and that was all it took for Julia to throw herself into his arms, drying her tears on his shoulder. He delicately patted her back and did his best to console her.

'I don't know what happened to make you so sad tonight, but if you'd allow me to make a suggestion, perhaps you should go and talk to your father about it. I'm sure it would do you a world of good. The two of you seem so close. You're quite lucky to still have him in your life.'

'That couldn't be further from the truth. The two of us close? We must not be talking about the same person.'

'I've had the pleasure of serving your father on many occasions, Miss Walsh, and I can assure you he has always been a perfect gentleman.'

'My father is anything but a gentleman! He's the most self-centred person I've ever met.'

'In that case you're right – it must not be the same person. The man I know has shown nothing but kindness. And, I should add, I've heard him describe you as his one success in life.'

This left Julia speechless.

'Go on, go and see your father. I'm sure he's waiting for you with open arms.'

'Right. Nothing in my life is what it once seemed. Anyway, he's sleeping. He was exhausted.'

'Maybe he got a second wind, because he just ordered room service.'

'Wait – my father ordered food?'

'That's what I said, miss.'

Julia slid back on her espadrilles and thanked the concierge warmly, going as far as to plant another kiss on his cheek.

'I can count on you to keep all this a secret, can't I?' he asked.

'I've never seen you before in my life,' said Julia with a straight face.

'And I can put that gown back in its bag without checking for stains?'

Julia flashed the scout's honour sign and smiled at the concierge, who told her to hurry along.

She went back across the lobby and took the lift to the sixth floor, but didn't get out. She hesitated for a moment before pushing the button to go and see her father.

Julia could hear the faint sound of the television from the corridor. She knocked, and her father swung the door open immediately.

'Julia. Might I say you looked stunning in that gown,' he said, lying back down on the bed.

Julia saw that the evening news was playing highlights from the exhibition opening.

'You left the others in the dust – the very image of elegance. I hope you've finally outgrown your days of wearing those ripped jeans. If I had known what you had cooking, I would have asked to come along. It would have been an honour to walk you down that red carpet.'

'None of it was planned. I was watching TV just like you, and I saw Knapp on the red carpet, so I knew I had to go.'

'Intriguing,' said Anthony, standing back up. 'For somebody who was allegedly out of town until the end of the month . . . Unless he's developed the ability to be in two places at once, I'd wager the man was lying intentionally. However, judging by that look on your face, your reunion wasn't exactly what you were hoping for.'

'I was right about Thomas being married. And you were right about him not being a journalist any more,' Julia explained, sinking into an armchair. She eyed the tray of food on the coffee table.

'Can I ask why you would—?'

'I ordered it for you.'

'You knew I would come knocking at your door?'

'Let's just say I know a bit more than you think, dear. The moment I saw you on TV – knowing full well you don't exactly have a penchant for glitzy affairs – I had a hunch something was happening. I even suspected your Thomas might have reappeared for you to run off in the night like that. At least that's what was going through my head when the concierge called to check with me about ordering you a limo. So I thought I'd provide a room service contingency plan in case the evening went south. Go on, eat up. It's only pancakes, nothing fancy. A little bit of maple syrup can't exactly mend a broken heart, but it can work wonders for your mood.'

◆ ◆ ◆

In the suite next door a certain countess was also watching the news. She asked her husband to remind her to call Karl the next day. After congratulating him on his stunning creation, she'd warn him she'd make his life hell the next time he promised her an exclusive design, only to find her one-of-a-kind gown gracing the gorgeous form of a woman half her age. Of course it would come as no shock to Karl that she was sending the gown back. Sumptuous as it was, she simply had no use for it now.

◆ ◆ ◆

Julia told her father all about her misadventure that evening: the unexpected departure for the cursed exhibition, the conversation with Knapp and her pathetic return to the hotel. What she left out was any explanation – or confession – as to why she had a meltdown after hearing Knapp's news. Learning Thomas had moved on with his life should have come as no surprise. She had suspected that from the beginning – how could he do otherwise? For reasons she couldn't possibly comprehend, the worst part was hearing that Thomas had given up journalism. Anthony listened to Julia without interrupting or adding even the slightest commentary. Swallowing her last forkful of pancake, she thanked her father for the surprise snack, which had been delicious, even if all the extra calories hadn't given her much peace of mind.

There was no point staying in Berlin. Signs or no signs, there was nothing left for her here. She just wanted to put her life back together. She decided to pack her bags before going to bed, and the two of them could fly out first thing tomorrow morning. This time it was Julia who felt a sense of déjà vu – and not at all to her liking.

In the corridor she kicked off her shoes and took the service stairs back down to her room.

◆ ◆ ◆

The moment Julia left the room, Anthony picked up the phone. Four o'clock in the afternoon in San Francisco. Perfect. The person on the other end of the line answered after the first ring.

'Pilguez speaking.'

'It's Anthony Walsh. Hope I'm not catching you at a bad time.'

'No such thing for old friends, especially one I haven't heard from in ages. To what do I owe the pleasure?'

'Actually I have a favour to ask, a little investigation if you're still up for that type of thing.'

'Up for it? I've been so goddamn bored since I retired, you could have called me to say you'd lost your keys and I'd be on the case.'

'Do you still have contacts with Homeland Security? Somebody with access who could provide me with some intel.'

'I think it's fair to say a couple of folks over there should still remember me.'

'Well, let's just hope they remember you fondly. Here's what I need . . .'

The conversation between old friends lasted a good half hour. Former detective Pilguez promised to get Anthony the information he was after as soon as humanly possible.

It was 8 p.m. in New York. A little sign on the door announced that the antique shop was closed for the night. Inside, Stanley was touching up the shelves of a late-nineteenth-century bookcase he had acquired that afternoon. Adam knocked on the window.

'God, not him again!' Stanley muttered, scrambling to hide behind a sideboard buffet.

'Stanley! It's me, Adam! I know you're in there.'

Stanley crouched down, nearly on all fours. He barely breathed.

'Stanley? I've got this . . . Château-Lafite?'

Stanley's ears pricked up, and he started rising from the ground, almost against his will.

'They're 1989! Two whole bottles!' cried Adam from the street.

Suddenly Stanley was at the door, swinging it open quickly.

'I'm sorry, I was working and couldn't hear you,' he said, ushering Adam inside. 'Hungry?'

18.

Thomas stretched and slipped out of bed, careful not to wake Marina, who was sleeping beside him. He went down the spiral staircase and crossed the living room of the duplex. Behind the counter of the bar, he grabbed an espresso cup and slid it into the machine, using a towel to muffle the noise before pressing the button. Thomas carefully opened the sliding doors and stepped on to the patio, soaking in the first gentle rays of sunlight pouring out across the rooftops of Rome. He glanced over the railing and down into the street, where a delivery man was unloading cases of fruit and veg in front of the little grocer's across the street from Marina's building.

He soon picked up the strong smell of burning toast coming from inside the apartment, followed by a volley of Italian cursing. Marina appeared, wearing nothing but a dressing gown and a sullen frown.

'Two things,' she said. 'First, quit flashing your bare arse on my patio. I doubt my neighbours really like that kind of entertainment during breakfast.'

'And the second?' asked Thomas without turning around.

'As for us, we'll be having breakfast at the cafe downstairs. There's nothing here to eat.'

'That's funny. I seem to recall us buying bread last night,' Thomas teased.

'Put some clothes on,' responded Marina, returning inside.

'Good morning to you, too!' grumbled Thomas.

An old woman watering her plants gave Thomas a friendly wave from her balcony on the other side of the narrow street. Thomas smiled at her and left the terrace.

It wasn't even eight, but the air was already sticky and hot. The owner of the trattoria downstairs was setting up his terrace, and Thomas gave him a hand bringing the sun umbrellas outside. Marina sat down and grabbed a croissant from a basket full of pastries.

'What do you plan on doing with your day?' asked Thomas, helping himself to a pastry. 'Are you angry with me because I'm leaving?'

'No. You want to know what gets me, Thomas? The way you always manage to say the worst things at just the right moment.'

The trattoria owner set two piping-hot cappuccinos on their table. He looked at the sky, calling out desperately for a storm to break the heat, and complimented Marina on her early-morning beauty. He winked at Thomas and went back inside.

'How about we try not to ruin this morning?' continued Thomas.

'Perfect. Finish your croissant. We'll go upstairs and you can shag me. Then you can jump in the shower while I act like your servant and pack your bags for you. A quick kiss goodbye on my doorstep, and then nothing for two or three months, maybe forever. Don't bother saying anything. There's no point.'

'You could come with me!'

'I'm a writer, not a reporter.'

'No, listen. Come to Berlin. We'll spend the night together, then tomorrow I'm off to Mogadishu, and you can come back here to Rome.'

Marina turned to signal to the cafe owner that she wanted another cappuccino.

'Wonderful idea. And as a bonus we get to say our goodbyes at the airport. You know how I love melodrama.'

'Come on. It wouldn't hurt for you to show your face in the news-room in Berlin for once,' Thomas added.

'Drink your coffee while it's hot.'

'If you stop moping long enough to say yes, I'll call and book you a ticket.'

◆　◆　◆

An envelope appeared underneath the hotel room door. Anthony winced as he bent to pick it up. He ripped it open and read the fax.

> Nothing yet, sorry to say. I'm a long way from giv-
> ing up. I hope to have more to tell you soon.

The message was signed *GP*, for George Pilguez.

Anthony Walsh sat down at the desk in his suite and scribbled a note to Julia. He called the concierge and ordered a car and driver, then left his room and made a quick stop at the sixth floor. Tiptoeing over to his daughter's bedroom, he slid the note under the door and crept off quickly.

'Thirty-one Karl-Liebknecht-Strasse please,' he told his chauffeur as he climbed into the back seat.

The black Mercedes pulled away from the kerb and into the traffic.

◆　◆　◆

After a quick cup of tea, Julia grabbed her bag from the wardrobe and began folding her clothes but soon found herself throwing everything in the suitcase in a sloppy pile. She stopped halfway through and walked over to the window. A misty rain was falling over Berlin. Down on the street below, a Mercedes had just driven away from the hotel.

◆ ◆ ◆

'Bring me your shaving kit if you want it in your bag,' called Marina from the bedroom.

Thomas stuck his head out of the bathroom.

'I can pack my own bag you know.'

'You certainly can. And you do a poor job of it. And I won't be there in Somalia to iron your clothes for you.'

'Marina, you didn't actually . . . ?' asked Thomas with a note of concern.

'Of course not. But I could have!'

'Have you made a decision?'

'About whether I should dump you today or tomorrow? Good news: you got lucky this time, you bastard. I decided I should say a little hello to our future editorial director, for the good of my career of course. Although there's absolutely no correlation with your departure from Berlin, it does mean you'll get to spend another evening enjoying my company.'

'That is great news. I'm thrilled,' he said with a smile.

'Really?' continued Marina, zipping his bag up. 'Now listen. We have to leave Rome by midday. And any fool knows not to stand between a woman and her bathroom.'

'And I thought I was the complaining one.'

'Maybe you're rubbing off on me. It's not my fault.'

In one fluid movement Marina pushed past him into the bathroom, only to reach back for Thomas, letting the sash of her dressing gown fall as she pulled him into the shower with her.

◆ ◆ ◆

The Mercedes parked in front of a row of large grey buildings. Anthony asked the driver to wait for him. He hoped to be back within the hour.

He made his way up a flight of steps under an awning and stepped into the building that currently housed the Stasi archives.

Anthony presented himself to the receptionist and asked for assistance.

He was directed down a hallway full of bone-chilling relics. Here and there display cases housed different models of microphones, video cameras and photography equipment. There were steamers for opening letters and gluers for sealing them back up after they had been read, copied and archived. A myriad of other objects lined the hall, equipment once used to spy on the day-to-day lives of a population held prisoner by a police state. There were pamphlets, propaganda manuals and an array of systems for eavesdropping, which grew increasingly sophisticated as the years passed. Millions of people had been spied on, judged and catalogued in the name of the absolutist state. Lost in his thoughts, Anthony stopped and gazed at a photo of an interrogation room.

◆ ◆ ◆

I know I was wrong. Once that wall came tumbling down, the change was irreversible. But who could know for sure, Julia? The people who lived through the Prague Spring? The Western democracies who turned a blind eye to countless crimes and injustices? Who could have known for sure that today's Russia would be free of its despotic leaders? Yes, I was afraid. I was terrified that the dictatorship would bring that rush of freedom to a screeching halt, and you would find yourself imprisoned in its totalitarian stranglehold. I was scared to death of being forever separated from my daughter – not by her choice but because a government made the choice for her. I know that you'll always hate me for it, but had things taken a sudden turn for the worse, I would have never been able to forgive myself for not coming and getting you out. I have to admit that part of me is happy I was wrong.

◆ ◆ ◆

'Can I help you, sir?' asked a voice from the end of the corridor.

'I'm looking for the archives,' Anthony stammered.

'You're in the right place. What can I do for you?'

A few days after the collapse of the Wall, employees of the East German political police, faced with the inevitable fall of their regime, began to destroy everything that might serve as evidence of their actions. But they couldn't just shred millions of pages of personal data collected over nearly forty years of totalitarianism. Beginning in December 1989, the people caught wind of the massive cover-up and seized control of the offices of the former Stasi. In every East German city, citizens took over and prevented the destruction of what added up to over a hundred miles of reports of all kinds, documents that were now available to the public.

Anthony asked to see the dossier of a certain Thomas Meyer, who used to live at Number 2, Comeniusplatz, in East Berlin.

'Unfortunately I can't help you with that request, sir,' the official in charge said.

'I thought the law guaranteed public access to the archives.'

'It does indeed. However, said law is also meant to protect our citizens against any intrusion into their private lives that might occur through the use of their personal information,' replied the employee with impeccable clarity, as though this was a fully memorized speech.

'Perhaps it's the interpretation of said law that's paramount. If I'm not mistaken, the main point of this law is to facilitate access to Stasi files in order to shed light on the influence the secret police had over the private lives of individuals,' continued Anthony, repeating verbatim the text engraved on a plaque hanging over the entrance to the archives.

'Yes, of course it is,' admitted the employee, who apparently couldn't quite grasp what this strange visitor was getting at.

'Thomas Meyer is my son-in-law,' Anthony lied with unflinching aplomb. 'Today he lives in the United States. I'm happy to report that I'll soon be a grandfather. As you can imagine, it's important for him to one day have a frank conversation with his children about his painful past. That's understandable, is it not? And you, do you have children, Herr . . . ?'

'Hans Dietrich,' replied the official. 'Yes. I'm the proud father of two lovely little girls, Emma and Anna. They're five and seven.'

'How wonderful!' exclaimed Anthony, clasping his hands together. 'I can only imagine how happy you must be.'

'I'm incredibly lucky, really.'

'Poor Thomas. The tragic memories of his adolescence are still far too vivid for him to come carry out this research on his own, you know. I came a very long way in my son-in-law's name to help give him the chance to make peace with his past and perhaps one day find the strength to walk these same halls with his own daughter by his side – between you and me, Hans, I'm sure it's a girl. I picture him coming back here with her, setting foot in the land of his ancestors, allowing her to find her roots. So, I implore you, Hans,' continued Anthony solemnly, 'as a future grandfather talking to the father of two adorable little girls. I need you to help me. I need you to help Thomas Meyer. Be the man who through sheer human generosity and understanding helps bring my future granddaughter that much closer to the happiness we all know she deserves.'

Anthony could tell his story overwhelmed Hans Dietrich, so he allowed his eyes to well with tears. That seemed to do the trick. Herr Dietrich offered him a tissue.

'Thomas Meyer, at Number 2, Comeniusplatz you said?'

'That's the one,' replied Anthony.

'Take a seat in the reading room. I'll see if we have anything on him.'

Fifteen minutes later Hans placed a metal folder on the desk in front of Anthony.

'I think I've found your son-in-law's file,' he announced, positively beaming. 'We're lucky it wasn't among the papers that were destroyed. The reconstruction of the shredded files is far from finished. We're still waiting for the necessary funding.'

Anthony warmly thanked him and then politely asked for a bit of privacy to study his son-in-law's past. Hans left him alone, and Anthony dived into the voluminous file. It began in 1980. The young man was the target of spying for a full nine years. Page after page listed his habits and movements, the people he saw and places he frequented, his skills, his literary taste, written accounts of his statements, both private and in public, his opinions and his level of commitment to the values of the state. It listed his ambitions, his hopes, his first brush with love and his romantic experiences and let-downs. No stone had been left unturned in dissecting Thomas's character. Lacking mastery of written German, Anthony had to ask for Hans Dietrich for help with interpreting the final page of analysis, at the end of the file, updated for the last time on 9 October 1989.

Thomas Meyer, orphan, was a student with suspicious ties. His best friend and neighbour from an early age, Jürgen Knapp, had managed to escape to the West, perhaps hidden beneath the back seat of a car. He had never returned to the East. There was no proof to confirm that Thomas Meyer had played a role in J. Knapp's escape, and the candour with which he described his friend's plans to the Stasi informant indicated his probable innocence.

The informant had discovered preparations for the escape, but unfortunately too late to stop Jürgen Knapp and have him taken into custody. Nevertheless the close ties between Thomas and the traitor, along with the fact that he never told the authorities about his friend's plans to defect, made it impossible to consider him a promising candidate for the future of the Democratic Republic. Given the facts cited in the dossier, there was no recommendation that charges be made against him, but entrusting this questionable individual with any important state position was out of the question. The report recommended keeping him under surveillance to ensure that he did not have contact with his former friend or any other person residing in the West. A probation period lasting until his thirtieth birthday was recommended before his status could be changed or his file closed.

Hans Dietrich finished his translation. Stupefied, he read and reread the name of the informant who collaborated with the Stasi for the report, not believing his own eyes. The man was unable to mask his repulsion.

'Who could even imagine such a thing?' said Anthony, his eyes fixed on the name at the bottom of the page. 'How wretched, awful . . .'

Hans Dietrich agreed. He seemed just as appalled.

Anthony thanked his host for his precious aid and generosity. The archive official nodded and hesitated a moment before sharing one last detail.

'I think you should know, given the context of your research, that your son-in-law has made the same discovery we have. A note in the file says he has already accessed his dossier.'

Anthony thanked Dietrich once more, from the bottom of his heart. He also assured him that he would make a contribution to the financing of the archives' reconstruction. He realized now more than ever how essential it was to understand the past in order to navigate the future.

As he left the building, Anthony felt the need for some fresh air to recover his strength. He sat on a bench for a few minutes on a small lawn near the car park.

Thinking back to all he had learned from Dietrich, he suddenly slapped his forehead and blurted out, 'Of course! Of course.'

He got up and returned to the car, sliding into the back seat and promptly taking out his cell phone to call San Francisco.

'I hope I didn't wake you up.'

'Of course not! It's three in the morning. Why would I be sleeping?'

'My apologies. But I think I've uncovered some important info.'

◆ ◆ ◆

George Pilguez turned on the lamp on his bedside table and looked for a pen and paper to take down notes.

'I'm listening,' he said.

'I have reason to believe that our man may have changed his last name, or at least made an effort to use it as little as possible.'

'Why?'

'It's a long story . . .'

'What about his current identity? Any leads on that?'

'Not a one.'

'Wonderful. You call me in the middle of the night just for that? Well, we're sure to crack the case now!' retorted Pilguez sarcastically before hanging up.

George turned out the light, crossed his arms behind his head and tried to go back to sleep. Half an hour later, his wife told him to get up and go to work. She couldn't take any more of his tossing and turning. This way, at least one of them could get some sleep.

George put on a dressing gown and stumbled into the kitchen, grumbling. He started to make himself a sandwich, liberally spreading butter on both slices of bread, celebrating the fact that Natalia wasn't hovering nearby with lectures about his cholesterol. He took the predawn meal to his desk. Some agencies never closed, so he picked up the phone and made a call to a friend who worked in immigration.

'If a person who has legally changed their name entered our country, would the original name still show up in our system?'

'What nationality?' asked the man on the other end of the line.

'German, born in the East.'

'In that case, yes. They would need to use their original name to attain a visa from our consulate. I imagine there would be some trace of it in our system.'

'Do you have something to write with?' asked George.

'Got my keyboard right here, buddy,' replied his friend Rick Bram, immigration officer at JFK Airport.

◆ ◆ ◆

The Mercedes drove back to the hotel. Anthony gazed out the window, watching the city pass by. The neon sign outside of a pharmacy went through a flashing progression of date, time and temperature. It was almost midday in Berlin, 21 degrees Celsius . . .

'And only two days left,' murmured Anthony.

◆ ◆ ◆

Julia paced back and forth across the lobby, her luggage at her feet.

'I assure you, Miss Walsh, I haven't the faintest idea where your father could have gone. He simply called for a car early this morning and hasn't been back since. I tried to contact the driver, but his phone is turned off.'

The concierge took note of Julia's bag.

'I wasn't aware of a change in your travel reservations. Mr Walsh hasn't made any such request. The last I was told he had decided to—'

'I don't need my father to decide for me! I told him to meet me this morning. The flight is at three, and it's the only way to make our connection from Paris to New York.'

'You could always get a connecting flight from Amsterdam . . . That would buy you some time. I'd be happy to arrange it for you.'

'Yes, please. Could you do that right away?' said Julia, searching her pockets.

Then, to the concierge's astonishment, Julia suddenly sighed and gave up, her head sinking down on to the counter.

'Is there a problem, miss?'

'My father has the tickets.'

'Don't worry, I'm sure he'll be back soon. There's still time. Assuming you absolutely have to be in New York by this evening.'

A black Mercedes pulled up in front of the hotel. Anthony got out of it and entered the lobby through the revolving door.

'Where have you been?' asked Julia, running up to meet him. 'I was worried sick!'

'Glory, glory hallelujah! You actually care about my whereabouts and my well-being. This is a historic day.'

'Or maybe you had me worried half to death about missing our flight.'

'What flight might that be?'

'We agreed last night to fly back today. Don't you remember?'

The concierge cut in on their conversation and handed Anthony a message which had just come by fax. Anthony opened the envelope and read it, looking over at Julia every few lines.

'Good Lord. A lot can change in one night,' he replied said jovially.

He waved the bellboy over to take Julia's bag back to her room.

'Come on, lunchtime. You and I have to talk, young lady.'

'Talk about what?' she asked worriedly.

'About me, who else? Oh, Julia. Only kidding. You should have seen your face!'

They sat down at a table on the terrace.

◆ ◆ ◆

The alarm clock woke Stanley in the middle of a nightmare. A splitting migraine kicked into overdrive as soon as he opened his eyes, as though to punish him for his excessively wine-soaked evening. He got up and staggered to the bathroom.

After seeing his face in the mirror, he swore to keep off alcohol until the end of the month. It seemed reasonable enough, since it was already the twenty-ninth. Aside from the pneumatic drill pounding away at his temples, it looked like the day was going to be a pleasant one. At lunchtime he could drop in at Julia's office for a walk along the river. Frowning, two thoughts came to Stanley in quick succession: his friend was still out of town, and she hadn't called or checked in the night before. He also couldn't remember a word from the drunken evening he spent with Adam. It was only a little while later, with his memory triggered by a large cup of tea, that he panicked about whether the word *Berlin* had somehow come out of his mouth.

◆　◆　◆

'Once a liar, always a liar. Or at least so one would imagine,' began Anthony as he handed Julia the lunch menu.

'Is that supposed to be directed at me?'

'The world does not revolve around you, my dear Julia. As a matter of fact I was referring to your friend Knapp.'

Julia dropped the menu and briskly shooed away the approaching waiter before he could even get close to their table.

'What are you talking about?'

'Take a wild guess. What else would I be referring to here with you in Berlin?'

'Just tell me what you know.'

'Thomas Meyer, aka Thomas *Ullmann*, is a reporter for *Der Tagesspiegel*. I know beyond a shadow of a doubt that he currently works every day with the same lying bastard who spun us that yarn.'

'Why would Knapp lie to us?'

'You should ask him yourself. I imagine he has his reasons.'

'How did you find all this out?'

'I have superpowers. Being reduced to a machine does have its perks.'

Julia raised an eyebrow at her father.

'Well, why not?' continued Anthony. 'You invent animals that speak to children. I can't enjoy the notion of possessing a few magic powers in the eyes of my own daughter?'

Anthony reached for Julia's hand, then thought better of it. He aborted the show of affection, instead grabbing a glass of water and lifting it to his lips.

'No! It's water!' screamed Julia.

Anthony froze with the edge of the glass right at his lips.

'I don't think that would be very good for your circuits,' she whispered, embarrassed at the looks from the surrounding tables.

Anthony's eyes widened.

'Why . . . you just saved my life!' he said, setting the glass back down with exaggerated care. 'Figuratively speaking of course.'

'Okay, forget superpowers. How?' Julia insisted.

Anthony looked at her for a long while and opted to leave out the episode at the Stasi archives. After all, the most important thing was the *what* and not the *how*.

'Now, using a pen name in a newspaper is one thing, but actually crossing a border is a whole other matter. We found that fateful drawing in Montreal, which, need I remind you, is only a hop, skip and jump away from the good old USA. Thus I took a gamble that he paid a visit to our homeland as well.'

'I stand corrected. Maybe you really do have superpowers.'

'No. Even better. I have an old friend who is a retired policeman.'

'Thank you for that,' murmured Julia.

'So? What's the plan now?'

'I have no idea. I'm just glad to know that Thomas is actually living out his dreams.'

'And what would you know about that?'

'All he ever wanted was to be a reporter.'

'Do you really think that's his only dream? Do you really think that, when he looks back at his life, he'll be content flipping through old newspaper clippings? Many men – so I've heard – come to realize in moments of great solitude that the success they spent their entire lives chasing after only served to drive them farther away from their loved ones. From themselves.'

Looking at her father, Julia could only guess at the sadness hidden behind that wistful smile.

'Let me ask again, Julia. What's our next move?'

'Going straight back to Berlin. That's the wise thing to do.'

'Don't you mean New York?'

'Yes, I do. That was a simple mistake.'

'Funny . . . just yesterday you would have called that a sign.'

'Like you said: a lot can change in one night.'

'You have to be sure you're getting it right, Julia. You can't move forward when your life is full of memories that feel like regrets. The foundation of a happy life is built on a few key certitudes. The choice before you now is yours and yours alone. I can't make it for you. Fact is I gave up on making your choices for you a long time ago. But let me just say: watch out. Loneliness can be a prickly thing.'

'Something you've had experience with?'

'Extensive experience, yes. I was alone for a great many years. But the mere thought of you would send my loneliness running for the hills. Let's just say I became aware of certain truths a bit too late. But who am I to complain? Most jerks like me don't get a second chance, even if mine only lasts a handful of days. And while I'm being honest, I have to tell you: I missed you, Julia. And I can't do a single thing to get back those lost years. I let precious time slip through my fingers, because of work. Because I thought I had an important role to play, was convinced I had obligations to attend to. But my only real obligation was to you. The most important obligation there is. But enough rambling. All this blathering on isn't really our style.

'Truth be told I would have liked to watch you teach Knapp a lesson, or even hold back his arms while you show him what happens when you mess with a Walsh, but I'm too tired for all that now. And besides, like I said: it's your life.'

Anthony leaned over and plucked a newspaper from a nearby table. He opened it and began to flick through the pages.

'I thought you didn't read German,' said Julia, her voice cracking.

'Oh. You? You're still here?' Anthony said dismissively, turning a page.

Julia folded her napkin, pushed back her chair and rose to her feet.

'I'll call you first thing after I see him,' she said as she walked away.

'Forecast says thunderstorms early this evening!' Anthony called out to his daughter.

But Julia was already too far away to hear, in the midst of hailing a taxi down the street. Anthony folded the newspaper with a sigh.

◆ ◆ ◆

The car pulled up at the main terminal at Rome-Fiumicino Airport. Thomas paid the driver and walked around to open Marina's door. They quickly checked in and passed through security. Thomas, bag hanging off his shoulder, glanced at his watch. Their flight took off in one hour. Marina was hanging around in front of the shop windows. He took her by the hand and led her to a bar.

'Anything special you want to do tonight?' he asked, ordering two coffees at the counter.

'I'd like to see your apartment. Ever since I met you I've been wondering what it's like.'

'Not much to see. One big room, a work desk by the window and a bed shoved up against the opposite wall.'

'Sounds good to me. What more could you need?'

◆ ◆ ◆

Julia pushed open the front door of *Der Tagesspiegel* building and gave her name at the front desk. She asked to see Jürgen Knapp. The receptionist picked up the phone.

'And tell him that I'll be here waiting in the lobby until he comes down, even if it takes all day.'

◆ ◆ ◆

As the lift slowly descended to the first floor, Knapp leaned against the glass with his eyes locked directly on his visitor. Julia paced back and forth in front of window displays showing mounted pages from that day's edition.

The lift doors finally opened, and Knapp walked across the lobby.

'Hello, Julia. What can I do for you?'

'You can start by telling me why you lied to my face.'

'Follow me. Let's go somewhere a bit quieter.'

Knapp led her towards the staircase and into a little room near the cafeteria, where he offered her a seat and searched his pockets for some change.

'Coffee? Tea?' he asked, moving towards the vending machine.

'I'm not thirsty.'

'Why did you come back to Berlin, Julia?'

'Don't tell me you're really thick enough to be asking me that.'

'It's been twenty years, Julia. How should I know?'

'I came for Thomas!'

'After all these years?'

'Tell me where he is.'

'I already told you. He's in Italy.'

'With his wife and children, and he's given up journalism, I know. Beautiful little story, except I can't tell which parts are true. I know he changed his name and I know he's still a reporter.'

'So why waste your time here?'

'I have a right to know. Why did you lie?'

'If you want us to start putting our cards on the table, I have a few questions for you first. Did you ever stop and wonder if Thomas actually wants to see you again? What right do you have to come barging back into his life like this? On a whim twenty years later the mood strikes you, and you come flying in straight from another decade! I'm afraid Berlin is fresh out of walls to knock down. No more revolution, no ecstasy, no wonder . . . All that madness is behind us. Get out of here, Julia. Leave Berlin and go home. Haven't you done enough damage here?'

'How dare you!' replied Julia, her lips quivering with rage.

'Oh, am I out of order? Because question time isn't over yet. Where were you when that landmine blew up in Thomas's face? And I didn't see you there, waiting for him at the gate at the airport when he arrived, injured from Kabul. I must've somehow missed you on the way to taking him to physical therapy every single morning. For the life of me I can't remember seeing you once. Your absence tore him apart. Do you even have the faintest idea of how much pain you caused? Of how long it lasted? Can you imagine that my friend, that idiot, his heart broken into a million pieces, went on defending you after he had every reason to hate you?'

Even with tears flowing freely down Julia's cheeks, nothing could stop Knapp now.

'Take a guess, try. Just tell me: how many years do you think it was before he accepted the truth and moved on? How long do you think it took him to get over you? When every damn corner of Berlin was haunted by a memory of the two of you together, memories he would recount to me at cafes, on park benches, along the banks of canals. And all the new people he met in vain, the number of women who tried to be with him, only to find themselves sabotaged by your perfume or one of the stupid things you said to make him laugh.

'I've heard it so many times that I've got you memorized. The feel of your skin, your bad moods in the mornings – which he of course found adorable for reasons I'll never quite get – your favourite things for breakfast, the way you did your hair, the way you put on your make-up, the clothes you liked to wear, the side of the bed you slept on. I had to hear the pieces you learnt at your Wednesday piano lessons a thousand times, because he continued to play them week after week, year after year, with the man's soul in tatters. I had to look at all your drawings, the watercolours of those stupid animals he knew by name. I can't count the number of times he stopped in front of shop windows at the sight of a dress, a painting, a bouquet and God knows what else, things that Thomas thought you might have liked. And all that time I constantly asked myself what you'd done to him to make him miss you so much.

'And when he finally started to get over you, I feared all it would take was running into somebody who looked like you to put him right back at square one. It was a long road for him. You wanted to know why I lied to you. Now you know.'

'I never meant to hurt him, Knapp. Never,' Julia sobbed, overwhelmed with emotion.

Knapp picked up a paper napkin and handed it to her.

'What do you have to cry about? Where are you at with your life, Julia? Married? Divorced maybe? Children? A recent transfer to Berlin?'

'Are you . . . enjoying being this cruel?'

'Oh please. Don't tell me you of all people are about to lecture me on cruelty.'

'You don't understand . . .'

'You'd be surprised. Let me take a guess. Twenty years later you just changed your mind. Well, you're too late. That letter, the one he wrote you right before leaving Kabul, I helped him come up with the right words – I remember it like it was yesterday. I was there when he came back from the airport the last day of every month, crushed. You made a choice, and he respected it like he said he would. If that's what you came here to find out, well, now you know. And you can leave.'

'But . . . I never made a choice, Knapp. I couldn't. Thomas's letter . . . I only got it three days ago.'

◆　◆　◆

The plane glided through the sky over the Alps. Marina had dozed off with her head on Thomas's shoulder. He lowered the shade on the window and closed his eyes in an attempt to sleep. One more hour before they would land in Berlin.

◆　◆　◆

Julia recounted the whole story without a single interruption from Knapp. While Thomas had mourned the death of a relationship, Julia had spent years mourning the loss of a man she believed to be dead. After her tale had been told, she rose from her chair and apologized once more for the pain she had unwittingly caused. She said goodbye to Knapp and made him swear never to tell his best friend about her visit to Berlin. Knapp stood frozen watching her walk down the corridor towards the stairs. As Julia started down the stairs, Knapp called out to her and added one last thing.

'I can't keep that promise. I don't want to lose my best friend. Julia . . . Thomas is on a plane coming back from Rome right now. He lands in forty-five minutes.'

19.

The taxi driver told Julia that the trip to the airport typically took about thirty-five minutes. She promised she'd pay double if he could get her there faster. At the second red light they stopped at, she suddenly opened her door and leapt out, advancing to the passenger seat and sliding in beside the driver just as the light turned green.

'Passengers stay in the back!' the man exclaimed.

'Unless I can tear off this mirror, I'm here to stay!' she said, lowering the sun visor for a look at herself. 'Go on, drive! *Beeil dich!*'

Julia winced at her reflection: swollen eyes, and the tip of her nose was still red from her crying fit. She wasn't going to show up after twenty years and expect Thomas to just take her into his arms with her looking like some kind of albino rabbit. She sighed – this was hopeless! A sharp turn ruined her first attempt at putting on mascara. Julia asked the driver to be more careful, but he only snapped back at her that he could either pull over so she could finish dabbing her face, or he could try and get her there in fifteen minutes. One or the other.

'Just keep driving!' she shouted with urgency, returning to her make-up.

The road was clogged with traffic. Julia begged the driver to use the right-hand lane for passing, despite the solid line forbidding it. When he explained that he could lose his licence, Julia promised she'd pretend to be giving birth if they were pulled over. The driver gave one look at her less-than-convincing belly and scoffed at the notion. In response, Julia stuck out her stomach, moaning and wailing theatrically with her hands pressed to the small of her back.

'Fine, fine, that's more than enough,' said the driver, putting his foot down harder on the accelerator.

At 6.22 p.m. she leapt out of the taxi on to the sidewalk before the car had even come to a complete stop. The entire length of the terminal stretched before her.

Julia searched around in a frenzy for the international arrivals area. A passing airport employee directed her to the far western end of the building. Breathless after her harrowing run, Julia scanned the arrivals board. No flights from Rome were listed. After a deep breath to brace herself, she took off her shoes and started running again, now in the opposite direction. Julia sprinted through the crowd of people waiting for arriving passengers to emerge from behind the sliding doors. She wiggled and bumped her way through the masses until she could claim a spot just behind the railing. The first wave of passengers came through the exit, the doors sliding open and shut each time a new group came from the baggage area. Tourists, holidaymakers, sales reps, business professionals . . . all of them dressed by function. People waved their hands in the air; some ran forwards to hug each other, others were happy to say a simple hello. She picked up chatter in French, then Spanish and a little later English.

During the fourth wave of people, Julia finally picked up traces of Italian. Two hunched-over college students walked arm in arm, looking like tortoises. A priest clutching his missal made a perfect magpie. A copilot and flight attendant amicably exchanging contact info must have been giraffes in a past life. A conference delegate stretching his neck and searching back and forth for his group was a worried owl. A little butterfly of a girl fluttered right into her mother's waiting arms. A father bear wrapped his thick arms around his wife. Then suddenly she saw him. Thomas's face shone from amid the sea of a hundred others, standing out from the crowd just as it had so many years before.

Twenty years had carved a few new lines around his eyes and made the cleft in his chin more pronounced, the effect only further accentuated by a few days' stubble. But those eyes . . . soft like sand, with that same gaze that had lured her across the rooftops of Berlin and turned her knees to jelly under the full moon in the Tiergarten . . . Looking at those eyes, she could see some things hadn't changed at all. Julia held her breath, stood on her toes and leaned out over the barrier. Just as she was raising her arm to wave in his direction, Thomas turned away, eyes drawn to the young woman by his side, who curled an affectionate arm around his waist. As they passed right by Julia, her heels and heart sank to the ground. The couple walked straight out of the terminal and disappeared.

'Do you want to come to my place first?' asked Thomas as he slid into the back seat of the taxi beside Marina and closed the door.

'Your apartment can wait. We should probably go to the office first. It's late, and Knapp may have already left. It's important that I pop in so he can see me, for the good of my career. Wasn't that the whole reason you convinced me to come to Berlin?'

'Potsdamer Strasse,' Thomas told the driver.

Ten cars behind them a woman got into a different taxi and headed for her hotel.

The concierge told Julia that her father was waiting for her in the bar. She found him sitting at a table near the window.

'Well, you look like you've seen better days. That bad?' he asked, rising to greet her.

Julia slumped into an armchair across from her father.

'That bad. Not everything Knapp said was a lie.'

'You saw him? Saw Thomas?'

'At the airport. Coming back from Rome . . . with his wife at his hip.'

'Did you talk to him?'

'He didn't even see me.'

Anthony called the waiter over.

'Would you like something to drink?'

'I'd like to go home.'

'Let me ask: were they wearing rings?'

'She had her arm around his waist. You expect me to waltz up and ask to see a marriage certificate?'

'Well, just a few short days ago someone had his arm around your waist – so I assume. I wasn't there to see it of course, it being my own funeral and all. Though, in a way I suppose I was there.' Anthony chuckled to himself. 'There I go again. But you have to admit it is a bit amusing.'

'I don't find it the least bit amusing. That was supposed to be my wedding day. And thank God that, come tomorrow, this absurd trip of ours is finally over. It's probably for the best. Knapp was right. What was I thinking, barging back into his life?'

'Perhaps you were thinking of second chances.'

'For who? For him? You? Me? The whole thing was a selfish delusion, bound to turn into a train wreck from the start.'

'In that case what's next?'

'I pack my bag and go to bed.'

'I meant once we get back to New York.'

'I'll have to take stock of my life. Pick up the pieces and try to fix everything that's broken. Find a way to forget all of this and start living my old life again. This time I don't have a choice.'

'Of course you do. The choice is clear: see this through to the end and leave Berlin with a clear conscience, or leave with a shadow hanging over you.'

'It's really something hearing you lecture me on matters of the heart.'

Anthony looked at his daughter attentively and scooted his chair towards hers.

'Do you remember when you were a little girl what you used to do every single night for hours on end, until you finally collapsed with exhaustion?'

'Yes. I read under the covers with a flashlight.'

'Why didn't you just turn on a light?'

'So you would think I was still sleeping. The whole operation was a secret.'

'And this flashlight of yours. Was it special? Magical perhaps?'

'Not that I know of.'

'And do you recall it ever going out? Dying, even once?'

'No, never,' replied Julia, confused.

'A flashlight that never dies. *Someone* must have been changing those batteries. I'm saying, how can you really know if you can't see the full picture? My sweet Julia, what do you really know about love? You've never loved anyone who didn't just tell you what you needed to hear about yourself. Look me in the eyes and tell me about your marriage, your plans for the future. If this unexpected journey had never happened, are you really going to sit there and swear to me that your love for Adam was unbreakable?

'How could you know the first thing about Thomas's feelings or where his life is headed when you don't have the slightest clue about the direction you're headed in yourself? And all this simply because a woman had her arm around his waist.

'Let's be frank, dear. How long did your longest relationship last? I'm not talking about Thomas, nor how long your feelings lingered on, but a *real* relationship. Two, three, four years? Maybe five? They say love lasts seven years for what it's worth. Go on, be honest and tell me. For seven years would you be capable of giving yourself to someone with no reservations, all that you are, no restraints, neither fear nor doubt, knowing that the person you love more than anything will eventually forget everything or nearly everything you've experienced together?

'Would you accept that all your care, every last move, gesture and touch, all you've done to prove your love, will be wiped clean from her memory and that nature's aversion to emptiness will fill the void with blame and regret? Knowing this is inevitable, would you nonetheless be able to find the strength to rise in the dead of night when your loved one is thirsty or has had a nightmare . . . to prepare her breakfast every single morning without fail, to make sure her days are full, that she's entertained, to read her stories when she grows restless? To go out, because she needs air, even when it's cold as hell. And at night, exhausted, would you come to sit at the foot of her bed to ease her fears, to tell her of a future she'll most likely spend far from your side? If your answer to each of these questions is yes, then forgive me for having misjudged you. For you do truly know what it is to love.'

'You're . . . talking about Mom?'

'No, my dear child. I'm talking about you. The love of a father or a mother for their children. Days and nights spent looking after you, protecting you from even the slightest danger, drying your tears, making you laugh, helping you grow . . . Do you know how many times we took you to the park in the dead of winter and how many times we lugged bags full of toys to the beach in the summer, the miles and miles we covered, words repeated endlessly until you learnt them? All this . . . before even your very first childhood memory.

'Try for a moment to imagine the love it takes to learn to live for you and you only, all the while knowing you would eventually forget your first years. All that we did, and for what? Despite the early years, you'd eventually suffer on account of our mistakes, and then one day inevitably you would move on. Proud of your freedom, leaving us behind.

'I know you're angry at me for not being there enough when you were young. But you can't imagine what it feels like to have your child leave home. Can you even fathom what that does to a parent, that rupture? I can tell you. You find yourself standing like a fool on the doorstep, watching them leave, trying to convince yourself that their departure is necessary and that you should learn to embrace the careless changing of the tides that sweeps your child away, and that puts distance between you and your own flesh and blood.

'So we close the door, and then we have to relearn everything. Learn to fill the empty spaces. Learn to no longer listen for the sound of your footsteps. Learn to forget the reassuring creaks on the stairs when you come home late and the sweet slumber of relief that would follow. When you left, I was all but certain I would never be able to sleep soundly again knowing you wouldn't be coming home, not then and not ever. You see, my dear Julia, a parent receives no prize and no reward for their endless dedication, and therein lies the very essence of what it means to love somebody. And we have no alternative, because *by God, how we love you children*. I know that you will resent me all your life for having torn you away from Thomas. So now I must once more beg your forgiveness . . . I should have never kept that letter from you.'

Anthony raised his arm to get the waiter's attention. Beads of sweat were gathering on his forehead. He took a handkerchief from his pocket.

'Forgive me,' he repeated, his arm still in the air. 'Forgive me, forgive me, forgive me.'

'What's wrong?' asked Julia, her concern mounting.

'Forgive me,' Anthony repeated three more times.

'Daddy?'

'Forgive me, forgive me . . .'

With that, Anthony rose to his feet, staggered and wobbled for a moment, then sank back down into his armchair.

Julia yelled for help from the waiter, but Anthony waved the man away, assuring them it was unnecessary.

'Where . . . where are we?' he asked in a daze.

'In Berlin, at the hotel bar.'

'But wh . . . what day is it? Tell me, what am I doing here?'

'Stop it! Just stop,' Julia begged in a panic. 'It's Friday. We came here together. We left New York three days ago, looking for Thomas, don't you remember? It was all because of that stupid drawing I saw in Montreal. You gave it to me; you wanted us to come here. You can remember that, I'm sure you can. You're tired, that's all. You have to conserve battery power. That may . . . sound ridiculous, but you're the one who said it first. You wanted to talk about us. All we've done is talk about me. Come on, focus. You can pull through this. We still have two days left, just for the two of us, like you said, to . . . to say all those things we never said. I want to know everything I forgot, to hear the stories you used to tell me . . . you know . . . the one about the pilot who gets stranded on the banks of the Amazon . . . and the otter that guides him back to safety. I can remember his fur was blue. That blue, the way only you could describe it . . .'

Julia took her father by the arm and gently led him back to his room.

'You don't look so good. Just sleep. You'll have more energy tomorrow.'

But Anthony refused to lie down on the bed, insisting the armchair near the window was all he needed.

'You know,' he said, easing down into the chair, 'it's funny how we always search for reasons not to love – fear of suffering, fear of abandonment – but the love of life, oh, how much you can take for granted until you realize that one day you're going to lose all of it.'

'Don't talk like that.'

'You have to stop projecting yourself into an imaginary future, Julia. There are no broken pieces to glue back together. There is simply life to live, the one thing that can't be imagined or predicted. And I can tell you it goes by at dizzying speeds. Don't go wasting your time with me in this room! Go trace the footsteps of your memories. You wanted to take stock? Well, go on. Do it. You were here twenty years ago. Now go and find those years you missed before it truly is too late. Thomas is in the same city as you tonight, and only tonight. Whether you see him or not, you're still breathing the same air. You know he's there, that the two of you are closer than you'll ever be again. Walk endlessly, stopping under every window with a light on and asking yourself how you'd feel if it was his silhouette on the other side of the curtain. And if by some wild chance it is him, you shout his name to the heavens! He'll hear you and maybe come outside. He'll say he's still in love with you, or he'll throw you out, but at least you'll know for certain.'

He asked Julia to leave him alone to rest. She shook her head and only moved in closer to her father. Anthony smiled.

'I'm sorry for that scare I gave you back at the bar. I shouldn't have put you through that,' he said with a guilty look.

'Wait. Are you telling me you were pretending to malfunction?'

'You can't imagine how much I missed your mother when her mind started slipping away. You're not the only one who lost her. I spent four years living by her side, while she didn't have the faintest clue who I was. Go! Have fun! It's your last night in Berlin!'

◆ ◆ ◆

Julia went back to her room and stretched out on the bed. There was nothing on TV, and the magazines on the coffee table were all in

German. She rose and decided to get some fresh air. What good was it to stay in her room? She might as well wander around the city and take advantage of one last night in Berlin. She fished around in her suitcase in search of a sweater. Towards the bottom, her hand brushed up against the blue envelope, the one that had long been hidden between the pages of the history book on the shelf in her childhood bedroom. She glanced at the handwriting on the front and slipped the letter into her pocket.

Before leaving the hotel, she went to the top floor and knocked on the door of her father's suite.

'Did you forget something?' asked Anthony as he opened the door.

Julia didn't respond.

'Don't forget: tomorrow, eight o'clock, I'll be waiting for you in the lobby. I reserved a car for us. We can't miss that flight. You have to take me back to New York, young lady.'

'Do you think that . . . love ever stops hurting?' asked Julia, still standing in the doorway.

'If you're lucky? Never.'

'Well, now it's my turn to say I'm sorry. I should have shown you this a long time ago. I wanted to keep it just for myself, but it concerns you, too.'

'What is it?'

'It's the last letter Mom ever wrote me.'

She handed the envelope to her father and left.

◆ ◆ ◆

Anthony watched his daughter walk away. He looked at the envelope she had given him and immediately recognized his wife's handwriting. He took a deep breath to steel himself; then his shoulders slumped, the strength seeping out of him. He sat down in an armchair to read.

Julia,

When you come into the room, I watch your silhouette against the light that streams in from the hall. I hear your footsteps as you step towards me. The lines of your face are so very familiar, but at times I have trouble putting a name to your face. Your scent is also very familiar to me; it's an enormous source of comfort. That fragrance is the only thing that helps me breathe – sweet relief in the face of this panic that has been choking me for so very long. You must be the girl who often comes early in the evening, and I know that night is drawing closer when you arrive at my bedside. You speak to me with a voice that is gentle and at peace . . . more at peace than my midday man, the one who comes to visit every day. I believe it when he says he loves me, because he seems to want the best for me. Everything he does is so gentle. Sometimes he gets up and looks out the window at that great light which shines beyond the tree line, then he hangs his head and cries. Why, I can only guess. I don't have the heart to tell him that I don't recognize the name he calls me by. The truth is whenever I smile at hearing him call me that name, I can feel a weight lift in the room. And so I find myself smiling at him when he feeds me as well . . .

You're sitting nearby right now, at the edge of the bed. You graze my forehead with the softest touch. I'm not afraid. I can tell from the look in your eyes when you call my name you're hoping I'll answer with yours. But there is no sadness in those eyes. That's why it makes me so happy when you visit. Every time your wrist comes close to my nose, I close my eyes.

The scent of your skin reminds me of childhood – my own, or yours perhaps? You are my daughter, my love. I know that right now, if only for a few short moments. So many things to tell you and so little time. I want to hear you laugh, my girl. I want you to run and go tell your father he should stop hiding by the window, and to dry his tears. Tell him I do recognize him sometimes. That I remember who he is and how we loved each other. Tell him I love him all over again each time he comes to visit.

Good night, my love.

Your mother

20.

Knapp stood waiting for them at the front desk. Thomas had called on the way from the airport to tell him they had arrived. After greeting Marina and giving his friend a hug, Knapp led them to his office.

'It's a good thing you're here!' he said to Marina, after the three of them sat down. 'I need you to help me with a problem. Your prime minister is coming to Berlin this evening, and the reporter I assigned to cover the event and the gala dinner in his honour is as sick as a dog. We have three columns allotted to it in tomorrow's edition. You have to get changed and leave right away. I'll need your copy before two a.m. to leave enough time for the subeditors. I have to get everything to the press before three. I'm sorry if this is throwing a spanner into your plans for tonight, but it's urgent.'

Marina rose swiftly and said goodbye to Knapp. Then she kissed Thomas's forehead and whispered in his ear, 'Arrivederci, my sweet idiot.'

As Marina walked off down the corridor, Thomas turned away from Knapp and rushed after her.

'Really? After all that you just get up and go because he says so? What about our dinner together?'

'You can't be serious. What, you're not at his beck and call, too? Remind me again: who is it that's flying out tomorrow for Mogadishu?

Career always comes first, before everything else. I've heard you say that a hundred times, Thomas. Tomorrow you're gone, and it's anyone's guess for how long. So take care of yourself. If the Fates allow, our paths will cross again somewhere out there.'

'Here. Take my keys. Come and write your article at my apartment.'

'I'll be more comfortable at a hotel. I can't imagine how I would concentrate at your place with so much to explore, so much to get distracted by.'

'I told you, the place is basically one big empty room.'

'Idiot. My very favourite idiot, but still an idiot. I was talking about getting distracted by *you*. Who knows? Maybe I'll change my mind and ring your doorbell tonight for a little treat. Bye now.'

Marina threw him a carefree 'Ciao' and walked away.

'Are you okay?' asked Knapp when Thomas came back, slamming the door behind him.

'You're a real pain! I only came back to Berlin to spend tonight with Marina. It's the last night before I leave, and you manage to take her away with some flimsy excuse about not having anyone else to cover that story. What's your problem? Do you have a thing for Marina? I thought you'd become such an ambitious bastard, you didn't care about anything besides this newspaper.'

'Are you finished?' asked Knapp flatly as he sat back down behind his desk.

'Admit it, you're a real pain in the arse,' Thomas fumed.

'Thomas, there's something I have to tell you. You might want to sit down.'

◆　◆　◆

The Tiergarten glowed in the evening light. Two old street lamps spread yellow halos across the canal towpath. On the surface of the lake nearby boatmen were tying vessels together, one to the next. Julia followed the path to the edge of the zoo. A little further on was a lookout point over the river. She cut through the woods with no fear of getting lost, as though she knew every last tree she passed. The Victory Column stood before her. She walked past the roundabout, and her feet carried her straight past the Brandenburg Gate. Then she stopped short, realizing all at once where she was standing. In that same spot almost twenty years ago a wall had once stood at the end of the row of trees. It was there that she had seen Thomas for the first time. In its place now was a simple bench beneath a linden tree, a welcome respite for passers-by.

'I was sure I'd find you here,' said a voice behind her. 'Same old Julia, same old wandering habits.'

Julia froze. She felt her heart tighten in her chest.

'Thomas?' she whispered breathlessly without turning round.

'How do you say hello in a situation like this? Shake hands? Hug?' he said hesitantly.

'You got me,' she said, still too petrified to turn and face him.

'When Knapp told me you were in Berlin, I didn't know how to find you. I thought about calling all the youth hostels, but there are so many now and we're no longer "youths" . . . Then it hit me. With a little luck I could wait here and you'd come to me.'

'Your voice is the same, maybe a little deeper,' she said, at last turning to face him with a fragile smile.

He took a step closer to her.

'If you want, I could climb that tree there. Drop down from a branch. Fall on top of you. For old times' sake.'

Thomas took a few hesitant steps forwards, then pulled Julia into his arms.

'Time goes by so quickly and so slowly all at once,' he said, holding her tightly against him.

'Are you crying?' asked Julia, gently caressing his cheek.

'No, that was . . . a fly that just flew in my eye. Are you?'

'I think those flies must come in pairs. Though I don't see any others around here.'

'Close your eyes,' whispered Thomas, his warm lips against her ear.

Then, as though no time and no distance had ever come between them, Thomas did as he had done every morning he'd woken up by her side. He gently brushed Julia's lips with his fingertips and planted the lightest of kisses on each of her eyelids.

'That was the nicest way to say good morning,' she said when he was finished.

Julia burrowed her face into the hollow between Thomas's neck and shoulder.

'God, you smell just the same way you always did. Just like I remember.'

'Come on, it's cold. You're shivering.'

Thomas took Julia by the hand and led her towards the Brandenburg Gate.

'Did you come to the airport earlier today?'

'Yes. How did you know?'

'Why didn't you say anything?'

'You were with your wife. I didn't really feel like introducing myself.'

'Her name is Marina.'

'Pretty name.'

'She's not my wife. It's more . . . casual – you know, nothing too serious. We're just sort of hanging up.'

'You mean "hanging out"?'

'Sure, whatever you say. My English still isn't perfect.'

'You get by pretty well.'

They left the park and crossed the square. Thomas led her to a cafe terrace. After they sat down, a long time passed with the two just staring at each other in silence, incapable of finding any words.

It was Thomas who at last broke the silence. 'It's kind of mind mind-blowing how little you've changed.'

'Oh, I've had my fair share of changes since the last time you saw me. Try me at six a.m., and you can get an accurate count of just how many years have gone by.'

'I don't need to. I counted every one.'

The waiter popped the cork of a bottle of Prosecco and poured them two glasses.

'Thomas, about your letter . . . I have to tell you . . .'

'Stop. I know. Knapp told me everything. If there's one thing I can say about your father, at least he sticks to his convictions.'

He lifted his glass and clinked it against hers delicately. Couples strolled across the square, stopping to admire the beauty of the Brandenburg Gate pillars.

'Are you happy?'

Julia said nothing.

'Where has life taken you?' asked Thomas.

'To Berlin, with you . . . just as lost as I was twenty years ago.'

'Why did you come back?'

'I didn't have an address to write you. It had already been eighteen years. I didn't want to risk it getting lost in the mail.'

'Are you married? Do you have children?'

'Not yet,' responded Julia.

'No children yet or no marriage?'

'Neither.'

'Does that make you single?'

'You didn't have that scar on your chin before,' she deflected.

'Well, jumping off walls is pretty harmless, but landmines leave their mark.'

'You've put on a bit of weight,' said Julia with a smile.

'Really? Thanks a lot!'

'No, it was a compliment. Seriously. It suits you.'

'You never got any better at lying. You're right, I admit it. I've aged. Are you hungry?'

'No,' said Julia, lowering her eyes.

'Neither am I. Do you want to take a walk?'

'I feel like everything I say is just ridiculous,' she murmured.

'No, it's not. You just haven't told me a thing about your life yet,' said Thomas sadly.

'I went back to our little dive bar you know.'

'I've never been back there myself.'

'The owner actually recognized me.'

'See? I told you: you haven't changed.'

'They tore down the old building where we used to live and put up something new. There's nothing left on our street except the little park across the way.'

'Maybe it's better that way. Our time together gave me the only memories I have of that place worth keeping. I live in the West now. That may mean nothing to a lot of people, but I still see the border when I look out the window.'

'Knapp filled me in on your life,' continued Julia.

'Oh yeah? What did he say?'

'That you run a restaurant in Italy with a whole horde of children who help you make your pizzas,' Julia responded.

'That fool . . . I wonder how he came up with all that.'

'He was remembering the hell I put you through.'

'I imagine I put you through a lot, too, if you thought I was dead.' Thomas gave a slight wince at his own words. 'That came out as very pretentious.'

'No. Well, yes, a little, but it's true.'

Thomas took Julia's hand in his own.

'We both followed our own paths. Life intervened and stepped between us. Your father had a lot to do with it, but in the end it almost seemed as though fate itself was trying to keep us apart.'

'Maybe . . . destiny did it for our protection. Maybe we would have ended up annoying each other and getting a divorce. You'd be the man I hate most in the world, and we'd never have spent this evening together.'

'Or maybe we'd have spent the evening together, arguing over how to raise our children. Not to mention some couples break up and stay friends. So, are you seeing somebody? Please don't nudge the question this time.'

'Dodge!'

'What?'

'You meant to say "dodge the question".'

'I have an idea. Follow me.'

The adjoining terrace was part of a seafood restaurant. Thomas slipped in and deftly grabbed a table right from under the noses of a couple of waiting tourists.

'Is that type of thing normal for you these days?' asked Julia as she sat down. 'It wasn't very polite . . . and won't they kick us out?'

'In my line of work, sometimes you have to be a bit assertive and take care of yourself. Besides, I'm friends with the owner and rarely have a reason to play that card.'

Right on cue the owner arrived and said hello to Thomas, then barked at him in an angry whisper, 'Next time be more discreet or you'll drive away my clientele!'

Thomas introduced Julia to his friend.

'What would you recommend for two people who aren't hungry at all?' he asked.

'I'll bring you some prawns. They're guaranteed to kick-start your appetite.'

The owner left. Before entering the kitchen, he turned and gave Thomas a wink and a thumbs-up, clearly impressed by his date.

'I work in animation,' Julia told Thomas.

'I know. I'm a fan of your blue otter actually.'

'You've seen Tilly?'

'Well, it's not like I've seen all your work, but like everything in my profession, word gets around. I heard your name through the grapevine; then I had some free time one day in Madrid and noticed one of your film posters outside, and decided to check out the film. The story wasn't the easiest to follow, what with my Spanish being so shoddy, but I think I got the gist of it. Can I ask you a question?'

'Shoot.'

'The bear character wasn't based on me by any chance, was it?'

'That's funny. Stanley thought maybe the hedgehog was you.'

'Who's Stanley?'

'My best friend.'

'And who's he to call me a hedgehog?'

'He's a smart guy and very intuitive. But most of all, I talk to him about you all the time.'

'Sounds like a nice guy. What kind of friend is that exactly?'

'A widower. Let's just say we've been through a lot together.'

'Wow. That's really sad.'

'We've had good times, too, though.'

'No, I was talking about him being a widower. Did he lose his wife a long time ago or—?'

'Not wife, boyfriend.'

'Well, then I'm even sadder for him.'

'That doesn't make any sense.'

'I know, it's stupid, but this Stanley seems even nicer when I picture him with a man. And who exactly inspired that weasel?'

'My downstairs neighbour. He runs a shoe store. Tell me, when you went to see my cartoon, what kind of a day were you having?'

'A pretty sad one after the final credits rolled.'

'I missed you, Thomas.'

'I missed you, too. More than you can imagine. But we should change the subject. As far as I see, they're fresh off of flies in this place.'

'Fresh *out* of flies.'

'Whatever you say. Bad days like the one in Madrid come and go. I've been through it hundreds of times, here, abroad . . . Still happens from time to time even now. But we really should talk about something else before you *accuse* me of boring you with my nostalgia.'

'Did you have any bad days in Rome?'

'How about you finally get round to telling me about your life, Julia?'

'Twenty years is a lot to catch up on.'

'You have someone waiting for you?'

'No, not tonight.'

'What about tomorrow?'

'Yes. There's somebody in New York.' Julia looked down at the table.

'Somebody serious?'

'We were supposed to get married last Saturday.'

'Why "supposed to"?'

'It was cancelled.'

'Wow. Was it him or you who—?'

'Actually, believe it or not it was my father.' The thought brought a little smile to her face, her gaze rising from the table.

'Still! After all these years he's still smashing your boyfriends' faces?'

'No, this time he took it quite a bit further.'

'I'm sorry.'

'That's probably not altogether true, but I don't blame you.'

'Well, truth be told, if anybody was going to hit your fiancé, it should probably be me. Yikes, I really am sorry – that time I was way out of order.' Thomas shook his head ruefully.

Julia tried to swallow back a giggle, but she soon gave in to the insatiable urge and burst out laughing.

'What? Why is that funny?'

'The look on your face,' continued Julia, still laughing. 'Like a kid next to an empty cookie jar with crumbs all over his face. No wonder you inspired so many of my characters. Nobody but you can make faces like that. God, I really have missed you.'

'Stop. Just stop saying that, Julia.'

'Why?'

'Because you were supposed to get married last Saturday.' Thomas was no longer smiling.

Just then the owner of the restaurant came to their table with a large plate of prawns.

'I have just the thing for you two,' he announced. 'Filet of sole in a fresh herb sauce with a side dish of grilled vegetables – just the job for your stubborn stomachs. How does that sound?'

'Look, I'm sorry,' said Thomas to his friend. 'I'm afraid we won't be staying. Would you mind bringing the bill?'

'Oh no you don't. I don't know what's going on between you two, but you don't leave my restaurant without tasting the food. So go ahead, keep on arguing, get it all off your chests, but leave your stomachs to me!'

The owner walked away to prepare the sole on a side table but kept his stern gaze on Thomas and Julia.

'I get the impression we don't have a choice. If you don't put up with me a little longer, it seems you're going to be in some real trouble with that guy,' said Julia.

'I get the same impression,' said Thomas, softening a bit. 'Please forgive me, Julia. I really shouldn't have . . . you know . . .'

'Stop apologizing all the time. It doesn't suit you. Let's try to eat, and then you can take me back to my hotel. I feel like taking a walk with you. Am I at least allowed to say that?' Julia asked with the faintest hint of pleading.

'Yes,' Thomas replied with a smile. 'So. Tell me exactly how your father managed to ruin your wedding.'

'Forget about him. Let's talk about you.'

Thomas walked her through the past eighteen years of his life, leaving out many key parts. Julia did the same. When they had finished dinner, the owner insisted they try his chocolate soufflé, which he had made especially for them. He brought out two spoons, but Julia and Thomas used only one.

With the moon shining brightly overhead, the two left the restaurant and took the long route back to Julia's hotel. As they passed through the park, they caught sight of the reflection of the full moon on the surface of the pond, where a few boats tied to a pontoon were gently rocking back and forth.

Julia told Thomas the old legend, and he told her about his travels while sparing her the details of the wars he had covered. She told him about New York, her job and her best friend while avoiding any and all talk of the future.

They left the park behind and walked through the city. Julia stopped Thomas right in the middle of a particular city square.

'Do you remember?' she asked.

'Yes. This is where I found Knapp in the middle of the crowd. Talk about an unforgettable night. Whatever happened to your two French friends?'

'I haven't spoken to them in ages. As I recall, Mathias runs a bookstore in Paris, and Antoine is an architect in London.'

'Did they get married?'

'And divorced, last I heard.'

'Look,' said Thomas, pointing to the darkened window of a cafe. 'That's the spot where we always used to meet up with Knapp.'

'You know, I actually found that number the two of you were always bickering about.'

'What number is that?'

'The percentage of East Germans who collaborated with the Stasi by passing along information. I happened to stumble across it a couple years ago in the library, flipping through a special edition of a journal on the fall of the Berlin Wall.'

'A couple of years ago? You were still thinking of that as recently as—'

'Only two per cent of the population. See? You can take pride in your fellow citizens.'

'My own grandmother was part of that two per cent, Julia. I went and looked at my file in the archives. I suspected they would have something on me due to Knapp's defection to the West. My own *grandmother* gave them information on me. I read pages and pages of details about my life, the things I did, who my friends were. Can you think of any stranger way of rediscovering all your childhood memories?'

'After these past few days? I could tell you some stories. But your grandmother might have done all that to protect you so you wouldn't be bothered.'

'Maybe. I'll never know.'

'Is that why you changed your name?'

'Yeah, the idea was to put the past behind me and start a new life.'

'Put the past behind you and everything in it? Even me?'

'We're back at your hotel now, Julia.'

She looked up to see the Brandenburger Hof Hotel sign lighting up the face of the building. Thomas took her in his arms with a sad sort of smile.

'There's no tree here. We can't say goodbye like this.'

'Do you think things could have worked out between us?'

'Who knows?'

'I don't know how to say goodbye, Thomas. Not even sure I want to.'

'I can't tell you how sweet, how wonderful it was to see you again. Like an unexpected present life handed me,' Thomas whispered.

Julia rested her head on his shoulder.

'Yes, it was so sweet. And so wonderful.'

'Of all the questions you haven't answered tonight, only one of them really worries me. Are you happy, Julia?'

'No. Not any more.'

'What about you? Do you believe things could have worked out between us?' asked Thomas.

'Probably.'

'Well, then you've changed more than I thought.'

'Why do you say that?'

'Because back in the old days, with that sarcastic humour of yours you would have said our life together would have been an utter fiasco. That there was no way you could have sat by and watched me get old and put on weight . . . and that you wouldn't have put up with me travelling for work all the time. Stuff like that.'

'I guess I've just become a much better liar.'

'That's the old Julia. The Julia I never stopped loving.'

'You really want to know if things could have worked? I can think of one way to find out,' said Julia breathlessly.

'What's that?'

Julia placed her lips on his. The kiss stretched on and on. Like two love-struck teenagers, they were oblivious to the rest of the world. She took him by the hand and led him through the hotel lobby, straight past the concierge, who was dozing behind the desk. Julia pulled Thomas to the lifts. She pushed the button, and their embrace continued to the sixth floor.

Their bodies reunited as naturally as they ever had in their most intimate memories. Sweat mingled with sweat under the sheets. Julia closed her eyes. His smooth hand slid down her stomach, and she reached up to clasp the nape of his neck. His mouth brushed from her shoulder down her neck and to the curves of her breasts. His lips wandered uncontrollably. She wove her fingers in his hair. His tongue went deeper, lower, and the pleasure rose in waves, bringing sensations from the past rushing to the present. With their legs intertwined and bodies wrapped around one another, no force could have torn them apart. The movements hadn't changed. Awkward moments were vastly outshone by the tenderness of familiar instincts.

The minutes stretched into hours. At last they lay at rest. Morning light broke over their languid bodies, stretched out and uninhibited in the warmth of the bed.

◆ ◆ ◆

In the distance a church bell struck eight. Thomas stretched and walked over to the window. Julia sat up and gazed at him, her sleepy eyes entranced by the interplay of shadow and light dancing across his body. Thomas turned round and looked back at Julia.

'God, you are beautiful,' he said.

Julia didn't respond.

'Now what?' he asked with care.

'Now . . . I'm hungry!'

'I noticed that bag on the chair is already packed.'

'Well, I'm leaving. This morning,' Julia stammered.

'It took me ten years to move on. I thought all this was behind me. I thought that fear was most potent on the battlefield, but now . . . I can tell you it's nothing compared to what I'm feeling in this room right now, being here next to you and knowing I could lose you all over again.'

'Thomas . . .'

'What do you want me to say, Julia? That all this was a mistake? Maybe it was. When Knapp finally told me you were in town, I imagined that time might have wiped away all those differences, the things that separated us – a girl from the West and a boy from the East. I had hoped that was the one thing that might have changed for the better with age. But I think our lives are still very different, aren't they?'

'I draw for a living; you're in journalism. We're both living the lives we dreamed of.'

'But that doesn't mean anything, at least not to me. You still haven't told me how your father ruined the wedding. Should I expect him to kick down this door and break my jaw again?'

'I was eighteen years old, Thomas. I didn't have any choice but to follow him. I was still mostly just a kid. And you don't have to worry about my father. He's dead. We buried him the day I was supposed to get married. That's how he ruined things.'

'Well . . . I'm sorry to hear that. And I'm sorry for your loss.'

'There's no need to be sorry, Thomas.'

'Why did you come back to Berlin?'

'You know why. Knapp told you everything. I got your letter a few days ago. I came as soon as I knew the truth.'

'Had to give it one more try? Just to clear the way before you get married. Is that it?'

'You don't have to be cruel.'

Thomas sat down at the foot of the bed. He took a deep breath.

'I had to learn to tame the loneliness over the years. It took an incredible amount of patience. I walked through cities all over the world just longing to find the same air you might have breathed. They say that when two people are truly in love, their thoughts are connected, intertwined. I often wondered about that as I laid my head down to sleep at night. I wondered if you were thinking about me while I was thinking about you. I came to New York even, walked the streets, hoping against hope I'd somehow run into you, absolutely terrified of the idea at the same time. I thought I saw you a hundred times. My heart would skip a beat every time I saw a woman who bore any resemblance to you. I swore to never fall in love like that again – it's too dangerous. Time has passed and . . . time has passed us by. You had to know that, didn't you? Before you even got on the plane.'

'Stop, Thomas. Don't ruin this. Please. What do you want me to say? Every time I looked up at the sky, day or night, I told myself you were looking down on me. So no, I never had the chance to make up my mind about us, because you were gone!'

'So, what, Julia? We stay in touch as friends? I call you when I'm in New York, and we have a drink together and reminisce about the good old days? You show me pictures of your kids – not *our* kids of course. I say that they look so much like you, trying to ignore how much they also look like their father. While I'm in the toilet, you'll call your future husband, and I'll let the water run so I don't have to hear him say, "Hello, baby." Does he even know you came to Berlin?'

'Stop it!' shouted Julia.

'What are you going to tell him when you get home?' Thomas asked, turning back to look out the window.

'I don't know. I have no idea.'

'See? Like I said. Same old Julia.'

'No. I've changed, Thomas, I have. But all it took was a sign. Fate led me here and made me realize that even if I have changed, my feelings haven't.'

Out on the pavement below, Anthony Walsh was pacing back and forth, checking his watch compulsively. He peered up at his daughter's window, his impatience visible even from a great height.

'When did you say your father died?' asked Thomas, closing the blinds.

'He was buried last Saturday.'

'Fine. Done. Don't say another word. You were right. Let's not ruin what we had. You can't love someone and lie to them. You just can't. We can't.'

'What do you mean? I haven't been lying to you.'

'Take your bag and run home,' muttered Thomas.

He put on his trousers, shirt and coat, not even bothering to tie his shoelaces. But when he turned back to Julia, he took her by the hand and pulled her into his arms one last time.

'I fly to Mogadishu tonight. I'll be thinking about you constantly every minute I'm over there. Don't waste your time on regrets. I pictured this in my head, being back with you, so many times. It was even more breathtaking than I could have imagined, my love. Just being able to call you that again one last time was more than I could have hoped for. Julia, you are the most beautiful thing that ever came into my life, the woman at the heart of my most cherished memories. You can't know how much that means. All I ask is that you promise me you'll try to be happy.'

Thomas gave Julia one last tender kiss, then walked out of the door and didn't turn back.

Leaving the hotel, Thomas walked by Anthony, who was still waiting impatiently by the car.

'She shouldn't be much longer,' he said, waving goodbye.

21.

Julia and her father said nothing to each other during the whole flight back to New York, save one question Anthony kept repeating under his breath: 'Could it really be that I messed up again?' The question left Julia perplexed. Mid-afternoon they arrived in Manhattan in the pouring rain.

'Look, Julia, you have to say something eventually!' Anthony protested as they entered her apartment on Horatio Street.

'No, I don't,' Julia replied, dropping her bag.

'Did you finally see him last night?'

'No!'

'Just tell me what happened. I might have some advice that could help.'

'You? That's rich.'

'Don't be so pig-headed. You're not five years old any more. And I'm nearly out of time.'

'I didn't see Thomas. Period. Now I'm going to take a shower.'

Her father stepped into the doorway, blocking her way.

'So, now what? Or were you planning on staying in that bathroom for the next twenty years?'

'Get out of my way.'

'Not until you answer my question.'

'You want to know what I'm going to do now? What do you think? I'm going to try to pick up the pieces of my life, or what's left of them. You should be proud – in one week you managed to ruin everything, to the point where some things may be damaged beyond repair. And don't give me that innocent look; you know exactly what I'm talking about. You spent half the flight talking about how badly you messed things up.'

'That's not what I meant.'

'What then?'

Anthony said nothing.

'That's what I thought,' Julia shot back. 'While I'm waiting for your response, I think I'll go slip into something really skimpy that shows off my curves, then give Thomas a call and see if I can get him into bed. We'll see if I can keep up all the lying, and maybe, just maybe, he'll still want to marry me.'

'Thomas. You just said "Thomas".'

'What are you—?'

'Thomas instead of Adam. You can't possibly tell me this was another simple mistake.'

'Get out of my way before I put you out of your misery once and for all.'

'Sorry, dear. Nature already beat you to it. And if you think you can shock me by going on about your sex life, think again.'

'First thing I'm going to do when I get to Adam's place,' she continued, looking her father up and down, 'is thrust him straight against the wall, tear off his clothes and—'

'That's enough!' shouted Anthony. 'Spare me the details, will you?' he added, calming down.

'Sure. If you get out of my way and let me shower.'

◆ ◆ ◆

Anthony rolled his eyes and let her pass. As soon as she had disappeared into the bathroom, he put his ear up against the door and listened as Julia made a phone call.

'No, no. There's no need to interrupt Adam if he's in a meeting. Just please let him know Julia is back in town and would like to see him tonight if he's free. He can pick her up at eight. She'll be waiting downstairs outside her building. If he can't make it, just give Julia a call.'

Anthony crept away from the door and moved into the living room, plonking himself down on the couch in front of the TV. He grabbed the remote and was about to hit the button when he realized he had grabbed the wrong one. He glanced at the little white button on his own remote control with a knowing smile and laid it down carefully on the couch beside him.

Fifteen minutes later Julia reappeared with a raincoat thrown over her shoulder.

'You're heading off?'

'Yes, to work.'

'On a Saturday? In this weather?'

'There's always somebody there over the weekend, and I have a lot of emails to catch up on.'

As she was preparing to go, Anthony called to her.

'Julia?'

'What is it now?'

'Before you make some foolish mistake, don't forget that Thomas still loves you.'

'And how would you know that?'

'We crossed paths this morning. He was very civil. He gave me a little wave as he was leaving the hotel. He didn't seem too surprised either. Perhaps he noticed me on the sidewalk from your window.'

Julia's heart dropped. She glared at her father, furious.

'Get out. When I get back, I want you gone.'

'Where? To that awful attic?'

'Back to your house!' cried Julia, slamming the door behind her.

Anthony grabbed an umbrella from the hook near the door and slipped out to the balcony overlooking the street. Leaning over the railing, he watched as Julia stormed off down the street. As soon as she had disappeared from view, Anthony left the balcony and entered her bedroom. He found the phone and hit redial.

He introduced himself as Julia Walsh's assistant. Of course he was aware Ms Walsh had just called and Adam was in a meeting. However, he needed to pass along an urgent message: Julia wanted Adam to come earlier than planned, at six o'clock, and to meet her upstairs at her place and not on the street in the rain. Yes, Anthony said, he was aware that was only forty-five minutes from now. All things considered, perhaps it would be prudent to interrupt the meeting and let him know. Also, there was no use in trying to reach Julia, since her phone had died and she was out on an errand. Anthony got the secretary to promise – twice – to promptly deliver his message. Anthony put the phone back down with a smug little smile on his face. Even more smug than usual.

Julia pivoted in her work chair and turned on her computer. Her emails loaded up on-screen, forming a seemingly endless scroll. The letter tray on her desk was also overflowing, and the voicemail light on her office phone was blinking frenetically.

She took out her cell phone, knowing exactly who could help save the day.

'Am I keeping you from your customers?' she asked Stanley.

'The only customers out in this weather are the type with gills! What a waste of an afternoon. Just horrid.'

'Tell me about it. I'm soaked down to my underwear.'

'Wait. You're back?' exclaimed Stanley.

'For about an hour now.'

'Well, you should have called sooner!'

'Think you could close that empty store and meet an old friend at Pastis?'

'Order me tea, piping hot – no cappuccino today. Or whatever you want. I'm on my way!'

Ten minutes later Stanley joined Julia, who was waiting for him at a table tucked in the rear corner of the old neighbourhood restaurant.

'Tell me everything. I'm assuming that no news from you for two days means you found Thomas, but judging by that look in your eyes it didn't quite go as you hoped.'

'I hadn't really hoped for anything.'

'Bullshit.'

'Brace yourself, because I don't know if you've ever seen pure stupidity personified, but you're about to.'

Julia told him nearly every last detail of her trip. She recounted the visit to the press syndicate, Knapp's poisonous lies, the truth about Thomas's double identity, the art opening in the borrowed dress and the last-minute limo that took her there. When she got to the part about the shoes she'd worn, Stanley let out a mortified gasp. He shoved aside his tea and made an emergency order for a glass of white wine. The rain outside fell even harder. Julia told him about her visit to East Berlin, the street where all the old buildings from her memories had been torn down, the vintage decor of the bar that somehow survived the sweeping changes, her intense confrontation with Knapp, the mad dash to the airport, seeing Marina and – at last, with Stanley on the verge of fainting – her fateful encounter with Thomas at the Tiergarten.

Julia continued: her meal on the terrace at the world's best seafood restaurant, though she had hardly tasted any of it; the moonlit walk around the pond; the hotel room where they had made love last night; and finally the last breakfast . . . or lack thereof. When the waiter came back a third time to check on them, Stanley threatened to stab him with a fork if he interrupted again.

'I should have come with you, baby doll,' said Stanley. 'If I had any idea what was going to happen, I would've never let you set off solo.'

Julia idly swirled a spoon in her cup of tea. Stanley looked at her intently and reached out to touch her hand, stopping her mid-swirl.

'Julia, you never take sugar. Feeling a little lost?'

'Sure, except for the little part.'

'Well, it may come as small comfort, but I can't imagine he'll go back to that Marina woman. Unlikely from my experience.'

'What experience is that?' replied Julia with a smile. 'Besides, by now Thomas is sailing through the clouds for Mogadishu.'

'And here we are in New York, drowning in the rain,' sighed Stanley, gazing wistfully out of the window at the endless downpour.

A few passers-by had taken refuge under a terrace awning. An old man held his wife close, doing his best to shelter her from the rain.

'I'm going to pull my life together as best I can,' continued Julia. 'I suppose it's the only thing I can do now.'

'You know you're right. Stupidity personified! You should count yourself lucky to have that kind of mess, and you want to "pull it together"? That's about as stupid as it gets, baby doll. Now dry those eyes this instant. It's wet enough with the rain, and I still have so many questions to ask.'

Julia wiped her eyes with the back of her hand and gave her friend a teary smile.

'Start by telling me, what are you going to say to Adam?' asked Stanley. 'For a while there I was worried he was going to show up twice a day for me to pity-feed him. He even invited me out to his parents' country house tomorrow. By the way if he asks? The food poisoning still has me down for the count. Do *not* blow my cover, baby doll.'

'I guess . . . I'm going to tell Adam as much as I can without hurting him.'

'Some might say the most hurt you can cause is through cowardice. Are you really going to give it another shot with him?'

'As awful as it sounds, I just don't think I have it in me to be single again. Not right now.'

'I thought you said you didn't want to hurt him! Sooner or later your plan is going to wind up hurting you both.'

'I'll find a way to protect him.'

'Can I ask you a very personal question?'

'Nothing's too personal between you and me.'

'The night with Thomas . . .'

'It was tender, gentle, magical . . . and heartbreaking the next morning.'

'I meant the sex.'

'It was tender, gentle, magical.'

'Then how can you not know what you have to do?'

'I'm in New York. So is Adam. There's a whole world between Thomas and me now.'

'Baby doll? You love somebody, I mean *really* love him, it takes more than that to keep you apart. You've got one life to live, and you better live it right.'

◆ ◆ ◆

When he heard the buzzer, Anthony got up from his seat and looked out the window to see Adam waiting in the pouring rain, with the gutters overflowing on to the sidewalk. The buzzer rang three more times in rapid succession.

'All right, all right already, I'm coming,' he grumbled as he buzzed Adam in and waited.

He heard footsteps echoing in the stairwell and stepped out to welcome his visitor with a broad smile.

◆ ◆ ◆

'Mr Walsh!' Adam cried, jerking back with a mix of shock and repulsion.

'Adam! To what do I owe the pleasure?'

Adam froze in place on the landing, jaw moving but not a word coming out of his mouth.

'Cat got your tongue, old boy?'

'You. You're. You're dead!' he stammered.

'Come now, no need to be crude. I know we've never been all that fond of each other, but that's perhaps taking it a bit too far.'

'But . . . you had a funeral. At a cemetery. I was there!' Adam said, faltering.

'Well, if you're going to carry on like that – as horribly rude as it is – best not do it on the landing. Come on in. You look pale as a ghost!'

Adam practically glided into the living room, beside himself. Anthony suggested he take off his dripping trench coat.

'I'm sorry but . . .' Adam said, trying to compose himself as he hung up his coat. 'I'm sure you can understand why I would be so surprised, considering I cancelled my wedding for your funeral.'

'*Your* wedding? I seem to recall Julia being involved as well.'

'My God . . . don't tell me . . . she couldn't have cooked up all that just to . . .'

'Find an excuse for leaving you? Don't flatter yourself. Our family may have overactive imaginations, but if you truly knew Julia, you'd know she'd never do such a thing. I assure you there's a plausible explanation for all of this. If you'd just pipe down for two seconds, I'll provide one or two—'

'Where's Julia?'

'Alas, it's been nearly twenty years since my daughter let me keep tabs on her whereabouts. To tell you the truth, I thought she'd be with you. We did land over three hours ago.'

'Wait, you were travelling together?'

'Of course. Didn't she tell you?'

'I'm not sure that would have been the easiest thing to explain. I was there when the plane brought your corpse back from Europe and even rode to the cemetery in your hearse.'

'Lovely. Next you'll tell me it was you who flipped the switch to start the cremation.'

'No. But I did throw a handful of dirt on your coffin!'

'How very thoughtful.'

'I . . . I'm not feeling so well,' Adam confided, his face turning an odd shade of green.

'Well, then go on and sit down instead of hovering there like a simpleton.'

He gestured to the sofa. Adam didn't move.

'You do still know how to sit down, don't you? Simply rest your backside on the cushions. Or did all of your neurons burst and fizzle at the sight of me?'

At last Adam gave in. He took a seat on the sofa – sitting down right on top of the remote control with the ominous white button.

All at once Anthony froze and fell silent. His eyes snapped shut, and he dropped to the floor, stiff as a block of wood on the carpet right at Adam's feet.

◆ ◆ ◆

'You didn't happen to bring back a photo of him, did you?' asked Stanley. 'I've always wondered what he looked like. Sorry I'm jabbering away like an idiot, but I just hate it when you're this quiet.'

'Why is that?'

'Because I know there's a whole lot going through your head right now, and I have no idea what it is.'

Suddenly Gloria Gaynor belted out 'I Will Survive' from inside Julia's purse, cutting in on their conversation.

She grabbed her cell phone and showed Stanley the caller ID: Adam. Stanley shrugged. Julia answered and was shocked by the sheer terror in her fiancé's voice.

'Julia. We've got a lot to catch up on. Maybe, just maybe there's a thing or two you'd like to tell me. But all that will have to wait. Because your father is passed out on the ground in front of me.'

'Okay, under different circumstances that might have been funny, but right now it's just bad taste.'

'I'm inside your apartment, Julia.'

'What are you doing there? You're . . . you're early!' she replied, tightening with fear.

'Your assistant called and said you wanted to meet earlier.'

'My assistant? What assistant?'

'God, who even cares? I'm calling to tell you your father collapsed and is lying motionless on the floor of your living room. Get the hell over here! I'm calling an ambulance.'

Julia shouted into the phone, giving Stanley a jolt.

'No! Whatever you do, don't do that! I'm coming right now!'

'Have you totally lost it, Julia? I shook the guy. He's not moving. I'm calling 911.'

'Don't! Don't you call anybody, you hear me? I'll be there in five minutes,' she replied, bursting to her feet.

'Where are you?'

'Right across the street, at Pastis. I'm on my way. In the meantime don't do anything, don't touch anything, especially not him!'

At a total loss Stanley whispered to Julia that he'd get the bill. As she bolted from the restaurant, he shouted after her to give him a call once the emergency had been dealt with.

◆ ◆ ◆

She raced up the stairs four at a time. On entering the apartment, she saw her father stretched out motionless in the middle of the living room floor.

'Where's the remote control?' she said as she came crashing into the room.

'What?' asked Adam, utterly confused.

'It's a little white box with one big button right in the centre. It's a remote control for Christ's sake!' she replied, urgently searching the room.

'Your father falls down, stiff as a board, and you want to watch TV? I'd better call more than one ambulance!'

'Did you touch anything? How did this happen?' asked Julia, rifling through every last drawer and cupboard.

'I didn't do a thing! Aside from talking to your father, even though we buried him last week. Pretty surreal experience I have to say.'

'Save the jokes for later, Adam! This is an emergency.'

'Oh, I wasn't trying to be funny. Are you going to tell me what the hell is going on here? Or pinch me and we can both laugh about this nightmare I'm having.'

'I thought the exact same thing in the beginning, but no such luck. Damn it, where is it?'

'Oh my God, please! What are you talking about?'

'Daddy's remote control!'

'That's it, I'm making the call,' Adam swore, heading towards the kitchen phone.

Julia zipped over and blocked his path, arms spread wide.

'Don't take another step. Tell me exactly what happened – exactly – starting from the moment you arrived.'

'It's just like I told you,' Adam fumed. 'Your father opened the door, I found myself actually apologizing for acting like I'd seen a ghost, and then he invited me in with the promise of an explanation for all this. He kept insisting I sit down, so I sat on the couch, and he collapsed mid-sentence.'

'Wait! The couch!' shouted Julia, knocking Adam right off his feet as she made a beeline across the room to the couch.

She frantically searched under all the cushions and in every nook and cranny, sighing with relief when she wrapped her hands around the precious remote.

'Okay, it's official. You've gone completely insane,' grumbled Adam, clambering to his feet.

'Please, God, let this work, please let it work,' Julia prayed, clutching the little white remote like her life depended on it.

'Julia!' shouted Adam. 'For the last time: what the hell is going on?'

'Shut up!' she replied, fighting back tears. 'There's no use trying to explain. You'll see it with your own eyes in a few seconds. Assuming this actually works.'

She closed her eyes, prayed to the heavens . . . and pushed the button.

Anthony's eyes snapped open, and he picked up right where he had left off. 'You see, Adam, old boy, one thing I can tell you about life is that it's never quite what it seems. Just when you think you're—' Anthony cut himself short when he realized he was lying on the ground in the middle of the room with Julia standing frozen over him.

He coughed and rose to his feet, while Adam stumbled back and collapsed straight into the welcoming arms of the couch.

'Oh,' said Anthony, glancing at his watch. 'Would you look at that? Seven o'clock already. I must've lost track of time.' He dusted himself down.

Julia gave him a scorching glare.

'Maybe I'll just go ahead and leave you two alone. I think it's better that way,' he went on. 'You must have a lot to catch up on. Be sure to listen carefully to my daughter, Adam. Be attentive, and don't interrupt. It all may sound a bit far-fetched at the start, but you'll see. If you buckle down and concentrate, you'll catch on in no time. I'll just grab my coat and leave you to it.'

With that, Anthony plucked Adam's raincoat off the coat stand, tiptoed across the room to retrieve the umbrella from the window and walked straight out of the door.

◆ ◆ ◆

She chose the shipping crate in the middle of the room as the starting point for explaining the unbelievable truth. Soon Julia herself was slumped over in a heap on the couch, with Adam pacing back and forth as she tried to reassure him.

'Even if you are my fiancé, how would telling you have changed anything?'

'I don't know. I don't even know if I am your fiancé any more. I don't know anything. You lied to me for an entire week, and now you come out with this elaborate fairy tale.'

'Adam. Imagine if your father knocked on your door one day after his death, and if through a crazy twist of fate you could suddenly spend a few more days with him. One week – and that's all you get – to say everything left unsaid. You're telling me you wouldn't leap at that opportunity? As absurd as it seems?'

'Whatever happened to hating your father?'

'Maybe I did once. But hard as it may be to believe, now I wish these six days could last longer. I spent most of the time talking about myself, and there are so many things I still want to know about him. About his life. For the first time I was able to see him through the eyes of an adult, free of all my childhood selfishness. My father had his flaws, but so do I. It doesn't mean that I don't love the man! On the way back I thought to myself that if I could be sure that my own children would show the same type of acceptance of me, I'd be less afraid about becoming a parent myself . . . and even a bit more worthy of it I guess.'

'My God you can be naive. Your father never stopped playing maestro, orchestrating every little part of your life from the day you were born. Isn't that what you told me on the rare occasions you actually talked about the guy? And if I buy into this fantasy you've cooked up, it means he has somehow managed to do the unthinkable and has continued controlling everything from beyond the grave! You and that *machine* don't have one thing in common. He's not even human! Everything he said could have been some prerecording. How in the world could you let him play you like that? The whole thing wasn't a conversation, it was a monologue.

'You earn a living dreaming up make-believe characters, but do you allow them to actually talk to the children? Of course not! It's an anticipation game, where you rig up what they want to hear and have them spout out something reassuring or entertaining. Well, with your father it was the exact same thing. He managed to pull the wool over your eyes one more time. Your little week of travelling together was a total farce, a twisted parody of a reunion. I mean, the guy's very presence was like a . . . like a mirage. Which I guess it sort of always was, just this time aided by technology. And you're so desperate for the love he never gave you, you walked straight into his trap. To the point of ruining everything we had, first with the wedding and now this!'

'Don't be ridiculous, Adam. My father didn't choose to die just to mess up our wedding.'

'Fine. But tell me, just where did the two of you go together, Julia?'

'What difference does it make?'

'Lucky you, you don't even have to muster the courage to tell me. Stanley did that for you. Don't hold it against him – he was fall-down drunk. You're the one who told me he couldn't say no to a good bottle of wine, and the one I brought him was flat-out irresistible. I can tell you I was ready to scour every last wine cellar in France to find out where you had gone, why you ran away from me and what I could do to get you back. I would have waited a hundred years to marry you, Julia. But now? Emptiness, nothing but emptiness.'

'Adam. I can explain.'

'You can explain? Little late for that. Maybe you should have thought of that when you came to my office to announce you were going on a trip. Or when I just missed you in Montreal, maybe then. Or afterward, when I called you day after day and you never even bothered to pick up or return a single voicemail. But no. Instead you run off to Berlin to seek out this man from your past, and you don't tell me a word about it.

'What exactly was I for you? A segue between eras of your life, a footnote between chapters? A life raft you could cling to until you end up back in the arms of your one true love?'

'Please, you don't understand,' begged Julia.

'If he knocked on the door right now, what would you do?'

Julia remained silent.

'You don't know. You really don't. How can I be sure if you don't even know?'

Adam headed to the door and swung it open.

'Tell your father, or his robot, that he can keep my raincoat.'

The door closed and Adam was gone. Julia listened to his footsteps, every last one, until she heard the downstairs door slam shut behind him.

◆ ◆ ◆

Anthony gave a hesitant knock on the door before entering. Julia was leaning on the windowsill, looking wistfully down at the street.

'Why oh why did you do that?' she murmured.

'Do what? The whole thing was accidental,' responded Anthony.

'Adam accidentally comes to my place two hours early, you accidentally let him in, he accidentally sits on your remote control and you accidentally end up sprawled out on my living room floor?'

'I admit, as far as interpreting the signs, those do seem rather ominous . . . Maybe we can call a fortune teller, get our palms read.'

'Cut the sarcasm. I'm not in the mood. I'll ask you one more time: *why* did you do that?'

'Just a little push, dear, to get you to admit the truth to him – and to yourself. Don't tell me that right now you don't feel a great weight has been lifted from your shoulders. You may be alone, now more than ever, but at least you can be at peace with yourself.'

'Okay, that covers the theatrics from earlier. What about the rest?'

Anthony took a deep breath.

'Your mother's illness stripped her of the ability to recognize me in the time leading up to her death, but I'm sure that somewhere deep down she never forgot how much we loved each other. I'll never forget, that's for certain. We weren't perfect, nor were we model parents – far from it. We often had no clue about what to do next. No matter how much we fought, we never – and I mean *never* – had a shred of doubt about staying together or about how much we loved you. Falling in love with your mother, winning her heart and having a child together were the most important choices of my life . . . and which led to the most beautiful things any man could ask for. Even if it's taken me so long to find the right words to tell you . . . it's true.'

'So . . . all this chaos, all the damage, my whole life in shambles . . . that was out of love?'

'Do you remember those little pieces of paper I told you about during our trip? The type you always keep near you – in your wallet, in your pocket or just in your head. Mine was the note your mother left in the tray the night I couldn't pay for our dinner on the Champs-Élysées. Maybe now you can understand why I dreamed of dying in Paris. Maybe your little piece of paper was that old Deutschmark you kept in your purse or one of the letters from Thomas that you kept in your bedroom.'

'Did you read those letters?'

'I wouldn't dream of it! But I noticed them when I slipped that last, fateful letter into your desk drawer. When I received the invitation to your wedding, I went up to your old bedroom. Standing in the middle of that little world made me feel closer to you, to all the things that I remember, that I'll never forget. I couldn't stop asking myself: what would you do when you discovered the letter? I thought about destroying it or actually posting it to you, or if the best thing to do would be to give it to you the day of your wedding. Alas, I never had time to make the right decision. But just as you said – if you're really paying attention, life can send you some astonishing signs. In Montreal I got to see part of your reaction with my own two eyes, but only part of it. The rest is yours and yours only. The fact is I might've actually just mailed you that letter if you hadn't so thoroughly burned the bridges that your own father didn't even have your address. Would you have even *opened* a letter if you knew it was from me? Besides, it's not like I had advance notice about dying!'

'You always have an answer to everything, don't you?'

'Not everything. The decision before you is one you must face alone. It's been that way for longer than you think. You could have turned me off at any time, remember? Just one push of a button. You could have said no to the trip to Berlin. You and you alone went to meet Thomas at the airport, and it was your own footsteps that brought you back to the spot where the two of you first met. I certainly wasn't there when you brought him back to the hotel! Julia, you can blame everything on your childhood, hold your parents accountable for every little problem you encounter and all the trials and tribulations of your life, blame them for your weaknesses and fears, but in the end you are solely responsible for all that you are and the choice of what you will become. And don't forget to keep your dramas in perspective – there are always families worse than ours.'

'Like whose?'

'Poor Thomas. His every last move betrayed by his own grandmother.'

'How do you know about that?'

'The point is no parent can live their child's life for them, but that doesn't keep us from the worry and heartache of seeing you unhappy. Sometimes that can even push us to action, to try and show you the way. Sometimes it's better to be wrong and tactless as a result of loving you too much than to sit idly by and watch you suffer.'

'If your intent was to "show me the way", you did a hell of a job of it. I feel totally and utterly lost.'

'Lost as you may be, you're no longer blind, now are you?'

'Adam was right. We never once had a real conversation during our entire week together.'

'Maybe he was, Julia. I'm not exactly your father – just what's left of him. But this machine has hopefully done its part to help you find a way out of your problems. I can't remember one time since we've been together that I haven't had some idea to help you along on your way. Maybe it's because I know you better than you think. Or maybe it's that regardless of how long it takes you to realize it, I simply love you far more than you think. And now that I've been able to tell you all this I can at last go gently into that good night.'

Julia looked at her father for a long time, then went and sat down next to him. They stayed silent like that for a while.

'Did you really mean those things you said about me earlier?' asked Anthony.

'When I was talking to Adam? What, were you listening through the door again?'

'No. Through the floor, up in your attic. I was worried the rain outside might cause a short circuit,' he said with a smile.

'Why couldn't I have gotten to know you sooner?' she asked him.

'It can take ages for parents and children to really know each other.'

'I wish we had at least a few more days.'

'I believe we just had them, my dear Julia.'

'What happens tomorrow?'

'Not to worry. Consider yourself lucky. You've already dealt with your father dying once; you're experienced.'

'I'm not in the mood for jokes.'

'Tomorrow . . . we'll see about tomorrow.'

As the night drew on, Anthony inched his hand towards Julia's. Finally he made the leap and took her hand in his. Their fingers tightened over one another and stayed that way, intertwined. Later, when Julia fell asleep, her head came to rest on her father's shoulder.

Anthony Walsh got up before sunrise, taking every precaution not to wake his daughter. He delicately shifted her body on to the sofa and draped a blanket over her shoulders. Julia grumbled in her sleep and rolled over.

After making sure she was still fast asleep, he sat down at the kitchen table with a pen and paper and began to write.

Once he had completed the letter, he set it down on the table. Then he opened his bag and took out a little stack of about a hundred other letters, all bound together by a red ribbon. He went into his daughter's bedroom and put them in one of her dresser drawers, careful not to bend the corners of the yellowed photograph of Thomas that accompanied the stack.

Back in the living room, he walked over to the sofa, took the white remote control, put it in the breast pocket of his coat and leaned over to plant a gentle kiss on his daughter's forehead.

'Sleep, my darling Julia, and know your daddy loves you.'

22.

Julia stretched and opened her eyes. The room was empty, and the massive crate was sealed once more.

'Daddy?'

She heard no reply, nothing but dead silence in her apartment. Breakfast for one had been perfectly arranged at the kitchen table, with an envelope propped up against the jar of honey between a box of cereal and a milk carton. Julia recognized the handwriting. She sat down and read.

> My darling Julia,
> By the time you read this, my batteries will have run down once and for all. I hope you can forgive me, but I wanted to spare you one more senseless goodbye. Burying your father once was quite enough. When you finish reading my last words, leave your apartment for a few hours. Grant your father one last wish and don't be here when they come to get me. Leave the crate closed and sealed as it is. Inside you'd only find me sleeping – peacefully at last, thanks to you. I can never thank you enough for these days you gave me, my dear. I was waiting for them for such a very long time. I'd always

dreamed of getting to know the mysterious woman you had become. I've learned one of the great lessons a parent can learn over these last few days – the importance of taking time to get to know the adult who stands where once stood a child, and to give that adult their rightful place. I'm sorry for all that you missed during your childhood. I did my best. I wasn't there for you enough, not as much as you would have liked. I wanted to be a friend to you, a confidant; in the end I was only your father. But I'll always be your father. Wherever I'm going, I will always take with me the memory of an infinite love – the love I hold for you. Do you remember that lovely story I told you about the power of the full moon's reflection in a puddle? That legend was true, and I was wrong to doubt it. It was just a matter of patience. In the end my wish did come true – the person I missed so much and longed to have in my life was you.

I can still picture you as a little girl, running and leaping into my arms. It may sound silly but you have always been and remain the best thing that ever happened to me. Nothing made me happier than the sound of your laughter and the hugs you gave me when I came home at night. I know that one day, when you're free from all that weighs on your mind, these memories will come back to you, too. I also know that somewhere deep inside you'll never forget those dreams you told me about when I came and sat at the foot of your bed. Even if I wasn't next to you, I was never as far away as you thought. Clumsy and awkward as I may be, I love you. I have but one more thing to ask of you: promise me you'll be happy.

Your daddy

Julia folded the letter. She walked over to the crate and gently ran her fingers along its surface, reassuring her father that she loved him too. With a heavy heart, she granted his last wish. She went downstairs and left a key with Mr Zimoure. She warned her neighbour that a truck would be coming to pick up a package at her place that morning and asked him to let them in. Without waiting for a response, she left and headed downtown towards a certain antique store.

23.

Fifteen minutes passed. Heavy silence still reigned over Julia's apartment. Then . . . a gentle click, followed by the sound of the crate creaking open inch by inch with painstaking caution. Anthony Walsh stepped out, dusted off his shoulders and walked over to the mirror to straighten his tie. He noticed the framed photo of himself and returned it to its place on the bookshelf, then turned to take one last look around the room.

Anthony left the apartment and went downstairs to the street. A car sat idly waiting for him there, right in front of the building.

'Good morning, Wallace,' he said, settling into the back seat.

'Good to see you again, sir,' replied his personal assistant.

'Is everything all set with the shipping company?'

'The truck is waiting behind us as we speak.'

'Perfect.'

'Shall we head back to the hospital, sir, as scheduled?'

'No, I think I've wasted enough precious time there already. We'll head to the airport, with a quick stop at home along the way. I'll need to change suitcases. And you'll need to get packed yourself. I've developed a newfound appreciation for company when I travel.'

'May I ask where we're going, sir?'

'I'll explain everything along the way. But do bring your passport.'

The car turned on to Greenwich Street. At the intersection, the window rolled down and a white remote control flew straight out of the car and into the gutter.

24.

New York hadn't enjoyed such a mild October since time immemorial. Stanley and Julia were going to have brunch together, just as they had every weekend for the past three months. On this particular morning a table awaited them across the street at Pastis. However, today was special: Mr Zimoure's autumn collection had just gone on sale, and for the first time Julia knocked at his door with no dire news or emergencies. Amazingly he had agreed to let her have the shop to herself a full two hours before the official opening time. And she wasn't alone.

'What do you think?'

'Turn around and let me see.'

'Stanley, you've been looking me up and down for half an hour. I really need to get off this platform.'

'Look, do you want my opinion or not? Turn around. Show me the front again. Isn't that a pity! Those kitten heels just aren't doing you any favours, baby doll.'

'Stanley!'

'You know I'm allergic to the sales rack.'

'Have you seen the prices in this place? It's the best I can do with my measly salary,' she whispered.

'Don't start with that again!'

'So. Do we have a winner?' asked Mr Zimoure, clearly exhausted. 'The two of you have single-handedly ransacked my entire store. I think I've taken out every last pair I have in your size.'

'No, not quite yet,' replied Stanley. 'What, pray tell, is the story with those ravishing pumps on that shelf over there? Yes, those ones up on the top shelf, the very last ones over—'

'Oh, I'm afraid I don't see those in Miss Julia's size.'

'What about in the back?' begged Stanley.

'I guess I'll have to go down and check,' sighed Zimoure, before going clomping down the stairs with heavy footsteps.

'I tell you, it's a good thing he's so distinguished and handsome, because the man is not winning any points for personality.'

'Sorry. Did you say "distinguished and handsome"?' Julia said with an incredulous laugh.

'Let's just say I've had a change of heart these past few months. Maybe we could have him over for dinner at your place sometime.'

'That's gotta be a joke. Right?'

'Well, you're the one always going on about how he sells the most exquisite shoes in New York.'

'Right. But what's that got to do with—?'

'I'm not going to stay a widower for the rest of my life. Is that okay with you, baby doll?'

'Of course it is . . . but *Mr Zimoure*?'

'You know you're right. Forget Zimoure!' said Stanley, his eyes wide, staring out the window on to the street.

'Wow. That was quick.'

'Don't look now but there is a drop-dead gorgeous man staring right through the window as we speak.'

'Wait, what?' Julia froze, too terrified to move an inch, not daring to glance behind her and have her hopes dashed.

'Well, he's had that delicious face of his practically pressed against the storefront window for the past ten minutes. He's staring at *you* like he's seen the Virgin Mary or something. But as far as I know, there's no Our Lady of the Three-Hundred-Dollar Pumps, not even a sales rack version. Don't turn around! I saw him first.'

With a lot of effort and trembling lips, at last Julia turned to face the man.

'Actually Stanley,' she said in a soft voice, 'I saw this one long before you.'

The overpriced shoes were left behind on the platform as Julia flew across the store, unbolted the door and ran out into the street.

◆ ◆ ◆

When Mr Zimoure came back up the stairs, he found Stanley sitting alone on the platform with a pair of pumps in hand.

'What, she left?' he asked, looking around, dumbfounded.

'Yes,' replied Stanley, 'but not to worry. She'll be back. Probably not today, but she'll be back.'

Zimoure sighed and simply dropped the box of shoes he had brought from the basement. Stanley picked up the box and handed it back to him.

'You sure do look exhausted. Come on, let me help you clean up this mess, and then I'll buy you a coffee. Or tea if you'd prefer.'

◆ ◆ ◆

Thomas brushed Julia's lips with his fingertips and placed the gentlest of kisses on each of her eyelids. She melted in his arms.

'I tried to convince myself I could go on without you, but as you can see I just can't,' he said, his voice thick with emotion.

'What about Africa? Won't Knapp be—?'

'I can't just run around the planet reporting the truth about other people if I'm lying to myself. What good would that do? Why race from country to country when the person I love is right here?'

Julia stood on her tiptoes, looking deep into his eyes. 'You don't need to say another word. Not another word.'

They kissed, a kiss that stretched on and on, the passionate embrace of two people so blindly in love that the rest of the world has simply ceased to exist.

'How did you find me?' Julia finally asked, nestling deeper into Thomas's arms.

'I searched for you everywhere for twenty years. Looking downstairs from your apartment wasn't much of a stretch.'

'Eighteen years. But believe me, that was long enough.'

Julia kissed him again.

'All this . . . and I still don't know why you even came to Berlin.'

'I told you, it was a sign . . . By total chance I came across that portrait of you at a street artist's stand.'

'But I've never had my portrait drawn.'

'Give me a break. It was you without a doubt – your eyes, your mouth, even that dimple in your chin.'

'And where was this? This mysterious portrait.'

'On the Old Port of Montreal.'

'Well, now I'm sure what you're saying is impossible. Because I've never even set foot in Montreal.'

Julia looked skyward and saw a cloud drifting over New York, taking form into a familiar shape before her eyes. She smiled.

'I am going to miss him . . . so much.'

'Miss who?'

'My father. Come on. I feel like taking a walk with you. You have to get acquainted with my city after all.'

'But Julia, you're barefoot.'

'That really doesn't matter,' Julia replied.

ACKNOWLEDGMENTS

Thank you

Emmanuelle Hardouin,
Pauline Lévêque,
Raymond and Danièle Levy,
Louis Levy,
Lorraine.

Susanna Lea and Antoine Audouard.

Léonard Anthony, Marie Garnero, Kerry Glencorse, Katrin Hodapp, Mark Kessler, Moïna Macé, Laura Mamelok, Danielle Melconian, Romain Ruetsch, Lauren Wendelken.

Chris Murray.

Antoine Caro.

Pauline Normand, Marie-Ève Provost.

Philippe Guez, Éric Brame, and Miguel Courtois.

Yves and Martyn Lévêque, Charles Veillet-Lavallée.

ABOUT THE AUTHOR

Having sold more than forty million books, Marc Levy is the most-read French author alive today. He's written eighteen novels to date, including *P.S. from Paris*, *Children of Freedom* and *Replay*.

Originally written for his son, his first novel, *If Only It Were True*, was later adapted for the big screen as *Just Like Heaven*, starring Reese Witherspoon and Mark Ruffalo. Since then Levy has not only won the hearts of European readers, but he's also won over audiences around the world. More than one and a half million copies of his books have been sold in China alone, and his novels have been published in forty-nine languages. He lives in New York. Readers can learn more about him and follow his work at www.marclevy.info.